THE GIRL FROM DIANA PARK

DAMIAN GREEN SERIES, BOOK 3

ALEC PECHE

GBSW PUBLISHING

Many thanks to GM Meyer and Honnie as my first readers for improving the big and small things in this story.

AUTHOR'S NOTE

Author's note:

In a reader review of other books in this series (Red Rock Island and Willow Glen Heist), a comment was made that the premise of the story was bad as such an island couldn't exist in San Francisco Bay. Guess what? It does exist and you can use the GPS coordinates below to find it on a map. At the time of my first book in the series I came across an article that the island was for sale and my imagination took it from there. If you should cross westbound on the Richmond-San Rafael Bridge, you'll find the island out your car window on the left side as you leave Richmond. It's rumored to be for sale for $5 million as of 2018, but as it's owned by three separate counties, it sounds like it would be a nightmare to try and build on. There is no house on it at the time of this writing which is just further proof that this is a work of fiction.

Latitude: 37° 55' 43.43" N
   Longitude: -122° 25' 50.16" W

2013

Jessica Roth had a terrible day at work. As a family law attorney, she'd been trying to file a motion by the end of the day. Her clients were in a difficult situation and needed a Conservatorship Stipulation and Proposed Order as soon as possible. She needed to do the first step and get it filed with the Santa Clara County Civil Court division. She'd made it with just minutes to spare before the office closed. The last-minute stop at the court had put her in a traffic mess, and she'd been late to pick-up her daughter Olivia from child care. Her husband Daniel worked in sales and was in China for a trade convention. She paid the late fee and still felt frazzled an hour later as she sat in Diana Park. Olivia had not been happy with her late arrival and Jessica had sought to make it up to her with a trip to her favorite park. She paused long enough to get out of her business suit and into a pair of scruffy sweats.

Now she sat on the rim of the swing set area alternating between watching her daughter and reading emails. It was fall and the sun had set and darkness, such as you got in a busy city, would arrive in the next twenty minutes. She'd give Olivia another ten minutes of play and then they would have a one block walk back home. Olivia had a swing set in her own backyard, but the park's jungle gym was bigger and better.

Olivia moved from the swings to the monkey bars and then on to the tree house and slides. She joyfully ran from the base of the slide to the stairs leading to the top of the playhouse and its slide. Jessica smiled at her and encouraged her on each apparatus. She wanted her daughter to burn off a little of the extra energy before they went back home, besides the fresh air was good for both of them. Jessica smiled and glanced down at her email for just a moment. As the daylight disappeared, it took a few extra seconds with each glance to focus on her phone screen.

Jessica glanced back up prepared to smile and compliment Olivia and suffered a little panic when she didn't immediately spot her. She shut her phone off and stood calling out "Olivia!".

She walked to play house atop the jungle gym expecting to find her hiding there, but it was empty. She called out, "Olivia, where are you?" a few times.

Then, in rising panic, she ran around the building in the middle of the park that was a pump house for the city water system and still there was no sign of her daughter.

She raised the hand holding her cell phone and dialed 9-1-1.

"What's your emergency?" the operator asked.

With tears of fear and panic in her voice, Jessica almost shouted into the phone, "My daughter is missing. I need help right now! Please come...."

CHAPTER 1

*D*amian Green looked out of the windows of his house situated upon Red Rock Island, his private island in San Francisco Bay. Later that morning he'd take his boat over to the Richmond pier and from there drive his truck to work. For lunch he had a craving for a Pete's Cheeseburger and so would drop in on his friend's bar. This evening, he'd steer his boat the other direction towards Ariana's house, on the other side of the Bay as Hermione had a soccer try-out for the upcoming high school season.

Ariana and Damian taught Hermione the basics of water polo before she tried out for that sport and she excelled. With soccer, they had practiced with her at a local field, and the three of them had flown to England for a vacation week between Christmas and New Year's and she had seen several Premier League games. It took time to develop the footwork of soccer and other girls in her school had played in youth leagues so Hermione was trying out for her high school team with a little disadvantage. Still, she was a natural athlete and she'd increased her running so she'd have the endurance to play for sixty minutes. He was anxious for her to succeed but hadn't seen any of the other girls play and didn't know how Hermione stacked up to them.

Ariana and Damian were raising Hermione until she was reunited with her parents. She was Hannah Sherwood when she'd fall asleep under a tarp in Damian's boat, which was parked at the marina. She'd woken up once he reached his island. She'd told a fantastic story about her parents being kidnapped and with a little research, Damian had found she was telling the truth. She renamed herself Hermione, after her favorite Harry Potter character and Damian began the search for her parents. She lived with Ariana, but Damian also had a bedroom for her to stay on his island home. She attended the local high school in Ariana's neighborhood and she'd been with them nearly a year.

Damian had been chopping the fresh fish he caught that morning for his cats, Bella and Bailey. They really did have the best diet of any felines in the world. They got the fish fillet and he discarded the head and tail into the Bay as food for whales, dolphins or sea lions that passed by his island. Cleaning up after the stinky duty, he got ready to leave after checking the weather forecast. If he traveled the Bay in low wind and sunny conditions he took a different boat than when the Bay was foggy or drizzling.

Thirty minutes later he was in his truck and on the way to his warehouse. He was up to ten employees as his company explored various inventions. He was close to bringing to market a solar battery internet connecting device that he intended to distribute to thousands of Peruvian farmers that currently had no access to the world. His team developed the solar battery and a satellite smartphone-like device except that it didn't have a telephone component. It was like a handheld tablet but smaller. What made it unique was the solar battery and the intuitive applications for the farmer in relation to crop production and weather. The side benefit was connecting them to the world, but really he wanted to improve the food production in developing countries to prevent death and disease from poor nutrition.

His warehouse was working on other inventions that excited him each day when he looked at the progress and the people of his team. Before he knew it, it was approaching the lunch hour and he still had a craving for one of Pete's cheeseburgers. He debated asking one of his team members to join him, but he was in the mood for a solitary meal. Ten minutes later he sidled up to a barstool and was pleased to see that Pete was running the bar. They spent a few minutes catching up with each other's lives and Damien checking in with Pete to assure himself that his software was still helping Pete manage the bar. Minutes later he was sinking his teeth into the cheeseburger he'd fantasized about all morning and it was as good as he remembered.

He finished his lunch and followed Pete back to his office to look at some pictures that he had taken that interested Damien. There was a corridor that connected the bar/restaurant with Pete's office, a storeroom, and the restrooms. His eyes caught sight of a poster on a bulletin board in the corridor. His eyes widened with alarm as he caught sight of the picture on a notice. He continued into Pete's office, his mind calculating how he would grab that notice off the bulletin board and take it with him. At the end of the conversation with Pete, he'd either leave Pete in the office or make a stop in the restroom in order for Pete not to see him remove the notice on the bulletin board. Damien didn't think he heard a word that Pete said; he was just waiting for the conversation to end so he could study the notice without interruptions.

Five minutes later, Damien found himself in the restroom watching his watch waiting for time to pass. At his designated time he opened the restroom door noted that the corridor was empty and proceeded to remove the poster in question and shove it into his jacket pocket. He waved goodbye at Pete as he left the bar and returned to his truck. He drove the truck a few blocks away and pulled over shutting the vehicle down. He pulled the piece of paper out of his jacket and smoothed it straight.

Studying the picture on the poster, he knew it was Hermione. His heart was racing as he thought about the next steps. Looking at the time, he decided to give Ariana a call.

"Hey Damien, are you calling to confirm the time you're supposed to be at my house this afternoon?"

"No, I just had a cheeseburger at Pete's for lunch, and I found a poster with Hermione's picture on it. I have to tell you that my heart is still racing from viewing the notice."

"Oh my God, why is her picture on a notice? Are you sure it's her? What does the poster say?"

"I'm texting you a copy of the poster, give me a minute," and seconds later he heard the swoosh of an outgoing text.

"Got it. How long do you think it was posted on that bulletin board?" Ariana asked after giving it an initial read-through.

"I don't know. It's been at least six months since I walked down that corridor at Pete's and the paper was curled and had the look that it had been there awhile. I could dust it for fingerprints."

"But you don't know who has touched the paper just walking through the corridor."

"Should we share it with Hermione?"

"We've always been honest with her," Ariana said. "There's nothing overtly bad with the announcement. Somehow I don't think it's her parents that posted it; it doesn't sound loving or desperate. In fact, it sounds like one of those 'Ten most wanted criminals lists'. It's interesting that Pete didn't make the connection between this picture and Hermione as he's met her several times."

"I think she was younger in this picture and her hair is completely changed and we men are not observant. Perhaps Pete doesn't see those notices anymore. He pays no attention to what's posted as long as it meets his decency standards."

"Have you seen this notice posted anywhere else in Richmond? It's sort of a strange place to post a notice. Most notices I've seen in bars relate to roommates or dating, not missing children."

"Are you suggesting that it was put there to attract my attention? Pete once called me an irregular regular visitor to his bar."

"I don't know what I'm suggesting, just trying to understand the poster and what it means."

"I was going to go to the office, but I'm going to leave now and return home to research this notice. I'll fingerprint it but I doubt that will tell me anything. I want to investigate the number on my untraceable computer. When should we say something to Hermione?"

"Let's tell her after soccer tryouts. I don't want that to interfere with her concentration on the soccer field," Ariana suggested.

"Okay. Ariana, can I just say how much I appreciate your help raising Hermione? I may be smart about many things, but I struggle every day trying to figure out what's the best thing to do or say with Hermione."

"Damian, you don't give yourself credit. We've shared her nearly a year and I haven't seen any missteps on your part."

"I've made her cry."

"You think that isn't normal for a teenager?"

"I suppose."

"I'll nominate you for father of the year if you survive teaching her driver's education."

"Haha. She'll probably be a level-headed human being about that too. We really lucked out trying to raise a smart, athletic, and resourceful teenager."

"Thank you for inviting me in to help raise her. She brings joy to both of our lives."

"Okay we best end this conversation before we become saps," Damian said with a smile in his voice.

"See you later."

Damian restarted the engine and put the car in gear. He drove back to the warehouse, checked in with his staff and left to return to his island. The staff was used to his odd comings and goings. Soon he had his boat inside his watercraft garage and his island was tightly locked up. He had a large cup of tea as he sat down to explore the notice that said, 'Looking for information' and then followed with a dated picture and description of Hermione. When Damian had found her cold and hiding in his boat one night as he returned to his island, her name was 'Hannah Sherwood', and she had long red hair. Her home had suffered a home invasion and her parents were kidnapped. She escaped to a 'safe room' and survived a week hiding as someone had stayed behind in the house looking for her. When she knew the man charged with finding her was sound asleep, she snuck out and eventually ended up in the marina where her family had a boat. That boat was missing, and so she ended up in Damian's boat asleep from exhaustion.

He'd called Ariana Knowles the moment he discovered the girl as he neared his island. Ariana had housed her overnight while Damian made a plan to go check out the teenager's story and her house.

It was all exactly as the girl had described including the abduction of her parents on security camera footage. Ariana was a widow, her husband having died from cancer before they could have children. Damian's wife and two girls had been murdered in a burglary attempt some eight years ago. Hannah was the same age as his oldest would have been and the adults gave the teenager the option to be turned over to social services with law enforcement's help finding her parents or she could stay with the two of them while they searched for her parents. After a search of Ariana's and Damian's backgrounds online, Hannah chose to stay with them. Her name was changed to Hermione Knowles from Hannah Sherwood. She'd cut and dyed her hair and added regular lens glasses to hide her appearance. Damian had used his computer skills to create a background for the kid and identity so she could enroll in the school system. He felt lucky to have her in his life and he thought they were doing a great job protecting the kid and giving her a caring and supportive home. Hermione excelled in school and in sports.

Now this poster was threatening their peaceful existence and it boded ill winds towards Hermione. He began by fingerprinting the paper. He'd just taken up fingerprinting shortly after Hermione joined them so he was by no means an expert, but he'd managed to hack into CODIS which was the national system for fingerprint identification. Rather than searching for fingerprints, he had instead downloaded their database anytime he was trying to match something. He sat back assuring himself the computer was beginning it analysis and he'd have a match in twenty to thirty minutes. He turned again to look at the paper trying to guess its age. Then his cell phone began ringing and he saw that it was retired Detective Natalie Severino and so he answered.

"Hello, Natalie. What's up?"

"I've got another not quite cold case, and I was hoping you could help. By the way, how are you doing? Haley says some of your inventions are getting close to going to market. Not sure what that means but she was excited about it."

"Yeah, we are close to being able to sell some of the inventions created in the warehouse. What's your not quite cold case?"

"It's a child abduction, the girl vanished without a trace five years ago. So the police wanted some fresh eyes and assigned it to me. It wasn't in their cold case files, but it's been a while since they have come up with anything new."

Damien's heart began pounding and he wondered what he would say to Natalie when she said they were looking for a child by the name of Hannah Sherwood.

CHAPTER 2

"The child's name is Olivia Roth and she would be nine or ten-years-old by now. She was in a park close to dusk with her mother five years ago. The file says that the mother glanced down at an email and when she glanced back up seconds later expecting to find her daughter on the gym slide, she was gone. She spent a few moments calling for her daughter and running around the playground searching, and then dialed 9–1–1. That story is for the most part verified by her cell phone records."

Damien's sense of relief was so acute when he heard the child's name that he missed the subsequent words from Natalie. He should have known not to panic as Hermione's home was not in Natalie's San Jose Police Department jurisdiction. He quickly resumed listening to what Natalie was describing.

"The file is pretty thick with investigative reports so if you have time tomorrow, I'd like to meet with you and go over the file to see what ideas you have from a technology perspective. Are you available?"

Damian thought about the search he was doing on Hermione's poster and the work he'd neglected that day in his warehouse and knew he wouldn't have time. But he thought of the parents of that child and knew he needed to find the time for Natalie.

"I'm swamped at the moment, so if you could come to the warehouse in Richmond tomorrow, I'll have sub-sandwiches waiting for you, and we'll take lunch to go over the file. Would that work?"

"Yes, that's fine, It will give me a chance to try and understand what Haley's working on if you don't mind me distracting her for a few minutes."

"I would never stand between a mother and her daughter-in-law. Spend all the time you want with Haley."

"Thanks Damian, she's lucky to be working for you. She always raves about how much she loves her job. Sometimes, I think she makes Trevor wistful as he loves his job, but not nearly to the degree that she does. She also really enjoys her co-workers."

"That's good to hear and tell Trevor he has nothing to worry about as far as his standing in her life. She raves about him here so much that her co-workers are rolling their eyes sometimes in front of her. It's all good. We have a good crew here."

Damian heard Natalie laugh and they soon ended the call after confirming a time for lunch. Damian made a calendar entry to remind himself to order lunch the next day. He had corporate accounts in restaurants locally and his staff took turns ordering lunch every day. He would take over the ordering the next day.

He returned to Hermione's mystery and his fingerprint analysis. He lifted six prints off the poster including his own. The computer had matched himself to three of the prints which was no surprise as he'd touched the page multiple time getting it off the bulletin board and folding it into his jacket. Two other names popped up - a couple he determined might be neighbors of the Sherwoods as they had the same street name in their address. He'd bet they called the number on the poster. The computer was still searching for one print, and the other identified as an employee of Pete's that he recognized the name of.

Damian moved on to the telephone number listed, but soon found it was a random cell phone number; the kind you bought at Walmart and activated without identifying yourself. What else could he do?

Then an idea came to him, he could at least track the location of the cell phone number even if he had no idea of who owned it. He just needed to identify the telephone carrier that the number belonged to. Telephones of all kinds sent out location signals trying to find cellular towers. It was a great feature if you were lost and needed someone to find you, but those same telephone carriers sold your data for profit since they collected it. He'd purchased access to those lists a few years ago and so began the search for the telephone's location.

When he landed on the right carrier's list, he was startled at what he found.

"Oh my God," he said to his empty laboratory.

'*What does the U.S. Court System want with Hermione?*' Damian thought.

He rechecked the address, and it was indeed the address of the U.S. Courtroom on Golden Gate Avenue in San Francisco. What did a judge want with Hermione?

He decided he needed to know what all was included in that building. Were Hermione's parents being held there? Were the three of them wanted for the kidnapping they had done of a Malaysian national? What services were in that building that might possibly want Hermione and why had the search for her been undertaken in such an odd manner. Damian did a reverse look-up to see what services were located in the courthouse.

It was a surprisingly lengthy list of occupants besides the courts. The agencies included the IRS, the FBI, the US Attorney, Homeland Security, a collection of different courts and the U.S. Marshals Service. Better that it was the FBI or the IRS after Hermione than a judge. He thought the FBI would protect her, and the IRS would leave her alone as she was too young to pay taxes. Also, he'd been monitoring her family home and knew the property taxes were paid on it, so she wasn't at risk of losing her heritage.

He glanced at the time and noted he needed to leave soon to head across the bay to Ariana's house in Belvedere. He wrote a program to crunch the data on the phone's movements based on it pinging cell phone towers. That might give him some clues as to who had the phone in their possession. He fed the cats and then left in his speedy two-seater boat to travel the eight or so nautical miles to Ariana's dock.

He walked up to her house from the dock greeting Miguel, her Portuguese Water Dog along the way. They had time a for a ten-minute chat to strategize the poster and the upcoming conversation with Hermione. Damian left the original poster in his lab and brought a copy with him. After the soccer try-outs, they planned to have dinner at a pizza parlor which was Hermione's favorite place, and she'd likely be hungry after all the running of the try-out.

Ariana grabbed her stadium seats as they would sit in the bleachers on the football field and watch. They knew that Hermione would be tested on her speed, dribbling the ball in and out of cones, and accuracy kicks in the net. She would also get a few attempts to take the ball away from other players. As opposed to swimming and water polo, they both worried about 'headers' in soccer causing concussions, but they settled in with the hope that she'd make the team as it was her decision to try.

Ninety minutes later they had their answers. Hermione had made the team, but not in the position they expected. Likely due to her water polo experience she exhibited the best goalkeeper skills of anyone on the team. It was a position that alternated between boredom, when the ball was at the other end of the field, and terror when a ball was flying at the net that she needed to block. It was clear from the tryouts that she had the best hands to grab the ball out of the air.

"I'm thrilled that's her position. She'll have far less opportunity to do headers in that position," Ariana observed.

"She's cool under pressure, so she'll handle that part of the game well."

Hermione came over to the bleachers, sweaty and dirty from making a few leaps to the turf to block balls and said, "Give me fifteen minutes, and I'll meet you at the car."

Then she stopped and looked at the two of them and said, "What's up? You don't look like yourselves."

They should have expected her astuteness, she was fabulous at reading people. She'd make a great goalkeeper as she would read the opposing players well and guess with accuracy where they were going to kick the ball into the net.

"It's nothing major. We'll talk about it after you've had time to shower. We'll see you at the car," Ariana reassured her and after staring at her substitute parents for a few seconds Hermione turned and ran into the gym.

"That kid is too smart, sensitive, and athletic. I couldn't be prouder of her," Ariana said her voice wobbling.

"Yeah, she is special. She seems so normal and well adjusted given what she went through with her parents and seems able to trust us to always do the best for her. Before we both descend into crying talking about how super she is and embarrass ourselves and her in front of the other parents, let's retreat to the car."

Ten minutes later, her short dark hair wet, Hermione joined them at the car.

"Hey sweetie, I forgot to ask - how do you like playing the goalkeeper?" Ariana asked.

"I'm excited that I made the team and I had my heart set on being a forward. But during the try out I could see that I had the best skills to be the goalkeeper. It's not that I can jump higher than the others, I'm best at reading their minds and guessing which corner of the net they were aiming for which allowed me to get into position to block it. The more I've thought about the position, the more I like it. What happened today that has you two worried?" Hermione asked launching immediately into the problem.

Whoa, was Damian and Ariana's internal response, the kid sure could change directions quickly.

"I went to Pete's Bar for lunch today craving one of his cheeseburgers," Damian started to explain.

He saw Hermione relax slightly as she responded, "He does have the best cheeseburgers. I get that."

"I went back to his office with him to look at some pictures that he'd taken, and I saw this poster on his bulletin board," Damian said handing the poster to Hermione in the back seat. "That's a copy. The original is in my laboratory."

There was silence in the car as Hermione studied the poster and the two adults waited for her next question.

"That's a dated picture of me from two years ago that I had taken for school."

"Yes I figure that's where the picture came from. Interestingly Pete walked by the poster I don't know how many times and didn't recognize you."

"I've lost a little of the kid fat from my face, and my hair color and shorter style have disguised me which is good. So what else do you know about this poster Damian?"

Kudos to the kid for knowing that Damian would go to work immediately researching anything he could about the poster.

"I copied fingerprints off the poster, and one pair belongs to what I suspect are old neighbors of yours since they lived on the same street as you - the Stevensons?"

"Yes, they were our next-door neighbors, but they didn't have any kids my age. What else did you find?"

They had pulled up to the pizza parlor and Ariana said, "Do you want me to get take-out or do you want to finish the conversation inside?"

"It's a noisy place, so I think we're good talking inside and the pizza is better when it's fresh," Damian said.

They walked in and after placing their order grabbed a booth and Damian listened to the ambient noise and then leaned in to talk with Hermione and Ariana seated across from him.

"I looked up the number on the poster and it's one of those phones you buy at Walmart with an activation card. There's no record of who purchased it. I used another system to find that the phone was physically located at the US Courthouse in San Francisco around 2:30 this afternoon. It could have belonged to a visitor to the courthouse or one of about ten agencies with offices inside. Oh, and there's one fingerprint remaining to be identified that my system was still running when I left the island."

"What are the agencies in this courthouse?" Hermione asked.

"Justice Department has several services, FBI, US Marshals, Passport Agency, and Homeland Security."

Hermione was quiet for a few minutes as Damian and Ariana sipped their sodas and waited for her to ask questions.

"Do you think someone is doing this for my parents or do you think someone is trying to use me to bring my parents out of hiding?"

"Good questions sweetie, I don't know," Ariana replied.

"I'm going to watch the movement of the phone to see if that clues me into who has it."

"You can do that?" Hermione asked doubtfully.

"Yes, the phone pings a cell tower on a regular interval looking for a connection and I have access to that data."

"Do you think that Ariana and I are safe at home?"

That was a question he hadn't thought of yet, and so he took a moment to answer Hermione's question.

"Yes....I think you're safe. I don't think that poster was put up today. I'll look at how long the phone has been pinging and that might give us a clue. My last trip to Pete's was several months ago and I don't remember if I walked down that hallway. The original paper no longer looks crisp; my guess is the poster has been on that bulletin board for weeks to months. To me that says that whoever is seeking information about you has no idea where you are so I think you're safe."

"Ok."

With that, Hermione seemed ready to return to a discussion of soccer and Damian and Ariana obliged her.

CHAPTER 3

Damian's computer had continued churning away overnight and he'd arrived at his warehouse knowing that it needed more time to churn the large amount of data he was asking for. Lunch had arrived at the building and Natalie arrived early for a tour with Haley as to what she was doing in the lab. Some of her co-workers had taken great pleasure in showing off their inventions as well. Once the food delivery was made, Damian joined the group to fill a plate and motioned for Natalie to do likewise and follow him into his office when she had her plate full to her satisfaction.

She was seated at a side table in his office with her lunch to the side of a rather large paper file. In between bites she told the story. A mother after a long day at work, a five-year-old happily playing in a park, mom watching and smiling with occasional glances at a cell phone. One minute she was there and the next, Olivia Roth vanished into thin air.

"The police were on the scene in less than three minutes of the girl's disappearance. The FBI joined the case in under two hours. Despite multiple police agencies and this thick file, no clues were found to the girl's location. Fortunately, there have been no unidentified young females that have turned up dead in this region since her disappearance. So the best guess of law enforcement is she's still alive. I'm developing such a reputation for solving cold cases thanks to you, that the department asked me to look into this abduction to see if we could solve it. It's not a cold case, rather it's a case that everyone feels bad about and perhaps your data brain can come up with some new angles to search."

Damian looked at the binder and knew he needed to read some of it so he didn't waste his time going over already searched parameters. Still, he looked at the data like it was bomb filled with parental emotions that would spill all over him and he didn't want to see into that Pandora's box. He wasn't sure how the police organized their files in a case like this.

"I assume the parents were cleared as far as having a role in the abduction?"

"Yes, other than being hard working, they were by the department's assessment, great parents devastated by the disappearance of their only child."

"Only child?"

"Yes."

"Did their marriage survive the strain?"

"No. How did you guess?"

"I can think of only one thing worse than having your child abducted as a parent. I could see it easily destroying a marriage."

Damian had experienced that one worse thing - his two girls were murdered and he also lost his wife from the same gunman. She wondered if he had thought about what if his wife had survived or what if his wife died, but he still had the girls. It was a question Natalie would never ask.

"Is there a part of that thick file that contains a summary of the leads that all law enforcement chased? I don't need to read all the interviews except the one with the mother."

"This is a copy of the original file, so I can just pull those pieces out and hand them to you."

"What's your impression of the case from what you've read so far? I assume you've read that entire file."

"Yeah, I did. You can read the parental panic and devastation. There are lots of photos. There were no prints taken as it's a public park."

"Did the parents ever register the child with the SJPD wherein they collect fingerprints? I remember when my girls were young we did something like that. Do they still have those programs?" Damian asked.

"I don't recall reading about that, just a moment and I'll look it up. If there are prints on records, they should be on a certain sheet in this file," Natalie said as she searched for the specific sheet.

There was silence as Natalie searched, then the crunching of paper as she sought to open the file wider.

"Hmm this is weird. The family did have Olivia fingerprinted and there's a record that the SJPD provided that service to her elementary school, but the detectives could find no record of the prints."

"Did they give a copy of the prints to the parents at the time they did them?"

"I don't know, I'll ask the detective who researched that question," Natalie said as she wrote the question down. Typically, she got any law enforcement questions answered for Damian.

"Can we make an appointment later this week to visit the scene of the abduction? Sometimes seeing the location inspires questions for me," Damian requested.

"Sure, what day works for you?"

Damian consulted his calendar and offered, "How about Friday about ten? I don't have any reason to go to San Jose, so I'll take a boat to that marina in Redwood City, and you can meet me there," knowing that Natalie's house was about twenty miles from the marina. It wouldn't save him time, but it would save him the aggravation of traffic. Out on the bay in a boat was a far less congested way to travel.

"Do you have an age-adjusted picture of Olivia?"

"Yes," Natalie said as she handed him a picture.

"I'm going to run this picture through facial recognition cameras in San Jose. Is there any research on kidnapped children as far as the kidnappers staying in the area with the child? I'm wondering where we should look for the child? Does law enforcement believe this was a random snatch, or was she targeted? What's the data on child abduction?"

"Good questions Damian. There's a briefing from the FBI in here. They have the 'Child Abduction Response Deployment' or CARD unit that's designed to arrive on the scene within three hours of the abduction. They set up a command post, bring in behavioral analysis experts, map out all sex offenders in nearby areas. They use protocols based on past investigations, coordinate forensic resources, and use the Bureau's computers to assist."

Damian spared a moment's thought as to why a search team was never activated for Hermione. He supposed it was because no one declared her missing at the time which was why this poster was so weird at least a year after her disappearance.

"Most local law enforcement agencies will deal with only one abduction in a decade so the FBI's role is to bring experience to an investigation. In Olivia's case, they coordinated an interview of sex offenders within a five-mile radius by the next morning."

Damian felt his skin creep over the thought of a sex offender kidnapping a young child and asked, "How many people is that?"

Natalie browsed the file and said "Forty-one within a five-mile radius."

"I'm losing faith in my fellow man. I assume they are all men?"

Again Natalie glanced down at the file and said, "Yes."

"Is there a profile?"

"Yes, but it's not specific enough to narrow the field of possibilities. The FBI eliminated the possibility of a family member abduction and Olivia being a runaway. In time, they couldn't eliminate the possibility that Olivia was in a home nearby, as they don't have the right to search homes without probable cause and being a neighbor is not probable cause. Many abductors stay close by the child's home."

"Do you have any ideas of where we could use big data to locate the girl?"

"While I don't pretend to understand your computing capabilities, I was hoping you could tap into cameras across the United States to look for her. I also wondered if you had a source of satellite camera footage from five years ago."

"Let's start with San Jose cameras as that will be a multi-day undertaking and then we'll spread our search from there. As for satellite footage of five years ago, I'll have to look into that as I've never tried to do that before. This will be a challenge, but a highly rewarding one if we succeed," Damian said.

"Depending on what you do as far as a legitimate search, you might create a new protocol for law enforcement regarding abducted children and where to look."

Damian nodded, thinking about the case. The first case Natalie brought to him had been a murder from thirty years ago, and the second was a bank heist. A child abduction case was fraught with many more emotions. Damian's heart had been frozen in time when his wife and two girls were murdered. He'd thought about suicide at the time it happened, but something stopped him. During that deep depressive time, he'd found a new reason to go on and created a separate software system that monitored the release of inmates from California prisons to assure himself that no convicts were ever accidentally released as had happened in his family's case.

He tuned back into Natalie and noted that she'd pulled particular sections of the case file for him and was paper clipping each section, adding a sticky note for identification. She must have noticed that his brain had disappeared for a time, and quietly waited for him to return to the present while organizing the reports for him.

She was just finishing, when Damian said, "I'll begin work on it later today and let you know if I discover anything before we meet on Friday."

Natalie nodded and soon departed Damian's warehouse.

Damian sat for a moment overwhelmed with his workload for perhaps the first time since his family died. He was worried about the poster for Hermione, and he needed to do office work. After hearing some of Natalie's and the FBI facts on child abduction, he felt a sense of urgency to find Olivia, and that was a massive data manipulation, and his employees deserved his time on their various projects. Fortunately, Hermione didn't have any soccer games for a week, so he could stay on his island and work his computers every night and video call her. He'd have to check in with Ariana to see if she needed help getting Hermione to practices. She did the lion share of caring for Hermione, but he wanted to help where he could.

CHAPTER 4

*D*amian stayed in the office just long enough to check on his employees and see if any needed his help. His employees were all independent thinkers and were used to the weird hours that he would come and go. They also knew that he gave time to Hermione's various sports team activities. He returned to the harbor, untied his boat and was back on his island in no time.

First, he checked the runs he had going on searching for the owner of the phone number and that run was ready. The phone had been active for two months; it was put into service around Thanksgiving. The phone pinged around the San Francisco Bay Area for the past two months except for a few days in Lake Tahoe. The phone frequently pinged at the address of the Federal Court House in San Francisco, and an address in Oakland which he suspected was home for whoever possessed the phone. There were other visit sites including Pete's bar and Hermione's family home in Shepard Canyon. From there Damian studied the times of arrival to the building in San Francisco, and the holder of the phone was pretty regular in his or her arrival times in San Francisco. Damian thought about watching the staff come and go to the building and see if he could spot the phone carrier. He had a device that would detect cell phones in an area by their number. He studied the readout again and noted he could go over to the building on Thursday in the morning and watch for the phone number. He debated watching what he thought was the home address, but when he checked it out on Google Earth, he thought he'd be obviously out of place on the street. The person was most punctual on that day of the week. He went over to the shelves of his lab and pulled out a device that would do just that. He needed to be at the courthouse by eight-thirty that morning, so he evaluated how he would get there. BART could be unreliable during rush hour and so he decided to take his speedboat over to the St. Francis Yacht Club, and then a taxi from there. He sat back and couldn't think of anything more he could do with the Hermione poster. It was time to move on to Olivia and see what he could do to reunite the little girl with her parents.

He started by reading the notes that Natalie had left with him. Then he moved on to looking for satellite images. He thought it highly unlikely that anyone kept images for that length of time, but who knew? Maybe spy agencies held on to old images, or maybe there was something near this park that was worth keeping pictures of. He also looked for cameras within a two-mile radius of the park. Perhaps he could find the girl on camera going in a particular direction. Damian researched the pricing and terms of a few satellite companies, then went to work on some cameras that were operational on the day of the abduction. Some city cameras had been in place for ten years he noted from the website. He also checked redlight cameras, used by some cities to generate revenue for running red-lights, but there had never been any in San Jose.

Damian then compiled a list of where surveillance cameras were commonly located in the United States and which of those locations catered to children. He added Burger Chef restaurants, the airport, Fantasialand, and a home security doorbell camera to the list. He planned to get footage out of all of these systems to look for Olivia. Then he paused a moment and questioned his actions. It would be better if he had permission to view the video rather than silently slipping in and accessing these company camera locations. Sometimes, Natalie couldn't use the evidence.

He went to a company directory to find the person he thought might help him. He recognized the name of someone that worked there and decided to see if he could gain his help. The contact knew him well enough that he might do him a favor and so he entered a phone number and listened to it ring.

"Hello?"

Damian was pleased he actually got through.

"Hey Mark, it's Damian Green. How are you?" Damian wasn't one for polite conversation, but he wanted to give Mark a chance to remember who he was.

"Hey Damian, it's been a while. Are you still the computer genius I worked with ten years ago?"

Damian let out a laugh, and said, "I am. I operate a small company with genius workers that are producing products to save the world."

"Yep, that sounds like you. What's up? You're not one to call and reminisce."

"I was hoping for a favor. I assist a retired detective with the San Jose Police Department with cold cases."

"Hmmm, that's a new image of you – walking around with a magnifying glass like Sherlock Holmes."

"Yeah, but that's not what I do. I just help on a technical basis with data."

"Ah, so you want some data from my computers. What do you need?" Mark asked. "Of course with your skills, you might have already been through my computer systems."

"My detective is working on a case from five years ago - a child abduction of a five-year-old girl. It was my idea to use facial recognition software to look for her at child-friendly locations like your amusement park. I also have a couple of fast food companies in mind that cater to children. I'm hoping she's spent the interim five years since she was abducted with a nice parent who has taken her to play rather than a sexual predator who's abused her."

"There's an ugly thought, let me see what I can do to help. It's my job to protect our guests and our company. I need to talk with our attorneys to see if there are any legal issues with us giving access to you for a noble purpose."

"Mark, I appreciate that and have an alternative, I'd be willing to send you the girl's age projected picture and my facial recognition software. You can run the picture yourself without giving me access to your data."

"Were you thinking of our Anaheim location or all of our locations worldwide? There are six parks."

"Wow, I didn't know that. I was thinking of only your California location as the FBI has a child abduction profile that says the majority of abducted kids are close-by their homes, so I wasn't going to search outside of California at the start."

"If we do this for you, we'll have to do it for all of law enforcement. So we will either have a reputation with parents as spying on their kids, or being wonderful for re-uniting stolen kids. Is there a way we can keep this out of the press? Maybe it's easier if you hack my systems which I know you're capable of doing. That way we look uncooperative."

"I see your point. How about if I give you the tools and you do a search. If it comes back positive then you and I can put our heads together to find another source of identification and leave your park out of it."

"I like that idea Damian, but if I came back with positive identification, I couldn't go back and erase the search. I have a boy of ten, and I would want my company to cooperate to return him to Vanessa and me. I think I'll still pass it by our attorneys. I have a good relationship with one of them and I think they'll try to work out a solution for both of us."

"That's all I can ask, Mark. Thank you. Would you like the picture and/or the software now?"

"That's a separate intriguing discussion. We should have that on our system for other corporate purposes. Do you sell your software?"

"I haven't, but I could. Because of the power of facial recognition, I didn't build it for enterprise-wide use. It would be something that you would want on only one or two desktops in your company, to prevent its misuse."

"Okay, I'll keep that in mind. I'll contact the attorney and we should be able to get an answer soon for you. I know you're wanting to ask how soon, but I have no guarantees and I'll keep you updated on a timeline."

"Thanks, Mark and here's my number," Damian added just before ending the call.

Damian spent a moment thinking about Mark's question of searching every amusement park or just the location in California. If they got no leads from this initial search for places in Northern California, then you would have to think about all of the state and all of America. Searching the world for Olivia Roth was a data nightmare he didn't want to think about. There was also the other problem of everyone having a genetic twin somewhere in the world. How many false-positives would his system find as they were using a computer-generated age-adjusted picture? Or there was the worst scenario, the child was dead and his search would never bear fruit.

Damian's perimeter alarms went off and he was dragged back into the present by the sound. Changing screens, he switched to his security system to see what had triggered the alarm. He'd had no unexpected human visitors in over a year. Whales and dolphins were programmed not to set off the alarms. He had water cannons in the cliffs of his island and in addition to that, he could use a high-powered water gun that dispensed pepper juice, and he had a drone that could drop purple smoke bombs and green-staining water balloons on an intruder. Usually, people obeyed his private property signs and stayed off the island, but he observed a single man coasting a small boat to his island, a larger boat anchored a safe distance away.

It didn't look like his boat was in any kind of distress, so what was the man's intention? He was Caucasian, 25-45, average height and build, wearing jeans, sneakers, and a jacket. He saw no weapons, although the man could have a knife or small gun sheathed around his ankle. The man was touching the screen on his phone, likely wondering what happened to his cellular reception. Damian kept a jamming system on to block cell phone usage within fifty yards or so of the island. Damian waited for the man to look up so he could capture his image on one of the island cameras. He watched and snapped a few shots at the perfect time. He then ran it through his facial recognition software and he soon heard a sound signifying a match.

The man's name was John O'Ryan and was a resident of New York. Damian's first thought was that his visitor got lost in the bay and then some alarming information popped up on his search screen and he picked up his cell phone to call Ariana.

CHAPTER 5

"Ariana, it's me Damian, but of course you know that."

"What's wrong, you're usually not flustered on the phone. Did something happen with the people looking for Hermione?"

"No... no.. it's you Ariana. I just had a man land on my island by the name of John O'Ryan. When I looked him up, I saw that you had a temporary restraining order issued against him a decade ago."

"What's he doing on your island? Did you blast him with your water cannons?"

"No, I am waiting to see what he is up to. Tell me why you got a TRO against this man while I watch his progress on my cameras."

"Before I met my husband, I went on a variety of dull dates and he was one of them. I had a habit of meeting people in a coffee shop for coffee or tea to get to know them. I knew within three minutes of meeting John that I was not interested in dating him. He was weird and had an intense focus on me. As soon as I could, I left the coffee shop and returned home. Fortunately, at the time I had a roommate as he followed me about thirty minutes later. He tried to force his way into the apartment and he professed his love for me. My roommate was on the phone to the police the moment she heard the knock and she stayed on the line with the dispatcher while I held John off with a kitchen knife."

"I was granted a TRO as soon as I requested it. When he threatened me, the police arrived and arrested him. What's he up to now?"

"He's hiking the cliff. I think I'll let him approach the house. The cats are inside and safe. I want to see what he does. I've loaded a water balloon with my green dye, and so I'll stain him as he leaves walking down the cliff. There's no reason to make a mess on my front doorstep, and his eyes will be focused on his footing."

"John O'Ryan is a bad man. Be careful. After the TRO was issued by the court, he threatened my roommate, sent me flowers, and unbeknownst to me, dropped a GPS tracker in my purse during our first and only meeting. So he knew where I worked, where I did grocery shopping, he joined my gym. It was awful."

"The nerve of the man! He knocked on my front door and when I didn't answer, he pulled out a lock pick kit."

"Be careful Damian, he's a really evil man."

"Don't worry about me. He'll shortly realize that there is no lock in the door."

"There isn't?"

"No, I use an electronic pass key. Okay, now the man is downright rude; he gave up on my door and is sitting down on one of my patio chairs to check his email."

"He won't get far doing that as you have his signal blocked, right?"

"Right, I'm tempted to blast him with the water cannons and drop green dye on him. It'll be a cold ride back to where ever he came from. I like the idea that I'll spot him sooner with that dye if I should see him in Richmond or Belvedere."

"I wonder how he found your island?" Ariana asked.

"I don't know, but as soon as I leave, I'm going to search my boats for trackers. I'm also going to find out where's he's been for the past decade and what he's doing in our neck of the woods. Ah, I think he's giving up and he's starting down the cliff. I've got my drone locked and loaded to dump on him after the water cannons finish."

There was silence on the phone and then she heard him say, "Take that you scumbag!"

"What's happening?"

"The water cannon knocked him down on the sand and as he lay face-up, I dropped two green dye balloons on him. He's just laying on the sand and hasn't realized that he's covered head to toe in bright green dye and my drone is safely back behind cover so he won't even know where the dye came from. He'll probably think it came from the cannon."

"Is he still laying on the sand? Maybe you should call the police," Ariana suggested.

"No it will take them too long to get here and besides I added something new to the dye. I've been experimenting with some-thing at the warehouse. I inserted tiny particles into the dye. Those particles have different optical properties meaning they absorb light differently and that makes them traceable. So now the dye he's wearing will glow in the dark and it will allow me to track John O'Ryan."

"Damian, you're so brilliant! What are you going to use that for commercially?"

"I'd plan to sell it to the shipping industry so companies could know where their boxes were, but the problem with that idea is that I'd need to make a new dye formulation for each package. Now that I'm working on an old case with Natalie on a child abduction, I'm thinking that it would be good to sell it to parents so they would know they could always find their children. I'd do a tattoo of some sort that would expire every five years or so. Beyond a certain age, the child wouldn't be tracked. It was just something I thought of in the last few days after reading about the two-thousand kids that go missing each day."

"Has he got up and left your island?"

"Yeah, he tried washing the dye off in the bay water, and ended up smearing over more of his body," Damian said with laughter in his voice. "He's shivering and huddling behind the windscreen on the boat as he heads toward San Francisco."

"Good. I didn't know you were working on a child abduction. How old was the child abducted?"

"Five, and Natalie called me about the case just as I was researching Hermione's poster. I had a few seconds of panic when she began describing the abduction thinking it was going to be Hermione, but then when she got to the age and the fact it was in San Jose, my heart rate settled down."

"I can imagine. I think I'm going to talk with the police here about John O'Ryan. Perhaps they can get a read on what he's been up to and how I should protect myself."

"I think that's a good idea. I'll share some video from my system that you can share with the police so they know what to be on the look-out for."

"Is anything that you did illegal?" Ariana asked.

"I don't think so. John's not injured and he violated my private property despite the warning signs. Mostly outside of your presence, I think they'll be amused to know they're looking for a lime-green man. Imagine that "be on the lookout" for notice."

Ariana laughed, "Thanks for helping me look at this situation with humor."

"You do have your alarm system engaged? Perhaps you should move over to the island tonight."

"I do have a good alarm system. Why don't you come here and we can take your evidence with us to the police tonight? Hermione is in school, then soccer practice for another ninety minutes or so. If you come immediately, that gives us an hour to speak with the police. I'll call them now to warn them we're coming in to make a report."

"Okay, I need to gather some equipment and download my security videos and perhaps I'll bring a sample of the green slime."

"Are you tracking John now?"

"No, it takes a special device and I have to grab it off the shelf. He hasn't come back towards my island, that's all I know. Once I get my boat headed toward your dock, I'll turn it on to see what he's up to."

"Damian, thanks and stay safe. See you soon."

Ten minutes later, he had all the equipment packed and in his speedster, he aimed his boat at Ariana's dock, then spent some time tracking John O'Ryan. He looked like he was steering straight at Angel Island, which meant he was likely heading to the harbor at Sausalito. Good, that put him closer to the Belvedere Police. At some point, his tracking system would have two targets as surely some of the green slime would roll off his clothing and skin and onto the boat, but he'd be able to distinguish the two signals as the boat would likely remain parked for a while. Minutes later he was at Ariana's house dropping his overnight bag and some equipment, and they were off to the police station to make a report.

CHAPTER 6

*A*riana and Damian arrived at Hermione's school a few minutes late and found her sitting on the wall next to the three arches that marked the entrance to her school. When she saw both of them in the car, she walked to the back seat door and opened saying, "What's up?"

"Can't we both pick you up from school on occasion?" Damian said.

"You don't usually do that. Is there a problem with that poster about me?"

"No, sweetie you're in the clear on this one. I had a single date with a man about ten years ago. He stalked me and ended up doing time in prison. He just tried to break into Damian's house, so he's staying the night while we figure out what to do."

"Why did you go out on a date with such a bad person?" Hermione asked.

"Because I didn't know he was such a creep. This was before I met my husband and I was using a website to find someone I might like. We had one meeting at a coffee shop and I knew within five minutes that I didn't like the guy, and so I cut the meeting short and walked away. Except he followed and the stalking began until he was arrested. Let that be a lesson to you someday if you use such a service."

"What did you do to him Damian? Did you blast him with your water cannon?" Hermione asked remembering the time she'd operated the cannon to keep some prison gang members from reaching Damian's house.

Damian grinned and said, "I did as he was leaving, then while he was face-up on the beach, I dropped a water balloon with green slime on him. I've improved the slime so that it contains micro-crystals that can be used for GPS. The Belvedere police are tracking him now. He parked the boat at the Sausalito marina, and if he approaches Ariana, he'll be arrested."

"You should lecture in my science class. Your stuff is so much more interesting than what they're trying to teach us in those textbooks."

Damian's heart warmed at the thought of Hermione wanting him at her school, but he said to her, "I don't think your teachers would appreciate me teaching hundreds of kids how to make green slime that they can use to track each other. I'd probably go to jail for morally corrupting youth."

"Yeah, you probably would," Hermione said with a sigh. "So what's our plan to defend Ariana?"

"Speaking of morally corrupting youth, we're not expecting you to stand in front of us with a wand casting a spell against my stalker. It's more an added layer of awareness about him since you're close to me, John will be threatened by you; that's how stalkers are," Ariana said.

"I hope the police arrest him soon, and this will be a non-issue," Damian said.

"How long does your green slime work?" Hermione asked.

"The dye stains about a month and I'm not sure about the micro-crystals. This is an experiment for me."

"Any guess as to how long it will last?" Ariana asked.

"The dye stains the skin layer and so you have to wait for the skin to slough off for the color to fade. The microcrystals aren't part of the skin so they could disappear as soon as the guy takes a shower I suppose. I really don't know how the crystals will interact with human skin. The good news is that the dye is on his face and hands so he'll have to wear make-up or a ski mask to hide the color."

"Do you have a second device to track him or do only the police have the tracker," Hermione asked.

"I have a tracker and he's on the other side of the Bay at the moment."

"How did he find your house?" Hermione asked.

"I don't know. I was going to search my boats for trackers, but I was in a hurry to get over here, so I didn't search any of them."

"Can you check the boat at Ariana's dock now?"

"Yeah I will," Damian said as Ariana pulled into her garage. Once they entered her house, he sorted through his duffle bag looking for his bug detector. Hermione followed him outside to watch.

"How does that work?" she asked playing fetch with Miguel while watching Damian.

"I left my cell phone inside the house because it would interfere. I turn off and unplug the sonar I use for this boat. Then this detector seeks out radio-frequency waves and the closer it gets to a source, the more it beeps. Here you use the detector, after I unplug the sonar," Damian said handing her a device about the size of a large cell phone, but thicker.

Damian unplugged all of the gadgets on his boat and took out their batteries. Then watched Hermione as she turned on the tracker and began searching the boat. He called out to her, "If you find something don't touch it as I might be able to get a fingerprint off of it. I'll just pry it off and drop it into a baggie."

She nodded and followed the beeping to a storage box under the seat. She picked up the cushion and opened the lid. She took out the life-preservers that Damian stored there and found a metal transmitter underneath. She pointed it out to Damian and said, "Want me to run in and get some salad tongs to pick it up with?"

"Good idea!"

Hermione came back with the specified kitchen item and picked up the metal device and dropped it into a baggie that Damian was holding out and asked, "Is it still transmitting now?"

"Should be. We'll cover it in a few layers of aluminum foil once we get inside. Whoever owns this tracker will have it's last known location, but after I'm done looking at it, I'll take it with me to a meeting in San Francisco or Redwood City this week and leave it there."

"This is pretty cool stuff. Can I get a job with your company this summer? I like this science stuff you do."

Damian had a flood of emotion hit him with Hermione's question. Pride, humility, awe, love, and pleasure. Swallowing he said, "Sure we'll work something out. We have to get you a boat safety class so you can commute to either my island or the Richmond Marina. Ariana and I will teach you and make sure we feel safe having you cross the Bay on your own."

She rolled her eyes at this, but Damian just smiled knowing they were back on normal footing despite the stresses of John O'Ryan and her poster. It was all he could wish for as a parent at the moment.

Ariana was working on dinner and smiled at the last words she heard after they came through the door into her house and added, "The Bay is huge with lots of traffic at times, we don't want you plowed under by a ferry. You can be pulled over by the Coast Guard and asked to produce identification that proves you are sixteen. Then you'll have to get from the marina to the warehouse. You turn sixteen in May so you may have your driver's license to get from the marina to the warehouse, but then you'll need a car. So I think that if Damian doesn't give you a ride to work, that you'll need to take a car service as I can't see buying you a car to leave at the marina. We'll have to talk about the whole car thing as we get closer to your birthday. Lots to figure out."

Hermione nodded with excitement and then asked, "How soon before dinner? I've got loads of homework tonight. I hate the start of each quarter as the teachers seem to pile on the work at the beginning."

"About thirty minutes," Ariana replied and smiled as she watched the teenager heft her backpack and head to her room.

Damian smiled at her departure and gave a brief thought as to how comfortable he was in Ariana's home with these two women. He wouldn't call himself a lucky man given his history, but he was a content and happy man.

"I'm going to go check your security system and I might add some motion sensors to your dock. There's a tracker in my boat and the only way it could have gotten there is if John O'Ryan was in his boat and dropped it my boat while it was parked at your dock, so I'm going to study your dock for ideas of how to prevent that in the future."

"Maybe once John is captured by the police, our lives will be calm again."

"Perhaps, but I haven't figured out Hermione's poster yet."

"OMG! In my fear over John O'Ryan, I forgot about Hermione's poster. What did you find on that today?"

"Not much, but I want to take a look around your land while I have daylight. I'll tell you about it when I return."

Gathering a few tools and with Miguel at his heels, he went back outside to look at the security system he'd modified a year ago when someone had been trying to kidnap Hermione. He felt like it would do its job to protect the women inside, but he wanted to check that all points were working and look at her dock. Then he thought again about the system and wondered how her stalker had known to take a boat to Ariana's dock to track any visitors rather than be caught by her security. He promised himself he would check the history on her system when he returned to the house.

Minutes later Ariana was opening the software screen on her computer.

"I was here on Monday of this week and Monday and Thursday of last week, so John O'Ryan had to have seen the boat one of those days and acquired his own boat on one of those days. Let's ask your system to show you all disturbances in the past week. You have it on all the time, right?"

"Ah, ….no. I usually only turn it on before I go to bed," Ariana admitted.

Damian wasn't that surprised. Hermione had not been threatened for several months and the man that had caused problems was permanently out of the country. Ariana tended toward the reckless side, so he could see her getting lax with her alarms.

"Not to scare you, but this John fellow could have been waiting inside your house. In fact, he might have searched your clothes and stuff."

Ariana shuddered at that thought and watched Damian run a report looking for motion on Ariana's property. She added an alarm to her phone to check that the security system was on. The first fifteen or so movements that Damian viewed were Ariana leaving or arriving home, or a delivery man. There was the odd animal that set it off – a squirrel running across her property, then finally he landed on a picture of John O'Ryan knocking on Ariana's front door. The intruder waited to see if anyone opened the front door then he pulled out the same pick set that he had at Damian's house and proceeded to let himself in.

Ariana let out a quiet string of expletives upon watching him enter her house and search it.

"I'm going to copy this activity and forward it to the police. I think that between the video of my house and yours that they have more than enough grounds to arrest him as well as seek the help of other police jurisdictions to capture him. Where was Miguel? I'm surprised he didn't greet Mr. O'Ryan."

Ariana was mortified watching John search her drawers and closets and even sniff the pillows on her bed.

"I had taken him to the groomer that day, thankfully. After dinner, I'm heading out to the store to buy new pillows. I can't sleep on those tonight. I swear I'll use that alarm system diligently from now on just to keep perverts like John O'Ryan out of my house. I've seen enough, you can keep watching while I finish making dinner," Ariana said in an angry voice that Damian had never heard from her.

He paused the video while watching her actions in her kitchen, then looked back down and hit play. It was probably a good thing she'd stopped watching as he was curious about what the intruder would do with Hermione's room. If Ariana was livid over watching the man in her bedroom, Damian knew she'd blow a gasket if she saw John in Hermione's room. As he predicted, John entered Hermione's room. He uttered an expletive under his breath as he watched the man take a small picture frame containing the photo of the three of them taken at Emirates Stadium in London where they'd watched Arsenal play soccer. John O'Ryan pulled out his cell phone and took a picture of the picture frame. He sped up the video after this now intent on finding out if there were any other visits and there were not. Checking the date and time of the man's visit, Damian noted he'd been here at Ariana's house while they were at Hermione's soccer try-outs. It was also when John dropped the tracker in Damian's boat. So, John had seen the boat return to the island and to the Richmond marina. He saved the footage and forwarded it to the Belvedere police and dialed the number of the officer that had taken their report.

"This is Officer Christopher Woodrow."

"Hi Officer Woodrow, this is Damian Green. I just forwarded

you video footage of John O'Ryan breaking into Ariana Knowles house. Have your officers made an arrest yet?"

"Not yet. Your green slime substance has sloughed off everywhere. The man used the outdoor shower at the marina and the men's bathroom to change into clean clothes. The address he gave the harbormaster for the boat rental belonged to a hotel and he was not a registered guest. We followed the signal to a second hotel where he showered and changed clothes and packed his belongings. With each washing, the signal has been weakening. Our latest tracking has him entering Muir Woods National Park. As you can see it's getting dark and the heavy tree cover is further distorting the signal. There is no camping inside the park, but he could be going through the park to the beach or just be planning on staying hidden."

"I know the green dye color will stain him for about a month, but I've no experience with the GPS micro-crystals and it sounds like since they don't adhere to the dermis layer of his skin, that my signal may end with his next shower. I think it's supposed to rain tonight and that will rinse away whatever he's sloughing off, although I think it's too cold to stand out in the rain and let that cleanse the dye off his skin. He placed a tracker on my boat and followed the GPS signal to my home so he may be aware that he's emitting a signal himself with the technology he has."

"Sausalito PD has a canine dog that we'll use in the morning, the woods are too dense and the weather is too lousy for a search in the dark," replied Officer Woodrow. "Unless he leaves the woods and shows up at your house tonight, I don't think we'll have any new news overnight."

Damian relayed the information to Ariana as he set the table for dinner. Once the three of them were eating, he told Hermione of his plans to visit San Francisco in the morning to find the owner of the cell phone.

CHAPTER 7

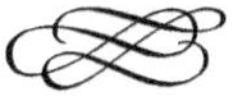

*D*amian dropped Hermione off at school the next day after a quiet night. He set out in his boat for the marina in San Francisco where he intended to dock his boat while he observed the court building for the holder of the cell phone.

He was fortunate that the weather was good with no drizzle as he would have been suspicious sitting in the rain. He had the GPS detector next to him on the planter box wall with earbuds on to detect whenever it made contact with a passing cellphone. Each time it beeped he would glance down at the display inside a bag to read the cell phone number that was displayed. Meanwhile, he practiced taking photos of the San Francisco City Hall which was a beautiful building in the background. He must have shot fifty practice photos before he got the beep from his device that matched the phone number he was looking for. This time his photo captured a man in a business suit walking into the court building. As it was a cloudy day, he wasn't wearing sunglasses and Damian got a perfect picture of his face.

His work done, he caught a taxi back to the marina and to his boat. In his lab, he ran the man's picture through his facial recognition system and discovered his name, James Spinnaker. Further research revealed him as an employee of Homeland Security, married with children living in Oakland. Damian took another look at the phone's pinging schedule and decided he would take a chance on approaching Mr. Spinnaker that afternoon to confront him about the poster. He could then circle back and assure himself that Hermione and Ariana were safe with John O'Ryan on the loose. In the meantime, he'd head over to his company and get some work done. Hermione's request to work there over the summer had him thinking about another employee of his – Lily and her son Jacob, who was thirteen going on forty.

He arrived just before lunch and sat down with his employees for a casual discussion.

After hearing the news of the day, he said, "Hermione asked if she could have a summer job here and it got me thinking about other kids. Lily, your son is too young to work for pay just yet, but if he's interested and if he turns fourteen by the summer, he could get a work permit to work here. I'd like to encourage future engineering brains. What would all of you think about having a teenager or two to assist you with your projects?"

"I'd love to have him work here," Lily replied. "He turns fourteen just before school lets out for the summer, so we'll apply for a work permit. I think kids could be useful in having us add features to our projects to make them more commercially appealing."

"So what would you have Jacob do here?" Damian asked.

"He could help me with testing my drone," replied Haley. "I have to do a lot of repetitive maneuvers either to fine-tune something or to test it as a solution. I'd love to have Hermione or Jacob take that load and do the testing for me."

"Are they safe? Could they get hurt here?" Damian asked.

Angus Walsh, his ex-con and logistics expert replied, "I think we have enough protective equipment to keep them safe. Haley crashes her drone, but we have the glass wall shield upstairs and that would protect a teenager. Of course, they could crash the drone into themselves or do some other equally stupid thing so we would want to choose the teenagers carefully, but I would enjoy encouraging some kid to go into engineering because of their work here. I think we should start with Hermione and Jacob as both kids seem level-headed and we can expand into other kids if it's a win-win for all of us."

"You're calling Jacob level-headed?" Lily asked with a laugh. "Look at these worry lines in my face."

"What mother doesn't worry?" Angus replied.

"Okay, I'll have Ariana begin getting the paperwork together so we can employ these kids and set up an appropriate wage for them. They can't work full time, and we'll have to figure out how to work them into our flow, but I'm excited about having them here."

"Damian, it's good to start small, but when you're ready, I have a ready-made source of new teenagers through my contact with probation groups. There are a lot of kids that would benefit by working here, and then there are hustlers in that group that I wouldn't let in the door of the warehouse."

"I appreciate your source and your honesty. When we're ready to expand, we'll need to pick your brain to develop our application process, but first let's have a positive experience with Hermione and Jacob.," Damian said and then signaling that it was time to change the topic asked, "What else is going on?"

After hearing about everyone's progress, he said, "I have a new project for someone. I had an intruder invade my island and I dropped a green dye water balloon on him. I've figured out how to make that dye stain for close to a month. I added something new to this balloon, a liquid filled with micro-crystals that act as a GPS tracker. We've learned the micro-crystals don't adhere to the skin, because the police and I have been tracking him and we've lost the signal. I'd like to develop a solution that will adhere for say five years and sell it to parents who want to use it to tag their children."

Damian noticed a variety of expressions on his employees' faces and so added further explanation.

"I'm working with a retired detective and Haley's mother-in-law, Detective Natalie Severino on a child abduction case. That's why she was here the other day. In looking at the grief these parents must be experiencing over the abduction of their five-year-old daughter, I thought this might be a solution for parents. I want an expiration on it as perhaps when a child reaches the age of fifteen or eighteen, the child would be beyond an age of abduction."

"I love that idea!" Lily said. "You need a compound similar to rhodium that decays in something like three years and then you just need to have it stick to the skin."

Lily had been looking at the ceiling thinking about the problem and returned her gaze to her colleagues, once she noticed the silence in the room.

"What!" she asked when looking at the expressions on their faces.

"How do you know about rhodium?" Damian asked.

"Oh, I was helping Jacob with the periodic table earlier this week and understanding the decaying of elements."

"You're one smart cookie!" Angus said.

"Thanks, I'd like to work on that project, but I also see problems if there's a substance that you can apply to someone to track their movements," Lily said.

"For the most part, all of us are tracked now because of our cell phones pinging off cell towers. Did you ever wonder where those morning traffic reports come from? The telephone company supplies data that shows how fast their company's cell phones are moving through a particular area from their phone's GPS pinging," Damian said. "I hear you though. It could be used by adults in a spat with one another. I think we would have to have it licensed to an organization like the FBI or the Missing and Exploited Children Foundation, for the substance to be applied.

That way it doesn't get abused. Let's find something that works, stays, and doesn't poison a child with radioactivity first, then we'll worry about its distribution."

Damian left his company planning to run back across the bay to catch James Spinnaker leaving work. If he changed his schedule and wasn't at the building, Damian would try again the next day. He felt an urgency to confront this man, but at the same time balanced that against the fact that the phone had been active for two months. He'd thought about checking his island lab computer to track the phone, but the man could leave his office just minutes after Damian checked his latest location. After spending an extra hour beyond Mr. Spinnaker's usual departure time, he gave up and returned to his boat heading over to Ariana's house.

"How was soccer practice?" Damian asked as soon as Ariana returned home with Hermione. He'd been sitting on the outside deck sipping tea and working his laptop awaiting their arrival. He and Miguel had been playing fetch, but now the dog was sitting down panting.

Hermione was wearing long sleeves and elbow padding and her knees were grass stained, "Let me take a shower, and I'll come back out and tell you."

Ariana came outside with her own cup of tea and said "She had a hard practice diving to the ground a lot today. They were practicing penalty shoot-outs. She's wearing her fair share of the turf from the high school pitch."

"She'll be sore tomorrow," Damian said. "We need to pour lots of fluid and some spinach down her throat."

"Spinach?"

"It will help with the bruising as will vitamin C."

"Okay, but I remember the bruises she got from water polo and I think she's just someone who bruises easily. Mostly I think she's satisfied with her performance. She could accurately predict which direction the kicker was going to try and kick it, but she can't cover the entire net, and in a few cases, the kicker didn't have enough control of the ball and went to a different place, than where the girl's brain was aiming."

"Not surprising at their age. Hey, while we're waiting for Hermione, I want you to work on a new project for the company. I want to set up a formal program for kids in high school to contribute to my company. We'll perfect the program with Hermione and Lily's son, Jacob, this summer and roll out a full program the following summer. We have to get permission from the state to employ kids, we'll need to set a wage, and find a way for them to contribute as well as learn. I feel almost as excited about this project as I do one of my inventions."

"That sounds wonderful and I'll put together a package for you! I have some ideas of where we could source kids to work for you. If it works, I'd also like to expand it to some of the start-ups I influence," Ariana said. She was a venture capitalist when she wasn't caring for Hermione or being the Chief Operating Officer of Damian's company. Fortunately, she liked the regulatory part of the business.

Hermione came through the glass doors and joined them asking, "Did you guys solve world peace while I showered?"

Ariana snorted and Damian replied, "We're a good team, but even Ariana and I cannot herd cats. How's soccer going?"

Hermione sighed sitting down to pet Miguel and said, "I wish I was taller so I had a greater reach. It's frustrating to know where the ball is heading and know I can't get to the edge of the net to block the ball. At least I practiced falling sideways to get more familiar with how to land and quickly pop up to block the next shot."

"How are they transitioning you to doing the same on the turf?" Ariana asked.

"They already did that. The school brought in an ex-goal-keeper from the San Jose Earthquakes and he taught me how to dive for balls on the mats and then we went outside and practiced the same thing on the turf. He was wonderful. So what else is going on? Do you know who put the poster up about me? Do you know where Ariana's stalker is?"

And there it was; that quick change of conversational topics that Hermione was famous for.

"We haven't had an update on the stalker, but it appears his GPS micro-crystals have worn off. All of the local police agencies are looking for him. The two of you are doing a good job keeping the security system on. I'll stay overnight until the man's caught."

"And my missing person poster?"

"The man who has the phone listed on the poster is James Spinnaker and he works for Homeland Security. I returned to the courthouse this afternoon, but I must have missed him. I'm going to approach him tomorrow morning."

"What are you going to say?" Hermione asked.

"I thought I'd start by calling him by name and say that I saw the poster about Hermione and traced it to him and I want to know why Homeland Security is looking for you."

"What do you think his answer will be?"

"I don't know. I'm hoping I knock Mr. Spinnaker off balance by approaching him in person rather than calling."

"If he says he knows where my parents are, what will you do?"

"I'll ask him to arrange a video call with them. If all goes well with the call, then I'll make arrangements for you to meet them," Damian said.

"Do you think that will happen? Do you think I'll be reunited with Mom and Dad?"

"I have no idea honey. I'm puzzled with why Homeland Security would have anything to do with your parents. Of all the agencies of the Federal Government, this would not make my top five list for contact with your parents as they're American Citizens."

"Okay, let me know what he says tomorrow."

"Will do, kiddo. What are your thoughts about this man and

the idea that he works for Homeland Security?" Damian asked trying to get some insight into what the teenager was thinking.

"We discussed departments of the Federal government in one of my classes and I remember thinking at the time that beyond the quiz, I'd forget about each of them until they impacted me. So if you say that finding my parents is not a part of Homeland Security than I'd have to agree with you and so why's this guy got a poster of me in Pete's Bar? Did you look anywhere else close to my hometown to see if there was a posting? I wonder if my parents' neighbors saw it in Pete's Bar or some other location in Oakland? If it's only in Pete's Bar than he knows something about you."

Damian was impressed with the girl's reasoning and said, "Forget being an engineer when you graduate college, you need to be a private investigator. Those are some excellent questions and you pose things I haven't thought of. This weekend, maybe I'll visit a few places in your neighborhood to see if I can find the poster elsewhere."

"Just trying to live up to my namesake – Hermione Granger; she and Harry would have investigated every angle."

Damian couldn't stop himself from leaning forward and hugging the girl as he said, "You do her proud."

Ariana watched the mush come into Damian and sought to rescue him from the wave of emotion she could tell was hitting him. She had moments like this every day in the wonderment of caring for this unique child.

"Dinner's ready, let's go inside and eat."

Much later, they settled into sleep in their respective bedrooms. Ariana was a light sleeper and awoke to a sound outside. She peeped out her curtains and gasped at lights staring back at her. She ran over to Damian's bedroom and shook him awake.

"There's something outside my bedroom window," she whispered when she knew he was awake.

He followed her into her bedroom, and he could hear the sound she was talking about, and he thought he knew what it was.

"Just a moment," Damian said as he returned to his bedroom to look for the tools he brought with him for his stay at Ariana's house.

He pulled out a high power water gun and asked Ariana to retrieve some honey from her kitchen. She was back in under a minute with a bottle of honey. Damian loaded it into the soap canister of the gun and then went to her bathroom window. He took the screen off the window and aimed and fired at the drone's propellers, while it hovered outside her window.

The thickness and stickiness of the honey soon gummed up propellers, and the drone started to fly unevenly. He watched the machine start to swoop like a drunk helicopter. He saw it lift over the house after a few attempts and it spun and dived lacking any motion precision. Honey wasn't meant to oil machinery. Damian smiled as he saw it falter and crash into the water just beyond Ariana's dock.

They hadn't turned the lights on not wanting to wake Hermione nor give the camera on the drone more light to see into the house with.

Looking at Ariana he whispered, "Unless I'm mistaken, your stalker's drone is forever dead at the bottom of the bay."

Ariana held up a hand, and they tapped lightly over a high-five and whispered, "That was brilliant! I thought you were going to shoot it with pepper juice, but honey makes so much more sense. Let's hope that was the only drone John O'Ryan owns. Thanks! Let's get back to sleep now."

She gave him a hug and moved to return to her bedroom as did Damian. Just before he gave in to sleep, he thought that Ariana's stalker must be close-by. Most drones required an operator to be within seven hundred meters of the drone so he was probably on the street above. He had faith that their security system would keep them safe.

CHAPTER 9

The next morning Damian was waiting at James Spinnaker's office building at the usual time he started. He waited half an hour beyond that usual time then got a taxi back to the marina to head south to the marina where Natalie was going to meet him. He'd head back to his island after the meeting and check on the location of the phone. If Mr. Spinnaker was inside, then he would go back to the building after his meeting with Natalie.

"Hey Damian, how's the week been going so far?" Natalie asked once she took a seat in her car.

Damian gave a few moments of thought of what to tell Natalie about his crazy week.

"It's been unusual. I had a stranger visit my island on the day you and I met. Turns out he's a stalker of Ariana Knowles from a decade ago."

"Wow, what did he want and what did you do?" Natalie asked not sure whether to be amused or worried for Damian. She knew he would have some crazy scheme for preventing access to his island that would make her laugh, but stalkers often did serious harm to their targets.

"I decided to watch him and he climbed up the cliff, knocked on my door, then pulled out lockpicks. Then he sat down at my picnic table and tried to play with his cellular reception. Meanwhile, I used my facial recognition software and saw his criminal record and connection to Ariana."

"So what did you do to him?"

"What makes you think I did anything?"

Natalie just looked over the top of her sunglasses at him and raised her brows as though to say, 'Go on and tell me what you did.'

Damian smiled and said, "I used my drone to drop my lime green dye water balloon on him. I waited until he was halfway down the cliff so I would have time to saturate him with water balloons, but this time I tried something new as well."

"What did you do Damian?"

"I added micro-crystals that perform a GPS tracking mechanism."

"So do the police have him in custody?"

"No, my product needs more work. John O'Ryan took a shower at the marina he rented the boat at and another shower once he got back to his hotel. He changed clothes and then headed for Muir Woods and then we lost his signal.

"I did a walk-around Ariana's property evaluating her security system, then I pulled out footage of her house and found that Ariana hadn't been turning her security system on and he'd visited a week ago and walked through her house. I think she felt the need to discard underwear that she'd seen John O'Ryan touch on the video. I'm staying at her house until he's captured. Last night at about two in the morning, Ariana heard a drone outside her bedroom, so I fired on it with a high powered water gun filled with honey. That gummed up the rotor blades and the thing dropped into the bay."

"It's never a dull day in your life," Natalie said, then felt a ping of pain thinking back to the day when his family had been murdered.

"It's certainly been unusual these past twelve months," Damian said and Natalie let out a silent breath she'd been holding over her last comment glad he hadn't taken offense or gone back to that horrific day.

"Well good luck with that."

"Actually, the two cases got me thinking about how to improve my invention with the micro-crystals. Lily is going to take the lead to figure out a technology that will stay for about five years so that children like Olivia can be tracked by law enforcement. We all wanted an expiration date on the product so that parents could choose at a certain age to let the technology expire as the kid becomes an adult. We would have the product applied only by law enforcement so that it can't be abused by adults. Then we'll need a machine that can track thousands of kids and decipher who the kid is that's missing."

"Wow, Damian that's brilliant! I like that you thought of the downside of the product and figured out a way to avoid that."

"We likely won't make money on the product, and it's a little Orwellian, but then I looked at the numbers of children that go missing daily, and it could be a real tool to keep children with their parents. First we have to figure out the technology."

"There's another advantage to you helping me with cold cases – you're coming up with new inventions."

"Speaking of cold cases and George Orwell's dystopia, I contacted a friend at Fantasia to see if they would let me run my facial recognition software through their footage to see if Olivia could be spotted at Fantasialand and this is him calling back."

Damian answered the cell and Natalie listened to his side of the conversation while she drove to the park where Olivia Roth was abducted. She could tell that Damian had been granted permission to visit the following week when he began arranging a meeting time.

After he ended the call, he said, "Sorry Natalie, I had to arrange that on my schedule. Can you make the trip with me to meet with their lawyers and IT people on Tuesday? I'll make flight arrangements, and I think we need a half a day, so we would leave at noon and return at five to the Oakland airport. You could have dinner with Haley and Trevor to avoid trying to head home at rush hour."

"Damian, you're such a nice guy that I forget what a mover and shaker you are. I'll meet you at your office that morning, and we can go together. I'll bring my retired detective shield and parts of the casebook with me in hopes of exerting emotional blackmail on Fantasia."

"I didn't know you were into emotional blackmail Natalie," Damian said with a grin.

"Whatever works, but is still legal," Natalie said parking the car.

Damian could see the sign for Diana Park.

They got out of the car and crossed to the park. Families were using the children's play area with kids on the swings, slides, and jungle gyms. As it was a school day, the kids all seemed pre-kindergarten in age. Moms and dads were playing with their offspring, and Damian saw the behavior of Olivia's mom by several of the parents. They would watch their child and smile or compliment them and then look down at the phone. Parents were giving them a suspicious look as they didn't like strangers watching their children.

"Let's walk around the park and you can recreate the kidnapping scenario for me. I sense we're making these parents uncomfortable. I want to see all the exits to the park, then we can return to the car and talk."

Natalie had her notes with her and said, "Jessica Roth was sitting on that bench," pointing to a bench inhabited by a mother rocking her infant in a stroller back and forth and watching another child.

"Olivia Roth started on the swing set and moved to that jungle gym to go down the slide. Jessica watched her daughter slide down several times when her cell phone pinged and she looked down at a message she'd been waiting for. Jessica opened that email and before opening the attachment, she looked up planning on smiling at her daughter's enthusiasm for the jungle gym. When Jessica looked up, she couldn't see Olivia and so she stood up and walked over to the jungle gym just to make visual contact with her daughter. She did a complete circle walking around the jungle gym and calling her name a few times, then dialed 9-1-1. Officers arrived in two minutes and found her frantically running around the park calling for her daughter. Within minutes five officers were searching for Olivia. Soon, the FBI arrived to assist."

"Remind me what evidence they collected from this park," Damian requested.

"Olivia dropped her sweater during one of her rounds of the jungle gym swing set. Her mom said she would slide down and then race around to the stairs to climb up it again," Natalie said pointing to the playset that Olivia used. "We got her DNA from the sweater as well as other items in the home. Dog sniffers were brought in, but they lost her scent one block over. The theory is that the kidnapper took Olivia out the back entrance of the park over there, and she had a car parked one block over. We'll go there once we're done here."

"Was Olivia's house that direction as well?" Damian asked pointing to the back exit.

"No, it's down that street," Natalie said pointing to a street that dead-ended into the park.

"There are no city cameras in this immediate area?"

"No."

"Did the FBI or the detectives ask area residents if they had security cameras?"

"I'm sure they did as that's standard operating principle. I seem to recall they found nothing in that area, but I'll re-check. Cameras were less popular five years ago than they are today."

"True," Damian said as he stood looking around the park. He could remember when he took his own girls to a park like this. They'd had a gym set in their backyard, but for variety they liked to come to the park. He looked around at the fencing and then came back to a spot, studied it and made a mental note to look it up later.

After further discussion, Damian felt like he'd seen all that was relevant to the case and he'd come up with some new ideas to chase in the case. They headed for Natalie's car with silence between them as Damian mulled over what he'd seen at the park and what he read in the file.

As they settled into the car, Damian took a look at his cell phone which had vibrated while they were leaving the park. He hit his cellphone screen a couple of times and watched something as Natalie started the engine of her car. It was an alarm from Ariana's security system.

"Drive as fast as you can! Ariana's in trouble! I've got to call the Belvedere police."

"Do you want me to drive to her house?"

Damian did some swift calculation thinking about the freeways and his boat.

"Take me to the marina, I'll get there faster by boat."

CHAPTER 10

*D*amian's heart stopped when he'd opened the screen and viewed different camera angles inside the house. He saw Ariana's stalker holding Hermione with a knife and Ariana unable to reach a phone to call for help while they were standing in her kitchen.

Natalie listened as Damian dialed the Belvedere police and identified himself.

"This is Damian Green and I want to report a home invasion and hostage situation at 375 Skyview Road in Belvedere. The suspect is John O'Ryan and he's holding a fifteen year old girl at knifepoint. Officer Woodrow is aware of O'Ryan. I can see the situation from interior cameras and have forwarded Officer Woodrow a snapshot of the interior."

"Officers are being dispatched now to 375 Skyview Road. Are you at the residence Mr. Green?"

"No, I was down in San Jose and was alerted by the security system alarm. I'm about twenty-five minutes away by boat. I'll be arriving at Ms. Knowles dock at that time. Please ask the officers to call me when they arrive on the scene so I can link them to the cameras of the security system."

"The first officer has arrived at the driveway. Several more are on their way with ETAs of one to ten minutes. The Marin County Sheriff is sending its Hostage Negotiation Team to the address."

"Can you give me the officer's email who is on the scene so I can link him into the security footage?"

That information was provided and the Operator said, "Officer Remington indicated that he has the connection to the video link and can see the hostage situation. A second unit is arriving at the scene and as soon as Officer Remington gives the report to the second officer, I will connect you directly to his cell phone."

"Thank you," Damian said. Natalie had written a note to Damian while he was talking asking if he wanted her to accompany him to Belvedere and after thinking about it for a few moments, he wrote back, "no". They would have enough law enforcement resources at the scene and as a retired detective out of her jurisdiction, she'd have little power to impact the situation.

He was roaring off across the bay minutes later glad that he'd used his speediest boat that day. The difference between his two boats equated to ten minutes which was a lot of time for this situation. Additional police resources had arrived at Ariana's house, but John O'Ryan was still holding a knife to Hermione's throat as Damian could see in the interior cameras. He briefly wondered where Miguel was. He was determined to reach Ariana's home before he lost a second family to a convicted criminal. Damian reviewed Ariana's house and thought of a plan. He checked compartments in his boat to assure himself of the available tools. Meanwhile, he had a headset on listening to the police outside Ariana's home. He'd been warned that he was not welcome at her house. Hostage negotiators had found in previous situations that having a family member participate in those negotiations rarely went well for the hostage. He had no plan to talk through a PA system or telephone to John O'Ryan or to show his face to police. Instead he planned to park his boat at a neighbor's dock and scale the side wall at Ariana's house. From there he hoped to work some of his inventions to save Hermione's life.

Ariana's kitchen included a separate butler's pantry off to its side. What John O'Ryan didn't know was that very pantry had a trap door in the floor that led down to a root cellar used in Victorian times to keep vegetables, fruits and meats cool. Damian took certain cameras offline of Ariana's security system so that neither the police nor Mr. O'Ryan would see him enter the root cellar from an outside door. Damian was most grateful for Mr. O'Ryan picking this particular room for the hostage situation as it was the only room in her house that gave him secret access.

He had a high powered water gun loaded with his most extreme pepper juice in his boat compartment. He was worried that Hermione was going to get the pepper juice splashed into her eyes and he carried two quart bottles of eyewash on his boat in case he ever got the juice in his own eyes. He would be prepared to immediately render first aid to Hermione, but he would rather treat her for eye trouble than a slit throat. John O'Ryan's back was to the butler's pantry. So he planned to sneak up behind him and simply tap him on the shoulder in hopes that he would look back in surprise with his eyes wide open at whoever tapped his shoulder. Ariana was facing the doorway to the butler's pantry and so would see his approach. He could only hope that she would hold her composure and not acknowledge his presence.

He was approaching the Belvedere Peninsula and could see police lights on the road above her house. He was glad he had reviewed her security system recently to understand the weaknesses of it. Specifically, he knew to climb over the north wall rather than the south wall of her property. The north wall was on the same side of the house as a cellar door entry to the butler's pantry. He'd never met her neighbors on the north side, but with all the police activity he doubted they would do anything immediately about a strange boat parked at the dock. Just in case, he wrote a note that he would leave on the boat's windshield.

He tied the boat up and could hear the PA speaker of the police at Ariana's. He took another look at the kitchen, to assure himself that he had the time to enter the house through the root cellar. Nothing had changed, and he was good to go with his plan. A minute later, he was over the north wall, duffle bag in hand, approaching the root cellar. He was grateful that the door to the cellar was partially covered by an oleander tree. It gave him cover from the police.

He knelt down next to the cellar door and went to work on the padlock. The door was both bolt-locked on the outside and had a latch on the inside. He needed to get through both series of steel to get in the house. Fortunately in his emergency set of tools that he kept on board the boat was a jar of nitric acid. In the past, he'd outfitted his boat and car with emergency kits, and this was the first time he'd used the nitric acid, and he hoped that the acid would work quickly to break down the steel. He also had other tools that he could use to make cuts into the steel to accelerate the effect. He rechecked the screen and Mr. O'Ryan seemed to be in the same position conversing with Ariana and Hermione was still unharmed.

With a little wiggling, he soon had the bolt broken open. He then went to work on the iron latch below underneath. Thankfully, it was an old house with none of the modern metals that would be hard to break. He dripped more nitric acid on the bolt and applied pressure to open the door. The old latch was slow to break and he debated adding heat to the acid when the latch broke open. He thanked his lucky stars that this cellar door was at some distance from the trap door that led inside Ariana's pantry. He was sure he wasn't making sounds loud enough to be heard through two doorways. He picked up his duffle bag and proceeded down the steps and into the cellar. Once on the cold cellar floor, he took off his shoes to ensure there would be no sound from his footsteps. He'd tried out the water pistol before he reached the dock and was assured it was in working order.

He crept to the stairway leading to the trap door to the pantry, careful to place his weight at the sides of the steps, testing each one to make sure he made no noise. Just before raising the door, he rechecked everyone's positions on the security camera. John O'Ryan had released Hermione and backed them into a corner of her kitchen, while holding up a knife to prevent either one of them from passing by him. As far as Damian was concerned, it was a better position as he was less likely to get the potent pepper juice in Hermione's eyes now, but the two women had to be excellent actors so as not to give him away.

He oiled the hinges, put gloves on his hands and then slightly opened the stairway door to look into Ariana's kitchen. She happened to look right at him and he placed a finger to his lips. She pulled Hermione into an embrace and whispered into her hair, "Don't look at the pantry."

Damian quickly and soundless eased into the pantry letting the door drop slowly and silently into place. He then stood up water gun in his right hand and ducked behind the door watching John O'Ryan through the hinges. He was telling Ariana that he would save her from the police outside and she kept him talking by asking him why he held a knife out to the two of them? John replied that Hermione was unnecessary and he wanted the two of them to go away. Damian had heard enough.

He moved from behind the door, a completely cool customer facing down a man with a large knife. As planned, he tapped John O'Ryan on the shoulder and fired his water gun at his face. He noted that Ariana dragged Hermione down to the floor and they turned their faces away. They listened to the agonized screams of John O'Ryan on the floor while Damian headed to the front door to bring in law enforcement. Damian knew that all of this activity would be relayed to the police outside as they had the same camera in the kitchen that he did.

As soon as he opened the door, he was nearly flattened by SWAT officers heading for Ariana's kitchen. Damian had the common sense to have left his pepper spray gun on the kitchen counter, but he told the officers passing him, "Be careful touching Mr. O'Ryan as he is covered in a very potent pepper spray."

Once the SWAT officer determined that John O'Ryan was completely subdued they called in the paramedics to treat Mr. O'Ryan.

"Give me a second, and I'll get you goggles to protect your eyes," Damian said as he went back to the pantry cellar door and went down the stairs to grab his duffle. Several SWAT team members were watching him suspiciously worried that he would spray them with the burning substance.

"Step away from the duffle sir," came a command from one of the officers.

Damian recognized that the tone of voice was deadly serious and so he backed away and said, "If one of you will look inside the duffle bag, you'll find several pairs of goggles to protect your eyes from the substance on Mr. O'Ryan's clothing and skin. There are also two quarts of eyewash in there to treat his eyes."

He hugged Hermione and Ariana now that the situation was under control. "Might the three of us go sit outside near the pool while you finish in here?"

Officer Woodrow of the Belvedere Police stepped forward and said, "I'll go outside with the three of you and begin collecting your statements." The officer looked at the SWAT team leader for affirmation and he nodded. No one wanted a teenage girl in the vicinity of a stalker screaming obscenities who had recently held a knife to her neck.

"Where's Miguel?" Damian asked.

"John locked him in Hermione's room. I'll ask Officer Woodrow to bring him out."

Damian stepped over to Ariana's outdoor sink and removed the rubber gloves he'd been wearing and washed his hands. The last thing he wanted to do was get the pepper spray in his own eyes. He'd been careful not to let his gloved hands touch Ariana or

Hermione's skin. Once the door was closed to the house, they were away from the moans and curses of John O'Ryan.

Damian sat between the two women, an arm around each of them. They both simultaneously kissed his cheeks and offered thanks to his intervention. Miguel came out with one of the officers and became a part of the group hug. Then they took turns hugging him back until they were settled next to him. Damian took a deep breath and thought *not today, not this time*. He couldn't save his first family, but he saved his second family.

A paramedic stepped outside and asked, "Sir, can you tell me what the substance was that you splashed in the man's eyes? I need it for my report to the hospital."

"It's pepper juice oil extracted from the Carolina Reaper, the hottest pepper juice available. It meets California requirements for pepper juice content, I just used a more potent oil than found in most sprays. The eyewash quarts are a saline solution, but I believe you carry baby shampoo to get the oil off the skin. He'll have his eyesight back in six to eight hours. Just be careful that you don't get the juice on yourself."

The paramedic acknowledged his words with, "Thanks for the goggles. It's comforting to know I can't touch my eyes. We'll return them later to you."

"No need. I'm an inventor and have lots more pairs in my lab. Keep them for your future safety."

CHAPTER 11

It was dark by the time they finished dealing with the police and the media. Reporters arrived on Ariana's street and they even had a news chopper fly over from a San Francisco news station. The three of them declined all interviews, looked around at the mess and instead decided to head to Damian's house after he installed a new lock on Ariana's root cellar exterior door. Down the road, they would be called into court to testify, but that was only if John O'Ryan was found mentally competent.

"I'm glad that it's Saturday tomorrow," Hermione said as she dropped her overnight bag on Ariana's boat. Damian moved his boat to her dock where it would stay overnight as they'd be back in the morning to clean up Ariana's house. Ariana's cleaning service normally came on Monday, but the pepper spray mess needed to be cleaned by Ariana and Damian to make sure no one else was harmed by touching the dried pepper juice.

"I'd have to agree with you," Ariana said covering her yawning mouth. "My adrenaline rush is gone, and I'm ready for bed at the early hour of six in the evening."

"I'll fix you both supper once we get to my place and then you can crash for the night," Damian said steering her boat out into the bay. It would be a twenty-minute journey and he bet the two women would fall asleep to the melodious sound of a boat engine, wind noise, and fresh air in under five minutes. He was tired himself, but was kept awake by his racing mind remembering the victory of saving this family this time!

He nudged Ariana and Hermione awake after he'd secured the boat at his dock on Red Rock Island. They followed him inside carrying their bags with Miguel bringing up the rear. Hermione threw her bag into the downstairs bedroom that Damian had made for her inside his laboratory. It wasn't spacious, but it had everything she needed after Damian added a second bathroom to his house in the lab. He still had only one shower, but at least he had two toilets and sinks which made Ariana and Hermione, his only guests, more comfortable. He'd also added a Murphy bed to his living room. It was a safe and quiet location where they could relax and not worry about their own safety.

The next morning as they journeyed back across the bay to Ariana's house, he thought about his plans for Tuesday.

"Hermione, do you have a soccer game on Tuesday?"

"No..... why?"

"I have a meeting with the folks at Fantasialand in the afternoon. How about if we fly down early and you can spend the day there with Ariana and I'll join you before and after the meeting. We'll discuss with the school that you need a break after yesterday's excitement," Damian said. Then looking over at Ariana paused and added, "Sorry, I should have asked you if that's a convenient time. Is it?"

Ariana gave it some thought and could think of nothing that could prevent her from taking the day off. She thought it was also a good idea for the three of them to take a happy break after being held at knifepoint.

"There's nothing on my schedule that can't be re-arranged."

Looking at Hermione, she asked, "What do you think kiddo? Do you want to skip school and visit the happiest place on earth?"

"Seriously? I've wanted to go there my entire life. Mom and Dad never listened to my pleas to go. I must be the only kid at school that hasn't been there," Hermione said, letting out a cheer of victory in the middle of San Francisco Bay.

Damian and Ariana smiled at the happiness in Hermione's voice. He made a note to contact Natalie to arrange a different flight for her.

"Do you want to be there when the park opens at 8am, which means you'll have to get up at about 3:30 to make a six am flight or would you rather get there at nine and stay until say ten or eleven at night? It'll be tough going to school on Wednesday."

"Are you kidding? I'm fifteen and I've never been to Fantasialand what do you think? Let's be there at eight and leave at midnight. I can sleep on the plane or really I can sleep the rest of my life!"

"Oh boy, you may not be exhausted on Wednesday, but I have a feeling that Ariana and I will be toast by late Tuesday night," Damian said pleased that Hermione was so excited to visit Fantasialand. He'd have to charter a jet to maximize their time at the theme park and give them all a better sleeping option while in the air. At least getting to and from the airport would be quiet at those hours of the day.

By noon, they had all evidence of a crime scene collection and pepper spray cleaned from the kitchen and rooms that John O'Ryan had visited or passed through while inside Ariana's house. Fortunately, Ariana had no carpeting in those areas or she would have been forced to tear it up. Life returned to normal and Damian made plans to meet the women at Ariana's house where they would drive to a private hangar at San Francisco Airport on Tuesday. With arrangements made and both women feeling secure with John O'Ryan in police custody, Damian left to return home and get some of his own work done.

He decided to visit Pete's Bar to relax and for a good burger and to see if a new notice was posted at the bar, then he planned to stop by his warehouse to catch up on some work there. He was happy to see there was not a new poster of Hermione gracing the hallway wall. While Pete was serving customers, he sat reflecting on the past five years he'd been visiting the bar.

"You look more introspective than usual Damian. Do you need my bartender's ear?" Pete asked.

"Actually I was thinking that I've been coming here for five years and for some reason this is a place of brilliant insights for me. Is it your cheeseburgers, your beer, or your companionship?"

"You varied a little over the years on your cheeseburger flavors, and had a variety of beers so it must be my companionship, or have you had the same result when I haven't been here?"

Damian thought for a moment and said, "I can't think of when I've been here and you haven't been. Don't you take any time off?"

"I start late and I don't close anymore. Your software program has allowed me to retain reliable staff and work fewer hours myself for more money. I have no complaints."

"Good."

"Actually your program is working so well, I've been scouting for a second location. I'm fifty years old, but I have my business in order and so I'm thinking about expanding. It seems like it would be the next step," Pete said and then with a worried glance added, "I'm assuming I can get your software at a second site?"

"Of course I'll install it at a second location. Could I talk you into putting your second location close to my warehouse? You'd get a weekly catering order out of that. I don't order from your bar because the extra fifteen minutes of travel time cools off the burgers too much no matter what containers you use," Damian said and then had another thought, "Have you zeroed in on a location yet?"

"No still searching."

"Do you have someone that can take over for you right now?"

Pete stared around his bar doing a calculation of the business expected and said, "Yeah for an hour or so, why?"

"I'm heading over to Richmond to my office to get some work done. I have a large three-story building and the top floor is completely empty while the second floor is hardly used. I could move my company upstairs and make space for you to open a new bar. I don't have enough employees to single-handedly support your bar so you'll have to check the neighborhood for commercial purposes. I'll finish my beer and we can go."

"Okay," Pete said as he turned to notify his employee of his absence.

Damian took the last swallow and gave Pete the address adding, "I wasn't thinking about renting the space out, this is a totally impulsive offer on my part, and you should feel no pressure to agree. I'll outfit your next bar with software where ever the location is."

"Of course you would Damian, you're a man of principles. Maybe a second restaurant location is the problem your brain solved at my bar today," Pete said with a grin.

"It might be my second spontaneous brilliant thought today."

"Second? What was your first?"

"Hermione and Ariana were held hostage yesterday, but they're fine now. I have a business meeting at Fantasia on Tuesday and so we're taking her out of school for her first visit to Fantasia-land. She's so excited by the prospect that she's moved on from yesterday's situation."

"Oh my God!" Pete said stopping in his tracks at Damian words. "Are they both okay? Were they hurt? Who took them hostage? What kind of people have you pissed off?"

"Hermione had a knife held to her throat, but she wasn't cut and Ariana's fine as well. Ariana had a stalker come back into her life after he was released from prison. He'll be back in prison for the remainder of his life I hope."

Pete resumed walking to his car, shaking his head, but planning to hear more once they arrived at Damian's warehouse. He didn't want to waste time in the parking lot as he had to get back to the bar.

An hour later, Damian shook hands with Pete giving him a lot to think about. Pete liked the building and had ideas of how to transform the space, and he would have signed a contract then to make this his second location, but Pete knew he needed to do due diligence on the traffic flow and needs of this area. Pete told him he planned to visit the location at a variety of times over the next two weeks as well as visit the food and bar joints closest to the warehouse.

Damian shook his head thinking about the impulsive offers he made that day Fantasialand and a second bar for Pete. It wasn't like him to make decisions like that without thinking them through. His life had changed dramatically since both Ariana and Hermione had appeared on his island, he'd become more spontaneous, perhaps he had to, as he included more people in his trusted circle, like Pete. He went back inside and spent some quiet as the CEO of his company. He checked the Project Management spreadsheet that Lily set up when she came on board. She worked with each of his employees setting up a timeline of tasks to be completed on the way to the eventual launch of any of the company's inventions. Damian had heard of such a system but had never used it, but now he was grateful that he could so easily understand where each of his projects was and where they were going. It helped his employees as well think twenty steps ahead of where they were. They all knew where they were going and Damian could see that he would likely have two inventions to try out in the world by the end of the year, pleased his products would be both commercially and socially viable in a few years. Soon he was back on the boat heading home after checking in with Ariana and Hermione. They'd had a quiet and peaceful day as her security system was doing a good job of keeping reporters away from their home.

CHAPTER 12

*D*amian was yawning as the three of them boarded the charter jet for Fantasialand. He remembered taking his own girls there twice. They were overtired by the end of the day but had a wonderful time there. He wondered how it would be for a teenager. He thought the magic would still be there.

Looking over at Hermione he said, "I like the disguise you're wearing. It changes your features, but doesn't look onerous to wear all day."

Ariana examined Hermione and had to agree. "I'm glad you suggested we change her appearance to hide her from the cameras. We spent some time yesterday using make-up to change the contour of her eyes and then I went to a theatrical supply place to get some putty to change her jawline. With her hair already changed and the ball cap and sunglasses it's good. Did you run her picture through your facial recognition system to see if it figured out who she was?"

"I did and I'm happy to report that none of the potential matches were Hermione."

"It's just unfortunate I won't have a slew of pictures to show my friends when I go back to school on Wednesday."

"Tell you what, after my meeting I'll know where the cameras are in the park, I'll find a few places you can take off your disguise and shoot some pictures. That is if Ariana is carrying spare putty for the repair to your disguise."

"I have some putty, but I think I'll be able to re-use the putty currently on her face."

"Good. Since the plane is in the air, let's see if we can catch a little sleep for the big day ahead!" Damian suggested as they finished shutting all of their window shades to make the cabin dark. A little over an hour later they were entering a car that would deposit them at the front gates of Fantasialand.

Damian hated to leave the two women as they were having so much fun. Ariana hadn't been to the park since being a child herself and he was having a wonderful time enjoying Hermione's pleasure in the park. It was her first visit to an amusement park in her life. Damian felt bad for not taking her before now. He vowed to get her to the other major Southern California theme park on her next school break. They needed to make up for lost time.

He appeared at the entrance just as Natalie arrived by taxi. They were soon joined by a member of the security staff that directed them through a backstage area and beyond to the administrative offices. Damian carried a powerful computer tablet containing his excellent facial recognition software. He was anxious to see if his strategy would work to find Olivia Roth. If it did, it would likely create long-term privacy problems for the park, but he wasn't going to think that far ahead.

Soon Damian was shaking hands with Mark Morante, a man he'd worked with over a decade ago.

"This is retired Detective Natalie Severino," Damian said making the introductions.

"You hear about cold cases on television, and you think of old murders. I can't imagine how it feels to a parent to have your child stolen and the weeks and months that go by with no information.

I'm glad you people never let up," Mark said shaking Natalie's hand.

"We don't ever stop an investigation into a crime, and we hope each time it's opened by a new detective that they'll solve what we couldn't. There's no professional jealousy, just a desire in our cores to solve a case and get a criminal off the streets. Damian has been a huge help with solving some of the old cases. His ability to sort through large pieces of data to find the needle in the haystack has helped me solve several other cases."

"Really?" Mark said looking over at Damian. "You're a man of many talents: genius, inventor, and now crime solver. Congratulations, Damian!"

"Yeah, well let's not waste your time. I have my software here," Damian said embarrassed by Natalie's and Mark's compliments. "If you could put me in front of your most traveled camera in the park and give me access to that camera's storage, I'll get to work."

"I thought I'd take you into our camera control room and you can look at the cameras and decide which is highly traveled, but yet gives you the full face image that you're looking for."

Damian and Natalie were shown into a room that looked like a network station monitoring a football game.

"Which area of the park do you find five to ten-year-olds? I assume roller-coaster type rides don't contain many girls under ten."

"You would be surprised where parents take their kids when they shouldn't. Most of the time the parent is selfish, wanting to ride a thrill ride themselves rather than for their child who is terrified. We have a lot of car and train rides that are slow with minimal drops," Mark said looking at his list of camera locations; he pointed out several monitors.

Damian thought the photo quality of the rider faces was good in five of the seven. Then another question hit him.

"Have all of these rides been in place for the past five years? Do you have footage going back five years on cameras fourteen, five, thirty-six, nineteen, and sixty-three?"

"Yes to all of your numbers. Some of those rides date back to the 1950s, although we didn't have cameras on the rides for several decades. If you're done picking your camera views, let's go to a conference room where I have a computer set up to pull footage for you."

"Mr. Morante, I really appreciate your cooperation," Natalie said excited that they might finally have a new clue in Olivia Roth's case. "I think I mentioned that as each detective looks at an unsolved case, they bring with them new forensic technologies in addition to a fresh set of eyes. I have the added advantage of Damian's computing power and the way he thinks about data as evidenced by our presence here."

As they walked to a conference room, Damian made a mental note to tell Hermione that she could avoid having her picture taken anywhere in the park as long as she was looking down at the camera. The cameras were all somewhat high overhead. He'd come to that conclusion after watching people in the security monitoring room.

Damian took a look at the files he'd be combing for face matches and they were indeed large. He decided he would speed up the first pass thru of the data by eliminating some faces that were definitely male, not children in Olivia's age group or kids with blond hair. Olivia's hair color was brown. Though he wanted to look at all five years, he started with one year at a time, and in particular the most recent twelve months. He set the program running, and it estimated that it needed twenty-four minutes to locate every child close to Olivia's physical appearance. That limited the potential number of faces down to just under a million; then his software went to work trying to match Olivia's age-adjusted picture to the pictures on the park cameras. It was a needle in a haystack that he was searching for. The three of them chatted about what they were doing for work and future plans to expand the Fantasia Park.

The computer signaled it had finished the facial recognition search and the three of them sat there dumbfounded at the result.

They had a match.

"Oh my God!" said an astonished Mark. "I honestly didn't think you would find a match at all or even so soon."

"Me either," agreed Natalie.

"It's the lure of Fantasialand. What parent, even a fake parent, can resist taking their young child here. To me, that bodes well for the child being kept in good conditions and not abused."

"Actually you can't link the two ideas. Remember that family of about twelve kids from Southern California. They were grossly abused, yet there was a picture of them at Fantasialand," Natalie said.

"That true," Damian replied a little less joyful at finding Olivia. He hoped she hadn't been abused beyond the act of kidnapping.

"So what are your next steps?" Mark asked. He knew he needed to get the lawyers of the company involved quickly, but he wanted to know which way Damian and Natalie were going to go.

"I think we need to collect all of the footage from all of the cameras as evidence collection," Natalie said.

"I'll want all of the footage on this day to determine who is with her at the park," Damian replied. "In this image for example, we can't see the full face of the woman that's with her."

"I can pull up the archive of that day, but before I do, let me check with our counsel. I don't want to violate any policies or privacy rights. Is there a way you can have your software identify only the girl in the picture and someone she's holding hands with. We don't want to be responsible for harassing good citizens simply because they're standing next to a child."

"My software can't do that, but I'd be happy to have you or your counsel go through the still frames first and eliminate any pictures that are likely random strangers rather than the woman that kidnapped the child. Let's try that first and see what we end up with; we can pursue other strategies if this first one doesn't work."

"Okay give me some time," Mark said as he left the room.

As soon as he left, Damian texted Hermione to let them know he was going to be longer than expected due to the discovery of the girl. He also let the teenager know how she could go about having her picture taken.

"Wow, Damian this is both exciting and nerve-racking. We might reunite the child with her parents within the next twenty-four hours. This will have implications for you and me. I'm sure that a lot of the brass in the SJPD will want to meet you and I bet the child abduction unit at the FBI will as well. You've written a whole new chapter on finding missing children. Fantasialand is in a difficult position. Do they add staff here to routinely look for every child abduction that might visit the park? How do we keep quiet about this so that abductors don't learn what they are doing? My mind is racing with a thousand questions," Natalie said in a rush.

"Natalie slow down. We'll figure this out together starting with a story to hide my involvement. I'm not going to appear at a news conference. As a detective you thought of popular locations that children go to play. You convinced one of those companies to allow you to look at the film for the past five years. It was a long process. You used facial recognition software that the department has available. Neither Fantasialand nor I wish to be at all connected to reuniting this child with her parents," Damian said firmly.

"Yeah I know you don't want fame and fortune from these cold cases that you solve, but you deserve some credit. Besides I bet Fantasialand will spill the beans on your role."

"I bet they don't. They don't want a reputation for finding abducted kids in their park. It would be a huge distraction from their mission. It would change the very nature of who they are. It's to them and my advantage to remain silent partners in solving this crime. This is non-negotiable."

Natalie heard Damian's resolve to stay as a silent partner solving cold cases in his voice. Besides, all they had done so far was see Olivia with a woman. They needed to track down the woman and hope the girl was still safe. She wondered when the department would be contacting the parents. Her mind was saturated with excitement for the parents to be close to being reunited with a child missing for five years.

"I hear you, maybe like a previous case, you can think of how I found the girl."

"Let's wait until we identify the woman seen holding her hand. If Olivia is living with a stranger, that relationship may give us a clue as to your cover story."

Mark eventually returned saying, "Oh boy, have we got a mess on our hands. We're excited for you, but is there any way you can keep our name out of any report you make about the case? Perhaps once you have the identity of the child's abductor, you can locate them on some other business or public camera?"

"Natalie and I were discussing that very scenario. Mark, like the company you represent, I absolutely don't want my name connected to solving this case. Both of us would be deluged with distraught parents across the globe that are still looking for their children."

"Yeah, well Fantasialand doesn't want to be viewed as a collection of criminal fake parents bringing their stolen children to have a little fun to make up for the fact they were stolen to begin with."

"I think there might be a long-term role with the FBI here to look for missing children, but that's for your employer to work out down the road. I'm just a basement hacker who was able to find one kid. I won't assist Natalie if she has other child abduction cases. While I might be prepared to sell my software to the FBI, I'm not going to make this my full-time job. Instead, I'm working on an invention that could be applied by police and allow GPS tracking of a child for five years at a time. It's not that I don't think having a child abducted is horrible – I do, but I'd rather be on the preventive side than searching for an abducted child."

"Do you think you'll be able to come up with a cover story as to how the abductor was identified that leaves Fantasialand out of the equation," Mark asked, worry evident in his voice.

"I do, and I think that once we identify the woman, we'll have our storyline that will leave you and me out of the discovery," Damian replied.

"Okay then, here are copies of the woman that I retrieved from the system," Mark said pulling a sheaf of papers out of a legal pad that he'd been holding.

Damian took a look at the pictures and said, "These are good shots. If you don't mind me using your conference room for a few minutes longer than I think we'll have her identity and our story."

Damian plugged what he thought was the best picture into his system and waited while it searched his software database. Four minutes later, he had a ding matching an image in the Department of Motor Vehicles website for Jennifer Shields with a San Jose address.

"Oh my gosh!" Natalie exclaimed recognizing the street name from her detective days. "That's in Olivia Roth's neighborhood. I've got to call this into the station so the woman gets picked up for questioning, and Olivia is secured by child services. What's my story?" she asked looking at the two men.

Mark didn't have an answer, so Damian suggested, "One of her neighbors lent you her front door video footage for the past two years, and you used the department's facial recognition software to discover Olivia and Jennifer Shields."

"That's a weak explanation that no one would believe," Natalie said.

"Then let your PR department come up with a better explanation. I want SJPD to get all the credit for solving this case. Surely your people can spin it to their advantage?"

"I agree with Damian, you must keep our name out of this story if you ever want our cooperation again."

Natalie knew in the face of such opposition she needed to convince her department not to reveal the sources of pinpointing who gave her the information. Actually, she could just show them the one picture of Jennifer Shields and Olivia Roth and refuse to provide her source. They might end her role as a retired detective, but she understood what Damian and Mark were saying, and her non-cop mind had to agree.

"Can you give me a copy of that picture," Natalie said pointing to the one in Damian's hand and then reached in her jacket pocket for the ubiquitous gloves that detectives carried. "Put these gloves on and print a copy of it for me. I want no fingerprints from either of you on the paper, and my superiors will have to live with me not saying where the paper came from."

"Mark, grab a sheet from the middle of your print stack so that no fingerprints are on it from when the printer was loaded," Damian suggested.

"I think I'll just open a new ream of paper while wearing these gloves and pull out a single sheet, that way I'm sure that no Fantasia employee's fingerprints are on the paper."

After Mark left to get Natalie's copy, Damian said, "Thanks for taking the heat on this one and not revealing your sources."

"Yeah, well my Lieutenant may guess that it's you, but he'll have no proof. I'm grateful the picture is timestamped." Soon she left with a Fantasia escort to find her way back to the main gate.

"Mark, thanks for your help," Damian said holding out his hand.

"Your welcome and I hope that little girl gets reunited with her parents soon. Say, if you need some kids to test your GPS film on, I'll volunteer mine. Getting to know, only briefly, this other little girl that was abducted from her family scares me."

"I'll keep that in mind. Can you have someone direct me to the Mt. Everest ride, I have friends there waiting for me."

"I'll take you there. I hadn't realized you were enjoying our park today."

"I'll really enjoy it now that Olivia Roth was located. I mean she's not safe yet, but she's close to being so."

"Do you think our names will be kept out of the story surrounding this child?"

"I do. Natalie doesn't want to lose my help on future cold cases and besides, she's a friend and wouldn't do that to me."

Soon after Damian made introductions with Ariana and Hermione, he watched Mark's back disappear behind a stage door.

"Was this visit to Fantasialand helpful? Did you find the little girl?" Ariana asked.

"Yes we did on camera. Natalie's on her way home with a time-stamped picture of the girl with her abductor – a neighbor."

"Wow," Hermione and Ariana said at the same time as they engulfed Damian in a hug.

Damian looked at them in surprise and said, "What?"

"You're a great man for figuring out how to reunite a child with her parents. Look at all you have done for Hermione and now this Olivia. Both were strangers to you."

"Stop, you're embarrassing me! And I haven't found Hermione's parents yet."

"No, but you stopped her from being reunited with thugs who aren't her parents and that's equally important!"

"Let just forget about all of that and enjoy Fantasialand until it closes today. If you like this park, we can come back again."

CHAPTER 13

$\mathcal{N}$atalie traveled from the airport straight to her Lieutenant's office and fortunately, the two locations were a little more than two miles apart. She knew she had about thirty minutes before he usually left for the day. She hoped he didn't have something like a dentist's appointment to take him home early.

She entered the detective division to a chorus of 'hellos' and walked into Lieutenant Shimoda's office. He was reading emails and she was happy to see that she wouldn't have to wait for someone else to leave first. She had in her hand two pictures; the age-adjusted sketch of Olivia Roth created by the police artist and the picture of her with a woman at Fantasialand.

When the Lieutenant gave her the case, he cautioned that it might be her hardest yet to solve, but he was secretly curious to see how Natalie's friend, Damian Green would approach the case. He thought they could all benefit from how the man thought about cases as he tried to solve them on purely a data basis.

He looked at the two pictures analyzing what he was seeing and exclaimed, "Oh my gosh, Olivia Roth is alive and would appear to be well. Where is she?"

"That's why I'm here LT, the woman holding her hand in the picture is identified as Jennifer Shields. She's a neighbor about twelve blocks away from the Roth house."

Shimoda went to his doorway and yelled, "Everyone to the conference room and Jenkins call up SWAT to report here as well. Five minutes everyone."

Natalie had loved working for the Lieutenant when she'd been a full-time detective for this very reason. He trusted her to bring legitimate information to his attention and didn't waste time giving her the third degree as to whether her information was correct. When he offered her the position of cold case solver, she'd said yes as long as he was her superior.

"I don't suppose you're going to tell me where you got that picture?"

"No, sir. I made a deal with the men that made this picture possible that I wouldn't reveal their names. They don't want to become a source for parents of missing children in the world and I respect that. They suggested a story I tell, and I was hoping with the help of our PR people we could craft a logical message about this case."

"Let's get the recovery of Olivia Roth launched, then we'll talk to PR. Tell me what you know about the woman in this picture. All I know at the moment is her name and address. I recognize the street name from when I was on the job. She's a neighbor of the Roths. Okay, our priority at the moment is Olivia's safe recovery. Let's get a computer search going on our abductor in the confer-ence room," Shimoda said as he ushered Natalie out of his office and toward the conference room.

Minutes later Natalie watched the detectives and officers of the department she used to work for assemble a plan to rescue a little girl with little advance notification. They debated contacting the parents sooner rather than later but wanted the little girl in their safe hands before they made that call. The plan was for Natalie to take immediate charge of the girl after SWAT recovered her, pending the parent's arrival. Natalie was cool with that task as she was sure the child would be shocked and distressed.

An hour later, Natalie found herself sitting on the sidelines as watched her fellow officers from a distance. She knew they were using infrared sensors to determine who was in the house. The last thing anyone wanted was the abducted child injured or killed during their operation. They'd quietly evacuated neighboring houses as soon as they detected two heat sources inside the home. The abductor appeared to be preparing something in the kitchen, while a smaller heat source was sitting in another room watching something, perhaps a TV or doing homework.

In their research on Jennifer Shields, they could find no record of a birth attributed to her. They hadn't had time to research school records or indeed any other kind of records as they'd been in place and mobilized to extract the girl and detain Ms. Shields. In the back of Natalie's mind was a tiny worry that Olivia Roth might not be the child inside, but those worries would end as soon as she saw the child. Every officer on the tactical squad had her picture. Another two officers had the contact information of Olivia's parents and they sat outside of each parent's residence waiting for the call to retrieve the parent. An ambulance was also parked at the end of the street as was the protocol for any SWAT operation.

SWAT had its officers in place surrounding the house. Another officer was charged with ringing the doorbell and getting Ms. Shields to step outside her home. The moment she stepped outside, she would be detained as they searched for the little girl. If the woman looked up and down the street, she would notice that something was amiss. No one was outside their home and no traffic was driving down the road. If she stepped out far enough, she would see a long line of police cars, but her view was blocked by plants around her front porch.

The operation went as planned and a child matching Olivia Roth's description was brought into Natalie's company pending the arrival of her parents. The little girl was crying from the fright of the officers in their SWAT gear. Natalie had brought a video game tablet with her as well as a book deemed popular among ten-year-olds. Natalie was just settling the girl down when the first parent arrived via police escort. It was her father and he approached cautiously afraid the little girl wouldn't remember him. An FBI psychologist had provided talking points for the police to talk to the father. Since she'd been abducted at an early age, she might not remember him, so he needed to tell her a story of a fun time they had together. He stood near his daughter and spoke to her in a soft voice,

"Olivia honey, it's your daddy," Aaron Roth said looking for signs of recognition and acceptance and only seeing terror and confusion in his daughter's eyes. At the same time, he searched the face he longed to see for the past five years. "Do you remember the sandcastles we built when we went to the beach a few years ago? We had a big castle with a fortress around it?"

Olivia was leaning next to Natalie listening to what the man in front of her was saying. He looked vaguely familiar like maybe a man at her church. She remembered the story he told and nodded.

"Do you remember when we went camping in the mountains, and we had an unexpected rainstorm that required us to close up the campsite and huddle in the car wet?"

Olivia leaned a little less into Natalie and the terror level in her eyes seemed to drop and she nodded.

"Do you remember trick or treating with me on Halloween? You were a big fluffy butterfly and I was an ugly bumblebee."

"You weren't ugly daddy, you were just trying to be a bee," Olivia said as she leaned into her father for a hug.

Natalie was wiping tears from the corner of her eyes, convinced that this child belonged to this man after those stories. She looked down the street to see a woman running toward them with tears streaming down her face. Natalie tapped the father so he could brace for the mother practically flying at them. She was sure that the mother had the same briefing as the father and so stepped into the woman's path saying, "Olivia, this is your mommy, and she's going to tell you some stories just like your daddy did."

Jessica Roth paused and knelt down to be below the level of her daughter's eyes and said, "Remember that Saturday when you and I went for manicures and pedicures? I got a boring color of red, but you had lime green glow in the dark fingers and toes?"

With this final memory the damn broke for the child as she was reunited with her real parents. There was a road ahead as these three rediscovered their lives, each other, and themselves. There would be psychologists to help, but first, they needed to get a statement from Olivia as to her experience with Jennifer Shields.

After a long emotional evening, law enforcement had surprisingly matching stories from Olivia Roth and Jennifer Shields. The girl had not been harmed or abused during her stay with Ms. Shields who had abducted her in revenge to Jessica Roth. She had no intent to harm the child, instead she wanted to cause the mother to have emotional distress. It seemed that Jessica Roth had been an attorney involved with the case of Tammy Shields, Jennifer's mother. Jennifer had been living abroad and hadn't realized that her mother had suffered from a sharp decline in her health. The county had been unable to reach Jennifer and forced her mother into a skilled nursing facility where she died two months later. Despite the evidence of severe and fast dementia, Jennifer blamed the government for her mother's death. She targeted Jessica Roth as she was the attorney that filed the paperwork on her mother to transfer guardianship to the government. She had stalked Jessica for awhile watching her routine and understanding what was important to her so that Jennifer could take it away as her mother had been taken away.

Everyone believed that Olivia Shields was Olivia Roth, but law enforcement went a step farther to confirm through DNA testing that they were indeed related. Olivia had been home-schooled and seemed to meet all of the child development milestones, and there were no signs of abuse. Jennifer Shields had no criminal history and her behavior was hard to understand. She said she quickly began to regret stealing Olivia, but couldn't figure out how to return the child without being arrested and so she'd lived with the ax about to drop on her head at any moment for the past five years. She'd been deep in grief over the death of her mother when she developed the plan to steal Olivia, and once she looked back at her theft of the little girl, she'd been horrified at her own behavior.

Natalie just shook her head over the senselessness of the crime and the damaged lives. She was happy to go home to her husband of over thirty years and her lucky family. Lucky because despite some of the horrible things she'd seen through her years as a detective, none of it had befallen her family.

CHAPTER 14

*D*amian and the two women arrived home at nearly one in the morning, but the bone-weary tiredness was worth it. Hermione declared the day, her best ever. That pronouncement was followed by immediate guilt.

"I don't mean to say that I didn't have great days with Mom and Dad."

"We know what you mean sweetie," Ariana said. "Fantasialand is rather special, and you had a wonderful time there as did Damian and I."

"If I'd known how much you would love the park and the fact that you had never been there, we would have taken you sooner," Damian said. "At the moment I just feel guilty over taking you out of school."

"Actually, I'm probably speaking for all of my classmates by saying we're willing to be held at knifepoint by a stalker every month if we know a trip to Fantasialand will occur over the next few days."

"I'd rather not risk your life again," Ariana said, "but since you're a teenager I get your meaning that you would sacrifice a lot for a visit to Fantasialand. We'll plan a trip again when you're not in school. Your teachers and soccer coach gave you this one mental health day, but they won't give you another unless it's for another tragic event, and Damian and I would be lousy parents if we allowed that to happen to you on a regular basis."

"Yes, I know and for your information, I'm fully recovered. I had no nightmares about your stalker last night."

"It's not always that easy. You might have flashbacks in the future, like maybe when I'm cutting up fish for the cats and see the knife."

"Maybe, but I haven't had any flashbacks from the men breaking into my parent's house and taking them away. I wonder where my parents are, but I don't relive the terror of running into the safe room."

"You're an amazing kid," Ariana said. "You'll be even more amazing if you're awake for school in five hours."

Hermione just smiled and headed to her bedroom, Miguel following her to take up watch at the foot of her bed.

Ariana gave Damian a hug and he exited her home walking toward the dock where his boat was parked. It had been a very long day for him, and she hoped he wouldn't fall asleep while steering his boat. Fortunately, he had the fast boat and would be home in less than fifteen minutes.

Damian steered across the dark bay. It was brisk and beautiful. A rare night with a full moon and no fog to spoil the view of the San Francisco skyline. The bright lights of the Bay Bridge on his right, the Golden Gate Bridge behind him, and the Richmond San Rafael Bridge were guiding his way home. He'd read the account of Olivia's reunification with her parents in a brief email from Natalie, and was very satisfied with his role in solving the kidnapping. He and Mark were happy that Natalie had been able to keep their names and methodology out of the press.

He felt the need to say a few words to Jen and his girls about his days' accomplishment. He stopped his boat a moment to look to the stars. The silence was calming and so gazed at the stars above imaging a star for his wife and two girls. He silently transmuted a message to them. They were loved, they were in his thoughts, he had a great day taking another little girl to Fantasialand, and most of all they'd be proud of him for finding the data to reunite Olivia Roth with her parents. He finished his message, wishing them a great future in heaven or on the stars wherever their souls were now located. He stared a few more seconds at the sky and thought he saw the stars in the Scorpius constellation twinkle back at him in acknowledgment. He laughed aloud at his imagination restarted the boat and continued his journey home to the island in a lighter frame of mind than perhaps he'd been in years.

After docking his boat and bringing it inside his watercraft boathouse, he walked through his lab and ascended the stairs. Opening the front door, he found Bailey and Bella nearby standing sentry duty on his island. He invited them inside for a fish dinner and twenty minutes later found them curled up on the window seat in his bedroom ready to tuck it in for the night.

CHAPTER 15

*D*amian went to the warehouse the next day. He knew he needed to visit the Superior Court building in San Francisco to confront James Spinnaker, but he lacked the energy to get up early to travel to San Francisco to be there at James Spinnaker's usual arrival time. After checking in with his employees, he had a team meeting to discuss Olivia Roth. He played a news station's coverage of the case.

"If we can get this dye right, we could prevent the agony parents and children go through during their separation. We need a way to create a code of some type that sends out a signal worldwide for five years, and that can be used where ever the child lives. So if a child is abducted to Mexico, Canada, Europe, or the Caribbean, our technology will still work. So imagine the factors here – unique to each child, works in all geographies, and stays in place for say five years."

"Does it work off satellite technology or cellular?" Chris asked.

"For it to work in all geographies it needs to be connected to a satellite I think," Haley replied.

"For the team that works on this, I don't want you to have any restrictions, so I would say it needs to work with satellites.

Parents want a guarantee that it will work in any location barring something like a cave or mine. We can't control for that. We also likely can't control for steel or other materials that block the GPS signal. Let's not create a design that will work in all situations all over the world rather let's design for the recovery of say fifty to seventy percent of the missing kids," Damian said.

"Speaking as a parent, I'd be happy to know that I can't lose Jacob to the world for the most common situations. I'd rather get a fifty percent product on the market and have some peace of mind now, then waiting five years and my boy's been in captivity for some reason, and I've not known where he is," Lily said.

There was silence in the room before Haley said, "I think those are pretty clear cut marching orders from Jacob's mom."

"You know Damian, I would take some of that green dye now and slather it on Jacob every day until a better product comes along."

"You're that worried?" Angus asked.

"I am. This world is filled with crazy people," Lily replied.

"Well the dye has only one signal, so I can cover one kid, but maybe I'll cover all of the kids whose parents work here. I can supply the product and for privacy's sake, I'll keep the signal detector pass-coded and in my safe so that I'm the only one watching the id's location."

"Since I'm the team lead and I need to observe the properties of the current version, I say that I get the passcode to the signal," Lily said.

Damian thought through her request and nodded, "Okay I'll turn the technology over to you and you can make arrangements to distribute the product to the staff that works here. I'll use my current bottle for Hermione, but I'll leave the recipe for you to manufacture and distribute while we work to improve the product."

Lily gave him a blinding smile and said, "Awesome. Thank you for trusting me. I won't let you down."

"I know," Damian replied quietly. Lily had worked for him less than a year and had served time for a bank robbery conviction. She'd done her time, was very smart and wanted to raise her son Jacob. He had no worries about her trustworthiness as she wanted a future as Jacob's mother.

The meeting ended shortly and he decided to hack into the phone company while he was at work to see what James Spinnaker's phone's usage had been recently. He thought about going over to the office building that afternoon, but that could be a complete waste of time. The cellphone carrier data showed he was far more consistent on his arrival time than his departure time.

It was interesting how the phone traveled around the bay area over the past couple of days. In addition to visiting a home in Oakland, Mr. Spinnaker also visited the Ports of Oakland and San Francisco. Damian wondered if those were meetings or if he had employees that he was supervising. He also made several visits to an address in the Mission District that looked like a thrift store.

Damian opened Google Earth to view the storefront and thought it was odd, but Mr. Spinnaker had an unusual job as a Department of Homeland Security supervisor. Maybe the Department was looking for space to expand offices. The more he thought about it, the more he felt he was wrong. It looked like a run-down building, not near any Homeland Security activity in San Francisco. Perhaps he should find out what the interest was at that location. It was the only site that was repetitively visited. Was it possible that this was where Hermione's parents were living?

He decided he would drop in on the storefront in the late afternoon to see what was happening there and to look for Hermione's parents. He needed that information before he confronted James Spinnaker in case it was a part of the scenario. He did a search of the address to see if anything came up in the news – perhaps a sale of the property or an announcement of a new business opening. Instead, he found police and news reports of an illegal casino. Did Homeland Security monitor illegal gambling operations? He looked at the data and decided it was likely that James Spinnaker was a gambler himself. Why else would he spend hours inside a dilapidated storefront. Still Damian planned to visit the site in the late afternoon. He'd wear some different clothing, sunglasses, and try to look like a tech employee gambling in the off hours. Checking the times that Spinnaker usually dropped by, he calculated he would have to leave in about three hours to make it to the location in question.

His phone rang and he connected the call. "Hi Natalie, it looks like your case concluded with an optimal ending."

"Yes it did. No one was injured, the child is safe with her parents and the suspect confessed. That's all a cop can ask for. I'm being pressured by the department to arrange a meeting with you so that we can revise our procedure of how we go about looking for lost children. I know you don't want to be identified, nor does Mark, but it's such a spectacular closing of a cold case that I'm having a hard time resisting the FBI and my chiefs."

"Well, keep trying Natalie. I'm still not interested in being identified."

"I knew you would say that, but you looked at this case from a completely different angle than any of us. You read the approach we take to locating lost kids. I think we could learn a lot by understanding how your brain works."

"Sorry Natalie, not interested."

"Okay, would you allow me to interview you tomorrow about the process you went through in thinking about where the child could have gone and how 'big data' as I think you call it, plays a role in locating kids?"

He sighed and said, "Okay, but you don't need to interview me. I'll send you the names of the computer resources that the FBI and perhaps the SJPD can use to find the next child along with a few thoughts."

"Thank you Damian. I know you didn't want to be involved, so I'm just trying to find a tidbit to throw at my colleagues."

"I understand the pressure you're under, but I'd rather spend all of my time preventing abductions than chasing after every missing child."

"Got it and thanks."

Damian sighed after he ended the call, but went to work creating the cheat sheet for Natalie's needs on where to look and who to hire. Thirty minutes later it was on its way to Natalie.

He was about to turn back to see if there was anything more he could learn about illegal casinos in San Francisco when he saw a call from Pete.

"Hi Pete."

"I know it's been less than a week since you told me about your first-floor warehouse space, but I'm ready to sign a lease agreement with you."

"Really, that was quick!" Damian said. "Did you have enough time to research the location?"

"Since we talked, I've been doing nothing but that! New condos are going up a block from your warehouse, and I spoke with people in the neighborhood to find out where they eat and drink, and there's a real need here. Just as important, you've been a great business partner for my liquor software and with an excellent partner I can build a business almost anywhere."

"Pete, this is a big venture, but you sound ready to march forward. Let me have Ariana draw up a business contract. I'll specify the square footage in the lease cost and a start date and we'll take it from there."

"Thanks, Damian, for suggesting your warehouse; it was a brilliant choice. Once I get your contract, I'll work out a plan for the opening of the bar."

"Sounds good. I could lend another resource to you once you're in that planning stage. Lily on my staff does project management and she could sit down with you and plan out what it will take to open the restaurant. Speaking of which, do you mind if I tell the staff about your second location?"

"Go ahead! Tell any of them that the beer is on the house tonight if they want to drop in and toast. They're exactly the people I want to appeal to with this new location, and it will be good to pick their brains, and I'll take Lily's help whenever you can release her for a few days."

Damian ended the call and called Ariana to tell her the news and to get the contract for Pete going. He'd told them about it at Fantasialand, and Hermione especially was looking forward to eating at Pete's when she did her summer internship. As it was the end of January, he was pretty sure the restaurant would not be open in time to serve her in June. Pete had permits and construction ahead, and all of that would take time."

It was time to leave to go and explore the casino and so he stopped by his staff before leaving.

"Guys, I have good news. We're moving upstairs within the month. Pete is going to build a second location of his bar on this floor." Damian announced but before he could finish there were hoots and cheers at the good news.

"How did that come about?" Haley asked grinning. "I didn't realize you were planning to rent the bottom floor of the warehouse, not that I'm not pleased! We need to have Ariana set up a deduction in our paychecks to pay Pete on a monthly basis as I'm sure we'll be hitting both the restaurant and the bar."

"I stopped in on Saturday to look at our progress on the various projects, but first I swung by Pete's for a cheeseburger. He told me he was looking for a second location and I just sort of volunteered the bottom floor here cautioning him to research the neighborhood as just the eight or ten of us can't solely support him. So he did the research and just told me he wants to build here. I'm a little worried that he didn't do enough research, but when we chatted he seemed to know this neighborhood and the changes that are coming. Lily, I offered him your services as a project manager to help him set up an opening date. I have to run over to San Francisco to do some research and so if you want to knock off early and go congratulate Pete, he said drinks for you guys are on him today."

With a hoot again for that bit of news, his staff wrapped up their desks and were gone in a burst of noise, filing outside and making carpool arrangements to visit Pete. He was smiling at the silence as he left the warehouse for the journey back to his boat. He'd make a brief stop at his island to grab a few things and be on his way to the illegal casino. He had a picture of James Spinnaker so he could recognize him if he walked into the storefront.

An hour later he was walking through the Mission District with the address up ahead on his right. As an actor, he sucked, so he was going to go in under the guise of being a video game addict. He thought he could portray that persona well. He stepped inside the gloomy room and looked for a computer to sit down at.

A man just inside the door grabbed his arm and said, "Hey man. I don't recognize you. Where are you going?

Damian looked down at the arm holding his, shrugged it off, and said, "I heard you have video games. I just want to play."

"You look a little old to be playing," said the bouncer.

"Oh yeah? Who's your best player? I'll take him on and beat him," Damian said knowing full well he could while he looked around him at the activity. People were sitting at computers but it didn't look like they were playing video games as they were using standard keyboards rather than mechanical keyboards. Most gamers preferred the color-coded and loud clacking of a mechanical keyboard over standard keyboards.

"Look, you need to leave. This isn't no public gaming cafe," the man said grabbing Damian's elbow to turn him around toward the exit door.

Damian broke his arm from the bouncer's grasp and said, "Hey, I heard about this place from Riot Games. They said that you had good players and I could bet in real money instead of bitcoin."

The bouncer shoved him into a chair and mumbled, "Sit here," and walked back through the back door. The guys at the desktop computers ignored him completely.

Damian took out his phone and checked email while he snuck some pictures in of the interior. He doubted they would be of use, but who knew?

The bouncer was gone so long, Damian almost forgot about him. He saw the movement out of the corner of his eye and noted the return of the bouncer. He slouched in his seat and tried to look hip although he had no idea what hip looked like.

"Follow me," said the bouncer.

Damian rose and casually walked, at least in his own brain, following the bouncer into the next room. He was pushed into a seat at a desk in front of another man, and the bouncer left. Damian sat there looking at the man waiting for him to speak.

The man was trying intimidation techniques on Damian, but they weren't working Damian just stared back. Finally, the man spoke, "What's your name? It'll cost you five big ones to go upstairs."

"Okay," Damian said pulling out five hundred dollar bills.

"Not so fast. Who are you?"

"What does that matter? I'm here to beat your best players."

"What kinda players?"

"Look, I told the guy at the door that I heard that you had good players here. I'm tired of beating everyone I play with and I want to go against someone tougher. If you don't want my money to enter the game or you don't have good players just tell me, and I'll go," Damian said making a move to take his money back.

The man slammed his hand on the money not willing to let the money go so quickly.

"What's your name?" he asked again, hand still on the money.

"Not important."

"How do I know you're not going to waste the time of my other gamers. You might lose in ten seconds. You're rather old compared to the usual age group."

"Are you going to let me play or not? I've got things to do; places to go. If you're not going to let me play then I'm leaving," reaching for his money again, but the man had not moved his hand.

"If you don't give me your name I can't log you in."

"Fine, it's Jack Dee Pie, " Damian said naming a popular gamer name.

"Sure, buddy what's your real name?"

"Just gave it to you. Tell you what I'll wait here and you can go ask your other players if they want to take on Jack Dee Pie."

The man laughed out loud and when Damian sat there stone-faced, he sighed got up sweeping Damian's money with him and left. Damian was tempted to search the guy's office, but he wasn't the person they were after, so he slumped and closed his eyes. He knew that if this was any kind of decent gaming hall, that the manager would be back in a flash to have Damian play. Damian's alter ego – 'Jack Dee Pie' was a top ten scorer in Minecraft and Terraria. In his years alone, before Ariana and Hermione had come into his life, he'd spend hours online, gaming though now he didn't play nearly as much. He'd never shared his picture online or appeared in public and so no one would know what he looked like and he'd forbid any picture where ever this gaming room was. All he had to do was wait for the return of this money manager and office goon.

Damian heard the door open behind him and the man approached. He stayed slumped, but looked up beneath the rim of his cap, not saying anything, but raising an eyebrow.

"You're apparently a famous man and no one has ever seen a picture of you so I don't know if you're the real McCoy, but the other players begged me not to let you in as you'd take all the money."

"What's wrong with that? I assume you'd get a cut too."

"Yeah, I do. Follow me."

He showed Damian up a flight of stairs to a dark room filled with guys and gals wearing headphones and sitting in front of their screens. They looked with apprehension at the person entering the room never having met one of the best gamers in the world.

Damian smiled and looked for an empty seat. He walked over to a console and sat down cracking his knuckles for effect, knowing the others were watching. He opened the program and said "game on, who wants to play? I've thrown five big ones in the pot."

He busied himself entering his login information after ensuring that he was running in an incognito mode and no one else could steal his information. When there was still silence he looked up and said, "Who among you is the best?"

The other plays all pointed to one man, and so Damian said, "Com'on aren't you dying to take me on? Think of the money and reputation you'll have when you beat Jack Dee Pie."

Damien knew the man would fall for that line from him. He also hoped he wasn't wasting his time and James Spinnaker would show up at this illegal gaming casino within the hour. If he didn't arrive within that time frame then according to his past behavior, he wouldn't be visiting today. He also hoped the police had no plans to bust this place or he'd be in a heap of trouble. He wished he thought of that before he came up with this hair-brained scheme.

Pretty soon he was giving his full concentration to the game at hand. He'd already overwhelmed three of the gamers and he was gaining a margin on the best player when he lost his concentration for a moment when James Spinnaker entered. Damian took a quick glance at the time and registered in the recesses of his mind that the guy had arrived within his usual time frame. He then rededicated his skills at defeating the gamer who'd gained some ground on him. Damian's fingers weren't necessarily the fastest, but his brain grasped strategy so fast that he could easily make up for his keystroke speed against other players. It was as if he had instant insight into the game designer's brain and could find the fastest way to defeat despite his keystroke speed. It was a case of cunning over speed.

In another twenty minutes, he had the final player close to a monumental defeat, he was just waiting for him to concede and then he'd concentrate on his new target. Damian heard an F-bomb from the location of where his final player was dying a slow death. He smiled and pushed harder and in another two minutes, he knew the last player had to concede defeat. Damian earned backed his five-hundred dollars plus took some of the other player's money. He looked up to see what Spinnaker was up to wondering if he was watching or playing his own game. He was into his own game and Damian discovered it was a different one then he'd just been playing. He also understood how the man could play it an hour at a time and walk away; he was playing against a computer rather than another human who would allow him to stop and start as met his schedule. Damian could see that Spinnaker was an addicted gambler as the game he played was rumored to have given an unfair advantage in the computer code to its own artificial intelligence. Once gamers understood that they deserted the game, but Spinnaker kept coming back on the hope that this would be the day he would beat the machine, except that there would never be a day he could beat the computer.

Damian untangled himself as soon as he could from the people and location of the gaming casino. He couldn't wait to be back on his boat in the fresh air of the Bay which was so much better than inhaling the despondent air of the casino. He'd kept his face away from Spinnaker as much as possible and for tomorrow morning he would confront him regarding the poster. He was reasonably certain that someone was using Spinnaker's computer gaming addiction to his or her advantage to find Hermione. Did whoever was behind Spinnaker actually know where Hermione's parents were or were they hoping to capture her to bring the parents out of hiding?

Looking at his watch, he thought that Ariana and Hermione were likely home from school and soccer practice.

"Hello, Damian. What have you been up to?"

"I've just left an illegal video gaming parlor."

"Are you still the king of the video world?"

"I am and I'm two-hundred richer! I hope I never enter that place again. The desperation of the other men and women there while they played was a drag to experience. There was no pleasure in playing. It took me about forty minutes to put away their best gamer after I coerced him into a game. No one wanted to play with me at first."

"Gee I wonder why?"

"Anyhow, Spinnaker did show up and he's addicted to a game that he plays against a computer which is a sure way to lose your money. I had no interaction with him, but that addiction makes him vulnerable. So maybe someone reached out to him there. I still don't understand the connection to Pete's bar."

"Did he get a look at you?"

"Only in passing. As I play a different game, he wasn't much interested in me. I also wore a ball cap, slouchy jeans and a plaid button down shirt – I was trying to look like a hipster."

He could hear Ariana laughing at the vision on the other end of the phone.

"That's too funny. You really are a computer genius and here you are wearing a costume to look like one! I wish I'd been a fly on the wall to watch this whole episode."

"It's a good thing you weren't there besides the bad atmosphere, the acting on my end was terrible. I actually said the words, 'five big ones' as an indicator of five hundred dollars. The things I do for Hermione!"

There was more laughter and he could hear Hermione's giggles in the background.

"Did you put me on speaker phone?"

"I had to share your vivid descriptions with Hermione so we could both be rolling on the floor with laughter."

"Haha. Well ladies, I'll head back to the courthouse tomorrow morning, and I'm glad I could provide some laughter at my expense."

"Stay safe Damian, and next time record yourself acting so we can enjoy it."

He just smiled and ended the connection.

CHAPTER 16

*A*s Damian made arrangements to leave his boat at the marina and call for a taxi in San Francisco the next morning, he reflected he'd possibly made more trips across the Bay journeys this past week, than perhaps in the entire first year he lived on the island. His island was designed to be self-sufficient, and he'd initially made arrangements with the harbormaster in Richmond for food and parcel deliveries to the island. Now he was off the island so much with his warehouse and to do things for and with Ariana and Hermione that he hadn't used the harbormaster's services in almost a year. He made a mental note to thank the man the next time he saw him.

A short time later he was in place and looking for James Spinnaker's arrival at his office. He knew the direction he arrived from and so it was just a matter of stopping the man. Damian was wearing completely different clothing than he was at the gaming casino including sunglasses, so he wasn't worried about being recognized.

Damian saw him walking towards the entrance to the building and said, "James Spinnaker, I would like to talk to you about the phone number listed on a poster for a missing child."

That stopped the man in his tracks as he quickly looked at Damian and then around him to see who heard Damian's questions.

"Yes?" he said guiding Damian to stand farther from the building entrance. His co-workers would likely pass by their conversation, and he didn't want it overheard.

"I know you're with Homeland Security. Why are you carrying a phone that connects you to a missing child poster?"

Damian watched the man switch through a bunch of responses in his head, he knew he had caught the man off-guard. It was evident he was searching for an answer to Damian's question.

"I can see I've caught you unprepared to give me the truth or at least a good lie. Who told you to post a missing child poster?"

"Ah, I don't know the person's name?"

"So why would a government employee be involved in the search for a missing child?"

"Who are you? I missed your name?"

"That's because I didn't give it to you as it's not important. Why are you searching for a child?"

"How do you know I'm looking for a child?" the man asked confused as though his brain was not thinking fast enough to figure out who Damian was.

"Because you're carrying a phone with a number related to a missing child announcement," Damian replied.

"How do you know I'm carrying a phone?" the man asked, not believing that Damian could know.

Damian pulled a phone out of his own pocket that he had purchased just for this occasion. He entered the number listed on Hermione's poster and a phone was heard ringing inside the man's briefcase.

"Oh."

"You work for the Department of Homeland Security. Since

when did that department start looking for missing children? It's not in your scope of responsibility."

In a hesitating voice, he said, "We sometimes look for children missing from people who have illegally entered the United States."

"The girl and her parents are United States citizens and you know that. What's another excuse for your department looking for the girl? Or does the search have anything to do with your department? Are you searching on behalf of someone else? Do I need to show the poster to your superiors along with the phone records and let them decipher what you've been up to?"

Damian was leaning into the man as he talked and Spinnaker had taken a few steps backward while they were talking. He was at the curb now and had nowhere to go to get away from Damian and his questions.

Spinnaker was looking worried as he had no idea who this stranger was and yet he seemed to know all kinds of information about him. He'd been slow on paying some of his debts at the casino, and the people he owed money to offered to forgive his debt if he would act as a go-between on a poster of a missing child. He'd been carrying the phone around for months and had received one call from an old neighbor of the missing child. Now he was confronted by an angry man who looked vaguely familiar, though James couldn't quite put his finger on where he knew the man from.

"Look, do you know where the child is? If you don't, we have nothing to talk about," Spinnaker said sidestepping Damian to head toward his office.

"Who hired you? Who's standing behind you wanting Hannah?" Damian was beginning to feel frustrated with himself for dealing with this man instead of notifying his superiors about his side job searching for a missing child for a friend.

"Do you know where the parents are? Have you met them?"

Spinnaker stopped and looked back at Damian and said, "Look I'll arrange a video call with her parents if you tell me you know how to contact the child. Are you hiding her?" Spinnaker asked suspiciously.

"You arrange that video call and if it's the girl's parents on the other end of the video then I might tell you where the kid is."

"Does she live with you?" Spinnaker asked.

"No she doesn't. Look, when you're ready to set up the call here is my contact information," Damian said giving the man a number tied to a phone that was in no way attached to him.

James Spinnaker nodded and turned away with Damian's card when he asked a final question that was bugging him.

"I saw the missing child poster in downtown Oakland. Where all did you put that notice up?"

"I put it up in every restaurant in Oakland because that's the closest major city to Shepard Canyon where the child lived."

Damian nodded and the two men parted ways. At least he had one question answered. No way was he going to expose Hannah to a video call. They, and Damian didn't know who the 'they' were, likely didn't plan to have her parents on the other end of that call. Of that he was sure.

There was nothing for him to do but head back to the marina and his boat and wait for the call to come through setting up the video call. He'd give the guy four days to call him, and if he didn't, he would provide the evidence he collected on the guy to his supervisor. In the meantime he wanted to find a fake Hannah Sherwood AKA Hermione that he could put on a video call.

He decided he would collect from Hermione all of the pictures she had of herself a year ago. He could transform them into a holographic image that would make it seem real like she was really in the room with Damian. He'd take the call on his island as they would be unable to trace him. He owned the satellite in the sky that he bounced his transmissions off of. He was both the owner and sole user of the satellite, and he could refuse any calls from any government agency to identify himself. He turned his boat towards Ariana's house as he needed the pictures now, but then Damian remembered that Hermione was still in school and he would have to wait for her to find the photos he needed. He wouldn't violate her privacy by searching her room for pictures. So he changed course again and headed toward Richmond and his warehouse.

Some days it felt so normal to walk into his office and work on inventions instead of dealing with one of Natalie's cold cases or some issue or sporting event with Hermione. He thought he would no longer have to worry about keeping the girl safe as the pharmaceutical company that was after her parents had dissolved and the CEO had gone to jail. His work with Hermione involved him searching for her parents. Their contact from Malaysia seemed to believe that her parents had escaped capture by getting off the boat they were being held on and swimming ashore. Damian had never been able to confirm that her parents were dead or alive.

He would clear his mind and give his employees his full attention today and see how he could move each of their inventions along.

They were all smart, but sometimes his second set of eyes saw some modification that would make their project work. He walked into the building and waved to everyone. He set stuff down on his desk and then returned to where his people were working.

"Did you go to Pete's last night?"

"We did," Haley said. "We're so excited to have Pete open here, and we all gave him hints on how to make his business successful. We'll all be his ambassadors in this neighborhood to see that his good reputation gets out."

"I'm going to sit down with him on Friday and create a project timeline to get him to the opening," Lily added. "There are things he doesn't know like how long construction will take and what delays he should expect from city planning. Besides my project management background, I waitressed for a few years, so I can give him input from that perspective to make it more employee and customer friendly."

"I told Pete if he needs another pair of hands to help with various aspects of getting the restaurant complete, that I can help him in the evening," Angus said. "I learned carpentry skills in prison since we made furniture for all the University of California schools."

"Sounds like you all are trying to do something to help Pete. Keep me posted if there's a way I can contribute that I haven't noticed. I want to spend my entire day with each of you one-on-one working through some of the problems you're having. Chris, you're first!"

With that explanation his staff hustled to their project cubicles as most of them were working on something that combined computer work with engineered movement or properties.

"Pete showed us the software and liquor dispensing system you designed for him. That was amazing," Chris said. "Sometimes the work we do here is abstract or it's in such a beginning stage that we lose track of the idea of a finished product that's useful and profitable."

"Thanks, Chris. Pete and I go way back and early on in our friendship, I noticed the turnover of his staff and his harassed personality. When he told me what the problem was with alcohol, I knew I had to design something that fixed the problem for him. The first system was ugly, there was lots of duct tape, and I got the purple colored glue for PVC pipes everywhere on the white pipes, but as I came to make changes to the system, it got better and better until I could sell it beyond Pete."

"Thankfully you have patience with us as we seem to be much slower than you in figuring out how to solve problems with the technology we design here."

"Chris, I don't have all the answers. When I started down the design road for Pete, all I wanted to fix was to stop the theft of alcohol. I don't know if Pete demonstrated the system for you, but it also tracks employees hours for payroll, liquor inventory, and it even sends orders to the distributors to make sure Pete has enough liquor to serve his customers, but not too much inventory that takes up space or uses up Pete's cash. So with this wave energy technology, we're starting by trying to bring electricity to poor and/or remote islands, but as we go on, we may get into battery storage and underground electrical systems because it's all connected."

Damian realized by the time he left that he needed to do this with his staff more often. The weekly staff meeting updates weren't deep enough problem-solving moments for him and his team. He'd cancel those and instead devote his time to in-depth, one on one meetings. For the third time that day, he headed across the bay, this time to Belvedere arriving just before Ariana and Hermione came home. He'd been sitting outside watching the boats on the bay as well as a gray whale that was having a blast splashing as the animal powered out of the water only to do a belly flop. He was smiling, lost in the glory of the day when he heard the door open behind him and soon he was surrounded by Hermione and Ariana.

Ariana smelled of a mild floral scent while Hermione was wearing grass stains on her clothes.

He put an arm around each of them and said looking out to the water, "Isn't it a beautiful day here. Look at the whales frolicking in the water."

The three of them sat there in silence watching the show by Mother Nature.

"Not that we aren't enjoying the scenery and your company, but there must be a reason you're sitting on my deck chairs rather than your own," Ariana said.

"Given the height of my island, sometimes it's hard to see whales, and I worry when they get in my neck of the bay that they might be heading up the river where they can get stuck. I much prefer watching the whales here where they'll be safe swimming toward the Golden Gate and beyond to the Pacific Ocean. Anyway I'm here for pictures. Hermione, I'm going to make a hologram of you, and I need as many pictures of you as you have just before we changed your hair."

"What's a hologram and why are you doing that?"

"I spoke with James Spinnaker and we agreed to arrange a video call with your parents. I'm not impressed with him, I think he's a pawn for someone else. So rather than have you there in person, I'll create an image of you as though you were there."

"That's a bummer and that's cool."

Damian looked at the teenager with his eyebrow raised clearly telling her to explain her comments.

"It's a bummer that it won't be my parents on the call and it's cool that you can create a 3-D image of me from pictures. How will you make me talk?"

"I don't think I'll have you talk, I'll set up the image so that you nod yes or no to any questions thrown at you. Once the people purported to be your parents come on screen and we see that they're not, the call gets ended."

"How can you tell if it is my parents?"

"I've seen the pictures you have of them and the video of the night they were kidnapped. I'm also going to have you around, but out of sight of the camera for you to verify that they're not your parents."

"Yeah! I can't wait to watch this. When is the call taking place?"

"I don't have a date and time yet, but we'll do the call from my island as our location will be untraceable. We'll do outside of school hours and against a blank wall so that no surrounding or background can be identified."

"Can they figure out who you are, Damian?"

"No, the camera on my end will have software in it that distorts my face enough that they won't be able to identify me. It changes the distance between my eyes which is a key identifier in facial recognition software."

"Okay. I'm sure you have this all figured out. Can you do a hologram now so I see what I look like?"

"I can give you a crude hologram tonight, but the one that I'll go with will be more nuanced."

"You should come to demonstrate this to my science class."

"Do any of the other parents lecture to your class?"

Hermione thought for a while and replied, "No, but they have arranged guest speakers to talk to the class. I guess I might get ribbed about you from the other kids."

Damian smiled and said, "That would be the normal and expected teenage response. Why don't you go get that shower to get the turf off you, then you can look for pictures, and after dinner, I'll show you the first hologram of yourself."

"Cool," Hermione said as she stood up and headed to her bedroom.

Ariana just leaned against Damian and said, "You're a special man, Damian Green. I enjoy being a parent to Hermione, but I couldn't do it without you. You smooth out all the curves of our existence."

"Now you're making me blush with your effusive praise. Stop. This could be the end of our days as parents, if I'm wrong and Hermione's real parents are on the other end of that call."

"I think you're right about it not being her parents and obviously Hermione does too. The whole thing is so shady that it doesn't feel like a reunion with her parents is possible."

"One question I got answered by Spinnaker was about Pete's Bar. He said he put flyers up in many places in Oakland as it was near Shepard Canyon. We would have a different problem on our hands if the 'they', whoever that is, specifically targeted locations they thought I would be at. This was all a lucky coincidence that I saw the poster. Then again, Hermione's old neighbors also saw the poster so I guess that's luck times two. Once we get to the end of all this, I'll share some information with his department about his gambling habit. It's the least I can do."

"It would be hard to let go of Hermione, but if her real parents are there, I'll have to do that."

Damian hugged Ariana, "I really think you'll be enjoying Hermione's company for the near future. This man doesn't ring true. Of more concern is who's behind James Spinnaker. I thought we were at the end of people wanting Hermione as a way to reach her parents. The kid doesn't know how to reach her parents, but whomever is after her this time, doesn't know she has no connection. Or they know where her parents are and think that by holding Hermione hostage, they could bring them out of hiding. Can you think of any other scenarios?"

The next day Damian was back at his warehouse working on his hologram of Hermione. She'd been fascinated by the crude one he created the previous night for her, and all three of them were amazed at how different she looked now compared to the hologram made from pictures that were twelve to eighteen months old. She was of an age that her face was going through rapid change. He even showed her how he could make her head nod in agreement. Now he was working on resizing her image so that her head was larger. He asked his employees but no one had experience with holograms, and so they had been checking in on his progress during the day. When asked why he was creating it, he said it was because he was doing a guest lecture at Hermione's school.

Lily made a note to ask Jacob's teachers to invite Damian as the work he was doing was fascinating even to kids. It was the first time she watched him create a project from scratch. Each of the inventions they were working on had been started by him, and so they had missed out on the early stages. It was fun to watch him flop as he tried things to make his creation better.

By the end of the day, Damian felt pleased with his hologram and called Ariana and showed her. She was sure it would pass on a video call as it looked like a younger Hermione. Now all he had to do was wait for the call to be arranged.

He left work early and returned to his island. Some days he loved sitting on a rocky outcropping on his island and fishing for the two cats. He was amused as they were near-by, ready to eat the fish as soon as they came wiggling out of the Bay. He was more fastidious and wanted to clean them for his pets. He collected enough for the next few days and made his way back into the house.

For whatever reason, he was feeling very introspective recently. He thought about the conversation he'd had with Jen and the girls out on the Bay a few days ago. He found himself thinking more and more about Ariana. Was he ready for a new relationship and was she? In the raising of Hermione, he had gotten to know her very well, and she had many qualities that he admired and frankly none that he didn't. Through Hermione and his business, their lives were entangled. Did he want to try and tangle them some more or might he wreck the other parts of his life if he pursued Ariana? The feedback he picked up from her was she enjoyed his company, but did she want more?

If he pursued a relationship how would they combine households? He could expand his house, perhaps add another story. His work was in Richmond, but Hermione went to school in Ariana's neighborhood and he wanted to keep her at the school as she was thriving. Maybe someday her parents would come back into her life. They'd both be happy for the girl, but they would deeply miss her. Would a relationship with Ariana survive without the sharing of Hermione?

He had no answers tonight; he was stuck in a waiting pattern for the video call to be arranged. He decided to pass the evening watching the Warriors game against San Antonio. This year they weren't as tough an opponent as they had been in the past. Without Tim Duncan, they weren't doing as well. The big guy hadn't played a lot of minutes in the last few years, but he was the heart of the team, and with his retirement, the team seemed to have lost its soul.

He was making some popcorn at half-time when the burner phone rang. He walked over to his coffee table and picked up the call.

"Yes."

"This is James Spinnaker. Am I speaking to Ryan Thompson?"

"You are," Damian said, having identified that as his name to Spinnaker.

"I'm ready to set up the video call with Hannah Sherwood. When can you arrange it?"

"You'll have her parents? I'll end any video call if I don't see her parents."

"Do you know what her parents look like?"

"Yes."

"When is Hannah available? Can she do a call right now?"

"No. how about tomorrow evening at eight?"

"Ah, ok. Is this the number I should call for a video call? Does your phone have Facetime or Skype or something?"

"Call this number tomorrow, and you'll see Hannah on the screen."

"Ok."

Damian cut the call then. He went down to his lab to look at the blank wall and a tripod to hold the phone. He checked everything to make sure no angles would be caught on the video call. He wanted a plain blank room and when he checked his hologram against it, it all looked real.

Picking up his phone he called Ariana.

"Did you forget something?"

"No, Spinnaker called so I'm inviting you guys to dinner at my place tomorrow and then we'll do the call at eight. You're welcome to stay overnight, or you can go home in the dark."

"I'll check the forecast, but as it's a school day, staying at your place will add thirty minutes to our drive. I'll bring Miguel, so we're prepared either way."

"Is Hermione anxious about the video call?"

"I would say she's more curious. She has complete faith that you're right at all times, and so if you say that it won't likely be her parents, then that's the expectation she has."

"Yikes! I'm frequently wrong. If I could see the future accurately, I'd be God I guess, and a billionaire."

Ariana laughed and replied, "I think we're both so different from her parents and so stable, not that her parents are mentally unstable, but just life stable that she can relax around us. Besides you are brilliant and have managed to get her on every sports team her heart desires and save her from bad people several times, so you are her superhero."

"Please Ariana, you're making me blush with the effusive compliments. I'm sure you're a Catherine of Aragon to her as well for how you handle these bad people, and you got Miguel!"

"Too-shay, it's all about the dog. You're right I win."

"See you tomorrow about six?"

"Yeah. Have a good night, Damian."

"Ditto."

'You schmuck!' Damian thought. He could have said sweet-nothings, and instead he said, 'ditto'. You'll have to up your romance skills if you decide to try and woo Ariana, he told himself.

He spent a few more moments thinking about the next day and then went to look at his refrigerator to see what he needed the next day to serve the ladies a meal. He'd grab a dessert on the way home from work tomorrow as well as some vegetables. The sole was biting at the moment so they'd have a fillet of sole. His menu complete he went back to the game, happy to see the usual third-quarter sweep by the Warriors taking place. He'd missed about half of the quarter, and while he had, the Warriors had put the game to bed.

CHAPTER 18

*D*amian had tried the hologram several times throughout the day and was anxious to have the video call and end the interaction with Spinnaker. Ariana had begun work for a lease agreement with Pete based on his space needs. He didn't need the entire bottom floor, so Damian would build offices in the remaining space and make the upstairs a series of labs for his staff to test ideas. He could set up some safer testing processes if he created individual labs based on different testing needs. As they worked on his child dye GPS system, they'd be doing chemistry experiments that required a ventilating hood. Haley needed a glass shield to protect her from the drone as she'd crashed it into herself a few times.

Finally, he left the office, making a stop for groceries, and he was soon loading his boat with supplies and heading over to his island. Once there he went through his usual routine of fishing, but this time he was fishing for the three of them rather than his cats. He could catch silver perch out of the bay quickly, but this time he was looking for sole and it might take him as long as an hour if the fish weren't biting. To make matters worse, it had started raining so he was covered head to toe in rain gear. Fortunately, Ariana's boat could be enclosed so they wouldn't get wet. He'd checked the weather before he went outside and the rain was expected to be light until the next day.

His fishing luck was with him, and he soon had enough sole for the three humans, two cats, and the dog. Everyone would eat well tonight. He was in the kitchen when he got the text that they were leaving Belvedere. He set his timer for ten minutes so he could head downstairs and put out his dock and help tie up Ariana's boat.

Working in the kitchen a while longer, he soon left to assist Ariana and Hermione with tying down their boat.

"Hello ladies," he said as Ariana steered the boat against his dock. They quickly secured the boat and ran inside to get out of the rain. It was a little heavier than when he'd been fishing.

"What's for dessert? I'm starved," Hermione asked.

"We aren't starting with dessert so how will that curb your hunger?" Damian asked.

"I figure I'll have to eat a nutritious dinner before I'm allowed dessert. So dinner's like soccer practice and dessert is the real soccer game."

"Nice simile, Hermione. It's key lime pie."

"Yum! Can you show me the finished hologram now?"

"Sure." Damian walked over to the computer on his laboratory bench and hit a few keys, then he had Hermione call him on his cell in video mode and look at her screen.

"O-M-G! It's me at a younger age. Make me nod yes."

Damian did just that.

"As much as I would hate having my parents in class, you really need to teach that to my high school class. It's so cool! What can you use it for in the real world?"

"Good question. People actually store data in holograms, and it's used a lot in the medical field to visualize organs, and Salvador Dali used it in creating art. There are some more abstract uses, but you'd have to know a lot more engineering concepts to understand."

"So can I ask my teacher if you can come to demonstrate this technology?"

"Sure, but the real question is which teacher?"

Hermione thought for a while about the subjects she was learning and said, "I think my physics class is the best choice. We're all a bunch of nerds and it would be nice to have a cool skill compared to the rest of the student body."

Damian laughed and said, "Let me know if you're successful talking your teacher into a demonstration. If he wants, I could meet him outside of class and go over what I would say and do."

"That's really thoughtful, Damian," Ariana said.

"I imagine every teacher has had a student ask their teacher if their parent can come to demonstrate something. Probably sometimes it works, and sometimes it doesn't depending on the subject and the parent. I think I could bring enough equipment for say six teams of students to divide up and make their own holograms which would be a practical lesson for the students."

"Damian, you are scary smart," Hermione said. "I honestly can't think of a moment since I've lived with you guys where I wanted to call you stupid in my head."

Damian was touched by the kid's off-hand comment and had to give her a hug. It was about the biggest compliment any adult could expect from a teenager. He looked over Hermione's head to Ariana and saw her blinking tears away. He motioned her to join the hug, but she shook her head, knowing the kid would move on to a different subject in a matter of seconds.

While he finished cooking dinner, Damian questioned Hermione in depth about her classes, in part thinking about his teen summer employment program and what he could have kids do. He'd never worked with that age group or anything close to it, and he wondered how he was going to find a balancing act between productivity, learning, and inspiration.

"So tomorrow is your first soccer game, right?" Damian asked.

"Yes."

"Are you ready for it?"

"I think so. I really need it. I can so predict where my teammates are aiming the ball that I block probably ninety-five percent of the kicks. I'm wondering what's going to happen when I'm faced with players I know nothing about. I'm hoping I don't let down the team."

"Remember that to some degree all of your teammates feel the same way. They know how each of you dribbles and exactly how much ball control each of you has."

"Yeah, but I'm the only player on the varsity team that has never played before trying out for the team."

Damian thought for a moment and said, "Your school uses a soccer ball machine, doesn't it? How do you do against its artificial intelligence? Are you as good at blocking those balls?"

"I'd say my percentage with the machine drops to about eighty percent. It's also a matter of whether I can get in place to block the ball. I head for the right place, but I'm not always tall enough or fast enough to block the ball."

"Who's your back-up?" Ariana asked.

"Back-up?" Hermione asked.

"If you were to get injured in a game, the game isn't over, your coach would have to turn to someone else to play goalkeeper."

"I hadn't thought about that, but he seems not to be training anyone else. Maybe he'll elevate the goalkeeper from the JV team."

"I'm sure he has a plan, but the fact that he doesn't have anyone else practicing suggests he has supreme confidence in you."

"Okay."

"We'll both be there to support you tomorrow," Damian said.

"I don't know whether that's good or bad. I hate for you guys to watch an epic fail on my part."

"You won't have an epic fail, Hermione. You have an instinct for the soccer ball and good hand and eye coordination. I daresay that after this season, college recruiters will be eyeing you for scholarships as you'd be a multi-sport athlete. You play for the school in multiple sports, but they only have to give you one free scholarship," Ariana said.

"Now you've really upped the pressure on me. I'll be disappointed if I don't get that kind of attention."

"Look I wasn't an athlete growing up, and I did just fine in college and you will too. We can afford your college tuition even if you decide never to play a sport again," Damian said.

"Is dinner almost ready? I'm starving. I might have to have dessert first."

"Nice try kiddo, but we're going to be mean parents and make you eat your vegetables first," Ariana said with a smile.

Damian handed her plates and silverware to lay out on his breakfast counter since he didn't have a dining table. Soon they were all eating and Damian and Ariana discussed the plan for Pete's restaurant inside Damian's warehouse.

"Do you think he'll have it up and running by the time I'm working there in the summer?"

"No. Pete has to get permits, hire a contractor and designer, pass inspections, and hire staff. I don't see it opening until a year from now," Ariana guessed, and Damian nodded.

"Okay, next summer. How long do you think this call is going to take?" Hermione asked.

Another abrupt change of subject for the teenager, Damian thought. He was a little less used to her frequent change of topics than Ariana.

"I'm guessing under sixty seconds. I'm expecting Spinnaker to call me and we'll only see each other on screen. I'll ask to see your parents first. He may demand that he see you first. If that happens, I will turn my head to the side and invite you over, but instead of you moving, I'll be turning on the hologram and moving you into the screen view."

"How can you have me walk into the screen?"

"I debated how I was going to do that and decided, I would have your hologram behind a screen, and I'll ask Ariana to move the screen revealing you. If he doesn't bring your parents immediately into his screen, we'll end the call. If he brings your parents into the screen and it's not really them, then we'll end the call. If you think it might be them, then let's have a question planned to verify their knowledge. What question should we ask?"

Hermione thought for a while and then said, "Ask them what I was going to name my dog if we ever got one. I nagged my parents for years about getting a dog, but I think they were worried that it might complicate our run into the safe room if we worried about a dog too."

"What's the answer to that question?" Ariana asked.

"Toto, I loved the Wizard of Oz because at times, I felt that we as a family were always looking for the Emerald City. I was Dorothy, and I had a dog named Toto."

"Okay," Damian said thinking about Hermione's constantly unsettled life with her parents always on the run.

They moved on to dessert and then went down to Damian's lab to do a few dry-runs of the call. The rain had trailed off, and so Ariana planned to head home after the call since Hermione had her first soccer game tomorrow. After Miguel barked at Hermione's hologram, they moved him upstairs as it wouldn't pay to have him barking during the call. Then they were ready to go.

CHAPTER 19

They were all seated in their places and Hermione's hologram was floating on air. Damian had decided just to use a large piece of cardboard to block the view of the hologram. Ariana who couldn't be seen, would slide it sideways at the right time. Hermione was seated off to the side where she could see what was on Damian 's screen but not be in view of the camera.

The phone rang and Damian connected the call, and they exchanged pleasantries while each brought the video side of the call to their screens.

When Damian could see Spinnaker on the other end, he waved and said, "I see you, but I don't see Hannah's parents or indeed anyone else with you there in the room. Where are her parents?"

"Likewise I don't see Hannah on your side. You show me Hannah, and I show you her parents."

Damian didn't want to roll over too quickly for this jerk so he said, "No, you show the parents first. I know what they look like, so once I verify their identity, I'll show you Her..annah."

Damian could kick himself for almost giving away her current name. If whoever wanted Hannah Sherwood knew she was going by the name Hermione Knowles, she'd be a lot easier to find.

"Look Ryan, I won't introduce her parents until you show me Hannah."

Good, Damian thought, Spinnaker seemed to miss his near screw-up on Hermione's name.

Damian nodded to Ariana, who moved the cardboard screen to reveal the hologram of Hannah Sherwood, almost two years younger than her current age.

"Okay, here's Hannah, now show me her parents or I cut the call right now as I never believed you had contact with her parents."

Damian watched as a man and woman came into view. He didn't believe they were Hannah's parents, just two people made up to look like them."

"I don't think you're the real parents. What was Hannah going to name a dog that you might one day buy for her?"

The couple looked blankly at Damian. He listened for Hermione to render an opinion on the image and he heard her say softly, "Those are not my real parents. They don't have the answer to an easy question, and they don't have the right mannerisms. Mom has a habit of twirling her hair while she talks and this woman isn't doing that."

"Hannah says you're not her real parents. Goodbye," Damian said cutting the connection.

The screen went blank and there was silence in the room for a few moments, then Hermione said sadly, "I wanted them to be my parents, but they weren't. It was just like you said Damian."

"I'm not always right kiddo," Damian said putting his arm around her shoulder. "They didn't seem desperately thrilled to be re-acquainted with you. That was my analysis of the couple's behavior. If I'd been searching for you for over a year, I'd have a look of desperation and excitement that it might really be you."

"Yeah, but then I wasn't real either," Hermione said with a grin. "Do you think they were holograms too?"

"No, they were trying to look like a couple by holding hands," Damian said turning on Hermione's hologram. "If I tried to put my hand on you, this is what it would look like," Damian said demonstrating, and his hand touched her shoulder, but then when he looked at Hermione it moved and ended up inside her skull.

"Whoops!" Hermione laughed. "You just accidentally touched my brain."

"Ouch," Ariana said. "That looks like your brains should start leaking out."

The three of them smiled at each other, glad for a reduction in the tension.

"So what are your next steps," Ariana asked.

"I'm going to let Spinnaker's supervisors know what he is up to in his free time. He seems open to bribery or extortion which is not a good position to be in if you work for Homeland Security. That will get him out of the equation."

"Are you going to find out who was behind him? Who was extorting or bribing him to do what he did?"

"Frankly, I don't know how," Damian said.

"Could you look at where his phone is right now and might that tell you something? Did he make any calls recently to set up this video call?" Hermione suggested.

Damian looked at her and smiled, "We're going to make a detective out of you yet. Perhaps you'd rather spend your summer with Retired Detective Natalie Severino, than at my business," Damian said clacking away at the computer keys to get answers to Hermione's questions.

Ariana had been watching the weather since the call ended to make sure it was still relatively safe to head back home in the dark. They didn't want to be caught by heavy rain or dense fog at night. The crossing looked safe at the moment and she wanted to get going as Hermione had had an emotional night and tomorrow was her debut as a soccer goalkeeper.

"We need to head home while the weather is decent. There's light rain and light fog, and it's not expected to get any more intense in the next thirty minutes. Damian, why don't you find the answers to Detective Hermione's questions and give us a call once we make it home. I'll run upstairs and grab Miguel."

As Ariana went up the stairs she heard Damian ask, "Are you really okay, kiddo? You're not crushed by the fact they weren't your parents, right?"

"No, you'd prepared me that it wouldn't likely be, so there wasn't as big a letdown as you might expect," Hermione said and then added after a pause, "You and Ariana have been everything I could have wished for in substitute parents, and so it's not like if those had been my real parents that they would have saved me from the Wicked Witch of the West and a serial killer for foster parents."

Damian had to laugh at what he and Ariana were compared to and said, "Well kiddo, we are at least better than that."

Shortly thereafter, he watched Ariana and Hermione push off from his dock and point the boat towards Belvedere. He pulled the dock in and locked up his watercraft garage for the night and went back to the computer to see if he could find the answers to Hermione's questions.

Once he had the answers to Hermione's questions, it was merely a matter of time waiting for Ariana to call once she made it home.

His phone rang, and he asked, "Was it a boring ride back across the Bay?"

"For the most part yes. We missed having to cross the path of the ferries returning to San Francisco. A few fishermen out but certainly no pleasure boats. What did you find on Spinnaker's calls? I have my phone on speaker so Detective Hermione can hear your answer," Ariana said, and Damian could hear the relaxed amusement in her voice.

"Spinnaker conducted the call from a yacht moored at Pier 39 in San Francisco. I'll go visit the location tomorrow to see who owns the boat. I should be able to get close enough on my boat to read the call numbers of that boat. As to who he called to set up the meeting – he used a burner phone, so I can't trace the owner, only that the call pinged off a cell tower in San Francisco. I think the boat ownership will tell us a lot."

"Can you go over tonight in case the yacht moves?" Hermione asked.

"I could and perhaps that's another good idea Detective Hermione. Let me get my speedster out and go see what I can find out about the boat, now."

"Sorry Damian, it's going to be a long night," Ariana said.

"Yeah, I'll probably be close to eleven getting home, but I would kick myself if the boat moved by the time I got there tomorrow, so it is what it is."

"Call or text us. We want to know you're safe."

"Of course I'll be safe, but I'll take a few tools just to make sure, I stay safe."

"Damian, can you tell which mooring contained the boat? I remember seeing a lot of boats there," Hermione asked.

"I can, and I'm going to take my cell phone number detector in case Spinnaker is still on the boat, though I don't know why he would be. The last I checked he was still on the boat, but I would think he would head home to his family."

They ended the call and Damian changed into all black clothing, and grabbed a few of his favorite tools. Ten minutes later, he had his dock back out, and he was getting into his two-seater speedster to head across the bay to the pier. He guessed, given the time of night, that it would be a thirty-five-minute journey in light rain. He'd checked the forecast before he got on the boat and knew the bay would remain calm for the length of time he expected to be on the water.

After an uneventful ride, he had slowed and was heading into the area where the yacht was parked. There were ferries docked for the night that during the day would cruise to Alcatraz prison full of tourists interested in visiting the rock. He slowed some more spotting lights on the yacht in question. He had his camera ready and took multiple shots with a long-range lens. He heard a big splash on the side of the boat, but no activity from any other boats parked at the marina. This side of the marina accommodated bigger boats and commercial ferries and a Neptune Society boat which were less likely to have activity on them at night. He was satisfied that he'd collected everything he could about the boat, and so it was time to turn around and head out. There were men on top of the boat watching out for it, which made Damian wonder who they were expecting an attack from. Then he noticed that a launch was lowered into the water and two men were getting into it. Perhaps they'd seen him taking pictures. It was time to go.

Damian went over the set harbor speed limit as he thought the boat might be chasing him. He passed a bunch of sea lions napping on the K-docks and set their floating platforms rolling. His boat was small, but the motor wasn't, and so its wake would shake up the sea lions' platform. He shortly heard them barking their unhappiness as his boat's wake wave hit their platform. Damian hoped his wave would dump a bunch of the sea lions into the harbor which would make it difficult for the other boat to navigate. You didn't want to hit one at any time as they were big enough to put a hole in a boat the size of his chasers. Sure enough, when he looked back, the sea lions were blocking the boat. The two passengers were trying to shoo them away, but they had no food to move the 450-pound creatures out of their way. Meanwhile, Damian disappeared into the darkness. He was grateful for the fog as it encompassed him as he passed Alcatraz on the way home to his much smaller island.

Once he got beyond the island he studied other boats out on the water and thought no one was chasing him. He made it home by just after ten, texting Ariana that he was home safe. He'd tell her about the chase the next day as they watched Hermione's soccer game.

As soon as he had the dock pulled in and the island locked up tight, he went to work in his lab trying to figure out who the boat belonged to. It was rented by a corporation and after walking through many documents online he arrived at another pharmaceutical house based in Malaysia. He thought he was done with corrupt overlords from that country but it seemed he was wrong. Hermione's parents must have angered more than one pharmaceutical manufacturer. He'd have to question her tomorrow to see if she knew anything more. The trouble was she was young and her parents had excluded her from many conversations about their dirty dealings with Asian drug manufacturers, yet the manufacturers were still after her to get to her parents. That meant they still thought her parents were alive but in hiding. Hermione had come up with some good ideas tonight about what to look for, maybe after they celebrated her first game, she would ask him some more interesting questions.

CHAPTER 20

*D*amian was listening to the news the next morning while eating breakfast when an item caught his attention, he heard the newscaster say, "A body had been found near Pier 39 floating, and nibbled on by the sea lions. He had no identification and police were seeking his identity, as his fingertips were part of what was nibbled on."

Oh my, thought Damian, he should call the police. But what was his reason to be in that harbor at that time last night? Maybe he should do it anonymously? But he really wanted that yacht harassed. Maybe he would make up a story that he and Ariana had been to a game to see the Giants and they dined after at Pier 39 because his boat was parked there? No, it wasn't baseball season or football unless you were in the playoffs. If they watched a Warriors game, it would be over in time, but there wasn't a game last night. If they were on a date, it was no one's first choice of dining locations. Any meetings in the city would be long over by that time of night, but maybe there was a convention at the Moscone Center he was attending, but he checked the meeting schedule, and he had nothing to do with the medical field so he wouldn't have a reason to be there. He just couldn't think of an excuse to be in that area of San Francisco, so he'd have to call the anonymous line. Darn, he also wanted to send them some pictures he took that were time stamped, but he'd after to do that on his encrypted system which would hide his identity.

He took some time to compose an email message of what he'd heard and who he thought the body was that they had retrieved.

I've included a picture of James Spinnaker, an employee of Homeland Security with a video-game gambling problem. I believe that's the identity of the body you found near Pier 39 this morning. I've also included the photos I shot of the yacht with the timestamps. When I thought I heard a large splash from the side of the boat, I assumed was a sea lion entering the water, not a man. If it turns out that the body was James Spinnaker then the people on the yacht tossed him over. The picture of him at a video-game machine in a building in the Mission District which I believe has been under your surveillance over the past few years.

After he composed the email, he studied it a minute and tried to think of anything to add but nothing came up. So he hit send, and the email was on its way to the detective division of SFPD. He wished he could show himself in person, but he'd been unable to think of a legitimate excuse for him being there at that time of night. He was tempted to stop by Pier 39 on his way to work that morning to see if the yacht was still there, but even if it had moved, the police and Coast Guard could trace a vessel of that size, and it couldn't be that far away.

Damian let his curiosity get the better of him and so on the way to work he swung by the harbor to see if the yacht was still there. He tried to see from the break-wall but it was too far away for him to be sure, so he slowly entered and navigated by the barking, smelly, sea lions on their platform. As he approached the section of the moorings where the yacht had been parked, he was delighted to see that it was still there and that police were on board. Even if they were routinely questioning every boat owner in the vicinity of the yacht, that was good enough for him. He turned around and headed away, hopefully before anyone noticed him. He'd moved his bumpers and fenders as he approached the break-wall to hide the call numbers of his boat in case anyone was looking. Damian wore sunglasses and a hat, sitting low in his speedster boat, there was nothing for any facial recognition to match if someone did get his photo. Soon he was back out in the bay with a big grin on his face as headed to the dock at Richmond.

He monitored the news throughout the day from his office to see if police were able to identify the body. Finally at about three, just before he was heading home to change clothes to go watch Hermione's game, there was news that the body was identified as belonging to one James Spinnaker. It said he left a wife and two children behind. Damian felt sorry for his family, but then again surely the wife knew of the gambling problem. The news was quick to point out that he was not on Homeland Security duty at the time he was murdered, and there were no indications that it was related to his work. Then they moved on to other news.

When Damian wrote the email to the detective division, he'd set up a fake email address to hide him and his location. Those attributes would stay in place until he permanently destroyed the account. He debated when he set it up if he should answer the police if they sent him any questions. He decided he would wait and see what if any questions were emailed to him before he closed the account.

After the brief stop at his island, he continued across to Belvedere. He was sidetracked thinking about a solar-powered boat as last night plus today's trips had drained the gas in his boat. Could he make a solar-powered boat? Given the number of rainy and foggy days that might not be a great idea. Maybe he could harness wind power and use it for a motor rather than for sails. As he was steering he did a quick internet search and discovered there were already solar-powered boats. Ariana's pontoon style boat really lent itself to covering the roof of the boat with solar panels. He would have to order a few kits and outfit all of their boats with the technology.

Once he resolved his boat's power needs, he returned to thinking about Spinnaker and how to reach Hermione's parents. How could he find them? Should he reach out to Spinnaker's supervisor at Homeland Security and tell them what he'd done in regards to Hermione?

Soon he and Ariana were driving to a distant high school. Hermione's first game would be as a visitor, but a net was a net and really she didn't need to worry about getting used to a different field. Damian described his night, then the email to the detectives, and his thoughts about where Hermione's parents were.

"I'm out of ideas to find her parents. They're either hiding on their own, hiding with the help of a U.S. Government agency, or dead. I think someone must have verification that they're alive for the attacks to keep coming for Hermione," Damian lamented.

"Have you looked at any court proceedings? Is any government suing these drug companies that Hermione's parents might be witnesses to? Is that why they're still trying to kidnap her?" Ariana suggested.

They'd arrive at the field where the match would be played. They could see Hermione guarding her net.

"Should we sit with other parents from her school or go sit by the goal net and yell support at her?" Damian asked carrying folding chairs and a small cooler for the two of them. When they were fans of Hermione's swim and water polo meets there wasn't as much choice as there seemed to be on the soccer field.

"Sit with the other parents. We don't want to look like we're there to guard our girl and besides they'll switch directions at the half. We don't want to ruin her concentration by being too close."

They set up chairs close to the mid-line of the field, and they each grabbed a cold iced tea. The weather was perfect, but they were very nervous about her debut as a goalkeeper. Ariana couldn't help herself about ten minutes into the match when Hermione successfully blocked a kick into the net. She reached over and grabbed Damian's hand to contain her anxiety for Hermione. Over the next half hour of the game it became a clear struggle for Hermione's team. They had far fewer attempts than the home team, but Hermione's goalkeeping was keeping them in the game.

They took a break at the half, and the coach had a conversation with the girls. Damian was interested in seeing if they changed their strategy in the second half. He hoped they got something going on the offense to give Hermione a rest. All of the action was at her net for the first half.

The whistle was blown and the second half began. Damian leaned over to Ariana and said, "Ah, the half-time speech worked. Look. Instead of all the players bunching up on defense to help Hermione, they're back to where they should be on the field."

Indeed as they watched, they saw the defense forwarding the ball to the offense to take it to the opponents net. It was there that they discovered that Hermione was the superior goalkeeper and they scored on their opponent.

They were folding up their chairs preparing to leave, a victory for Hermione's team on the scoreboard when Damian said, "Hermione has a good coach. His halftime speech changed the game to the girls' favor."

"Yeah, I didn't see him yell at any of the players throughout the game. Instead he ran alongside complementing them on each kick, and calling the ball mistakes simply bad luck. It was a second-half rout! Hermione might have found her sport. I wonder how she feels about this versus water polo or the more individual sport of swimming?"

They stopped for some tea in town at their favorite tea house, knowing that the Hermione would likely have at least thirty minutes before she was ready to go."

"Would you mind if I outfitted all of our boats with solar panels?" Damian asked.

"Do we have to get different motors that run on electricity then?"

"I envision a dual system that reverts to gas when solar power runs out. In fog filled San Francisco Bay, you might only be able to use your boat about half the year if we relied only on solar."

"Will it be ugly?"

"Not for your boat as we'll just cover the canopy with the panels. My boats are another story, and I suppose they'll be ugly. My boats are worst because they spend time inside the watercraft garage when they could be soaking up the sun."

"Why don't you put panels on that side of the island and have them charge up your boats? You have more sunshine where you are than Belvedere has."

"That will work. You're full of brilliant ideas today!" Damian said smiling into Ariana's eyes.

Then he got serious and asked before he lost his nerve. "Have you thought of us dating?"

Then he could have kicked himself for such a stupid question.

"Yes, I have. I like you as a human being and you're a great father to Hermione."

"But it isn't Hermione that's gluing us together, is it? If her parents came back tomorrow, would that be the end of us seeing each other?" he asked knowing the answer on his side but not knowing what she was thinking.

"Don't forget I'm your company's COO, but despite Hermione and work, I think our lives would be growing together, perhaps at an even faster rate than they have. Perhaps the complications of Hermione and work have slowed that down by interfering with us getting to know each other as personal partners rather than business or parent partners."

Damian glanced at his watch and knew they were running out of time as they needed to go pick up Hermione. They began the motions of clearing up their tea, when he asked, "Let's go on a date, then. Where and when?"

Right Damian, that was a romantic question.

But Ariana knew her man, this was a real desire of his, and that was all she needed to know.

"Let me look at my schedule, and I'll give you a date. As to the where, how about we go to dinner and a concert, I'll find the musicians and where they're playing, then you can pick a restaurant. I'll see if Hermione wants to stay at my house or yours, or spend the night with a friend. She's too old to need a babysitter."

"Sounds like a plan," Damian said as they pulled up to the school to find Hermione sitting on the entrance wall.

Hermione got into the car, and they both said, "Awesome job, Hermione!"

She looked at them and said the coach had said the same thing.

"Seriously, the first half was awful, your entire team spent the time crowded by you in defense. Then your coach said something at the half, and they started spreading out so they could play offense and then they found out that the other goalkeeper needed some work," Damian said.

"That's almost exactly what the coach said at the half break. He told the team that I had proved I knew what I was doing as a goalkeeper with all of my blocks and ball pick-ups, and now they needed to do their job, and so they did. I almost felt like sitting down at one point, but that would have been the ultimate insult to another team and I probably would have caught an unsportsmanlike penalty for that, so it was a great day for me. It was also good for Meghan and Ashley as they both scored goals once they figured out the opposing team goalkeeper wasn't very good."

"This is only the first game, but I'm thinking you might be a better soccer player than swimmer or water polo player," Ariana said.

"That's only because I'm a goalkeeper. If I actually had to move the ball up and down the field, I wouldn't have even made the JV team."

"You got some ball control, you kicked it out to your team-mates a few times," Damian said.

"Yeah, but it's mostly luck that the ball goes where I want it to go. I need to practice doing half field kicks to get the ball farther from my net. At least now that we've had a real game, I know what skills to practice. I'm really good at figuring where someone is going to kick, and I've got good reflexes, I just need to practice the big kicks, little kicks to my teammates, and jumping high. I didn't think I wanted the goalkeeper job at first, but now that I've played it, I love it."

"It also helps that you're above average in height. You're soon to be sixteen and you're five feet eight. You might end up at five feet ten by the time you're done growing. Are your parents tall?"

Hermione had to think about that for a moment and said, "Mom is five-feet-eight and dad is six-feet-one."

"Five-feet-ten just might be your final height. It's better to be on the taller side of things, so we'll hope for that height for you."

"The average female Olympic swimmer is five-feet-nine, so I'd be good for that sport also."

"Just don't do gymnastics, that's for shrimps like me," Ariana said. She was at Hermione's current height permanently but had been shorter as a teenager.

While they were talking they settled into their favorite Mexican restaurant. Hermione mentioned that morning she wanted a burrito for dinner if her team won. If they lost, they could just eat at home. Ariana had laughed that her breakfast nook was the designated spot for losers.

"So what happened last night? Ariana said you went to visit the boat at the pier."

"I did. Your urging made me get off my duff and boat across the bay at nine o'clock last night. There was a light mist when I left my island, but it stopped just beyond Alcatraz Island."

"So what happened then?"

"It was a big yacht, and there were men on the top level watching, but James Spinnaker's phone was still showing as being there. I took some photos of the boat and its call numbers when I heard a big splash off the side of the boat. Then I noticed the men were in the process of lowering a boat into the water and seemed interested in me. So I took off by the K-docks at high speed which created a wake that dumped some of the sea lions into the waterway. That was sufficient to block their boat and I went home with no further incident."

"So then what happened?" Hermione asked somehow knowing the story wasn't at an end.

"This morning I heard on the news that a body had washed up at Pier 39 and authorities were trying to identify it, but the sea lions had nibbled on parts of it. So I thought that might have been the splash I'd heard the previous night. I sent them an encrypted message with the timestamped pictures of the boat, the time I heard the splash, and James Spinnaker's name, picture and work address. Then I watched the news all day, and the body was identified by this afternoon as him."

"Did the sea lions kill him?"

"I don't think so, they generally don't attack humans, and if he was alive when he hit the water, he should have been able to swim and get out, but if you're dead why not try a taste of the fingers."

Hermione twitched her nose in disgust at that visual, but then smiled and said, "He was a bad man so I'm allowed to laugh at the visual on how he was nibbled at after he was dead!"

"The police haven't sent me a follow-up email perhaps because I said no one would answer it and it was untraceable. I went over there on my way to work and saw police officers on the yacht, but I couldn't tell if they were collecting evidence or merely interviewing boat owners close to where the body was found."

"So what's your next step? Who owns the boat?"

"Hermione, you are quite the detective thinking through these questions," Ariana said.

"It's what my namesake Hermione Granger would have done

in a Harry Potter story. She would of course also do magic, but every spell I've ever tried hasn't worked."

Damian was smiling as he said, "Well I've never had a magic solution work either. The boat belongs to another pharmaceutical company which begs the question, how many companies did your parents anger?"

Hermione tried to think back to the moves her parents had made over the years and what companies her father worked for. Had her mother worked at one point? She remembered a nanny as both parents were working and they weren't living in the United States.

"Mom worked when I was seven or eight. We were outside of the United States, and I had a nanny because both of my parents were working. I think we were in an Asian country."

"How soon did your mom quit work before you moved to Shepard Canyon?"

"Maybe a year or so."

"You wouldn't by chance remember the name of the company she worked for?" Damian asked.

Hermione thought for a moment and said, "No, though I think I would recognize it if I saw the name."

Damian mentioned the company name that owned the yacht and Hermione thought about it for a moment then said, "Do you know what the company's logo looks like?"

"I remember mom bringing home something from the company with a design on it."

Damian typed away on his cell and brought an image up. Hermione studied it and then nodded.

"Mom had an umbrella with the company's logo on it, so she must have worked for them. Are you telling me now a company that my mom used to work for is after her? I thought they were only after my father!"

"Let's hope this is it, that there is only one company per parent that want to kidnap or kill them," Damian said.

"So what are you doing now?"

"Where would you go next, Hermione? What would you look up?" Ariana asked.

Hermione thought for a while and then said, "I guess the question is what has changed? Mom stopped working for the company five or six years ago. Why come after us now."

"Brilliant. You ladies are brilliant!" Damian exclaimed. "I hadn't thought of a new angle yet. When I get back to the island tonight, I'm going to look for news on the company and specifically for any lawsuits against the company that your mom might serve as a witness for. Do you remember what your mom's role was for the company?"

Hermione shook her head no.

"That's okay, I'll search an old company directory and see what I can find. Did your mom use her real name for her job?"

"I don't know. I didn't pay attention to those kinds of details."

"Do you remember your parents telling you to call them something different? Like maybe your father went from Stephen to Jason?"

"Let me think about that question, I don't remember a name change."

"Okay I have work to do. Ariana, how's the contract going with Pete for his restaurant."

"We've actually already signed it. He's so excited to get this restaurant up and going. He's had the plans of what he would like for like five years, and your warehouse fits his vision, so he has an architect submitting them to the city for approval and he's already interviewing contractors. You need to move out of the way perhaps as soon as the end of next week, as he could begin demolition even though the plans aren't approved yet."

"Yikes, that fast? I had Lily sit down and do a project timeline with him because she's so good at that and to help him stay organized, but she never mentioned we needed to move out of the way that quickly," Damian said.

"Probably because she thinks you're planning just to move your modular furniture upstairs and there's already an office up there."

"Actually I was going to upgrade the space in terms of safety, so I guess I need an architect quickly. I want to add a ventilation hood for whoever works on the green GPS goo and a glass shield for Haley so that her drone can't crash into her and any other safety enhancements that people think of. Guess I'll be working on that tomorrow. We can still get out of Pete's way, but I'll take some time to upgrade the space upstairs. It will be a work in progress."

"I've got a paper due tomorrow so can we go home now?" Hermione asked. "Besides I'm getting texts from my teammates that I want to respond to. We're all reliving the glory of the game."

Damian nodded glancing at his watch as he got up to leave. They all had a lot of work to do over the next few days. He was glad Hermione didn't have another game until next week.

CHAPTER 21

*D*amian headed back to his island with a head full of things to follow up on. He was busy thinking about Pete's restaurant and Hermione's parents' problems, and then he remembered that he and Ariana were going to go on a date! How weird was that? It was nearly two decades since he tried to date a woman and man was he rusty. He didn't know how people did it today going on first dates with virtual strangers that they met online, yet that was the source of some one-third of all marriages in the United States. At least he already knew that he liked Ariana's looks, brains, and moral fiber which was likely more than most internet daters knew on their first date.

He might drive himself nuts obsessing about where his relationship might go with Ariana, but at least he felt alive and human, full of expectation and contradictions. He shook his head to clear his mind and hunkered down to work.

As Ariana suggested, he did a search on the pharmaceutical company that owned the boat concerning court proceedings and saw the problem for the company. Apparently, they were the manufacturer of a mesh used to repair the sagging of bladders that caused incontinence in women. The company supplying one of the chemical components of the mesh started to worry about the long-term consequences of using that particular compound inside the human body and cut off the supply. The manufacturer searched for the product around the world to replace the original chemical and found a company in China that had a supply of that compound. That company told the pharmaceutical company that their product contained the compound they were looking for and they had purchased a large supply – tons of the material from a company in Texas that bought it from the original company but had lost the import paperwork. Some people working for the mesh manufacturer were pretty sure that they didn't have the right chemical to make their mesh, but someone higher up hid all of the documentation and went forward with implanting the mesh in upwards of one million women. Now that substitute compound was causing the mesh to crack inside the human body leading to pain and other problems for the women who had it implanted.

Damian leaned back and thought wow, now that's a motive! If Hermione's mother was involved in that chain of trickery about four to five years ago, and one million women want to sue your company for using a bad chemical, and this bad corporate news tied up a company in lawsuits, then maybe the company might want to silence some of the staff that were involved in the original search for the product.

Sad how both of Hermione's parents ended up with pharmaceutical companies that wanted to silence them about the terrible practices they had that affected real patients' lives. Now Damian understood why Hermione's father had extorted his pharmaceutical company as they were both done working in their respective fields, yet they were probably brilliant scientists based on Hermione's smarts – she had to have gotten her brains from somewhere.

So where were Hermione's parents hiding? Damian was convinced they were alive and hiding. If they were in the United

States and that was likely as that was where the class action suits were filed in the courts, then probably some branch of the Justice Department was hiding them or the team of lawyers that had filed the class action lawsuit. How could he reach out and figure out if they were in protection of the government? After they got off the boat and swam ashore, they would have had to contact some law enforcement agency that put them in protective custody.

He did some quick research on the internet about witness names and found that they were called 'discovery' and were not included in jury transcripts, so there seemed to be no database he could legitimately use to find witness names. So he had two choices, hack into the Department of Justice documents looking to discover notes kept on the part of their attorneys, or he could hack into the United States Marshal Service which would be charged with keeping her parents safe until the trial. Damian could see a billion dollars at stake from the class action lawsuit, and some people would find that was worth killing for.

Damien cracked his knuckles, leaned forward, and began hitting the keyboard. It was time to hack into the Department of Justice computer systems. Somewhere in there was a list of people they were protecting. He spent a few hours trying to navigate his way through the various departments and their computer files. Over the next few days, Damian searched for a list of people that the Marshal Service was protecting. He saw names likely in code at one point. Somewhere there had to be a legend that matched people's original names to their code names.

He continued searching off and on over the next week. It was slow going because the Department of Justice and US marshals service were big servers and he didn't want to be caught looking into their files.

He met up with Ariana and Hermione for another soccer game. It was becoming apparent that Hermione might be the best goalkeeper in all the local high schools. Her kicking skills were average, but her ability to guess where the ball was going made all the difference between winning and losing. While Damian and Ariana were watching the third match she gave him the details of their date.

"I've been thinking about our date and where to go. How about if we stroll through the art galleries of Sausalito and then have dinner in that town somewhere. There are many good restaurants so we can just pick one at the moment that suits us," Ariana suggested.

Damien smiled, "That sounds like a plan. I don't need to purchase any art but I've always been curious about the galleries in Sausalito and you're right about them having many good restaurants."

"OK how about this Friday? Hermione has a sleepover with some girlfriends. It's not that I worry about leaving her alone, rather as we figure out the relationship between you and me, I'd rather not have a complication of her expectations," Damien nodded in agreement with the plan and they finish watching Hermione's soccer game.

"So how's the search for my parents going?" Hermione asked after they sat down at a local restaurant.

"It's more complicated than my usual hacking job. I'm looking into the servers at the Department of Justice, and I have to hide who I am and where the computer is located that I'm using and I can't spend much time inside there. I'm trying to find a list of people that the US Marshals Service is protecting hoping that your parents might be on that list. But if they were wise, they wouldn't keep a list of their protectees by their names just anywhere. If I were them, I would have a legend where you call a certain person or persons in protective custody by a code name rather than the real name."

"How do you stay safe from the government when you're accessing their computers?"

"Good question. You have to start by bouncing your computer to various satellites around the world. Then you have to make sure you never spend more than ten or fifteen minutes at a time. So each time I access the server, I use a random generator to generate a name consisting of letters and numbers, and I use a different one each time."

"Is there a chance of you getting caught?" Hermione asked.

"Of course there is! That's why I am taking so many precautions and why it's going so slow. If I were to get caught, it means spending time in a white-collar prison."

"Is there any other way to get the information on my parents?"

"If there is, I haven't figured it out. Perhaps you could put your thinking cap on and think of something else I can do to find your parents."

"Could you just call the head of the Marshal Service and ask him if they're protecting my parents?"

"I could, but the risk is that we might lose custody of you and we might even go to jail for taking care of you with no legal basis as the Marshals Service tries to figure out what our connection to you is. There are many in this world including the police who would see how we have taken care of you as criminal behavior."

"Oh. Okay. Don't call them directly!" Hermione exclaimed. "Don't take this wrong, but you guys have been better than my real parents at raising me. It's not that my parents weren't kind and loving, but you couldn't find a more unstable lifestyle than what I had with them. I feel like my entire childhood was spent hiding from someone and moving a lot."

"Oh sweetie!" Ariana exclaimed. "I understand what you're saying, but let me just say that Damian and I are thrilled to be your fake parents, and I think I speak for both of us when I say that even if we were your real parents, we wouldn't do anything different in caring for you."

"Well, I think we would do fewer computer searches about the evil people chasing your parents, and I would sneak into fewer houses," Damian said smiling.

With a group hug, they went their separate ways, Hermione to work on homework and Damien to head back across the bay.

After a few more days of looking for a list of people in protection at least and perhaps a legend with everyone's name, he gave up. Instead, he decided to focus on a person on the email server through which a lot of communications presently flowed. Maybe that person would be willing to say whether Hermione's parents were in protective custody. As he told the teenager, there was a massive risk in contacting them if her parents weren't in protection. Maybe he could think of a strategy to keep the three of them hidden behind a wall until the Marshals Service revealed whether they knew the whereabouts of her parents. Then he got a surprise email in his inbox.

CHAPTER 22

'*Are you looking for the parents of Hannah Sherwood?*'

The email arrived in his inbox overnight. It was the account he used to report the details on the splash he'd heard when James Spinnaker was thrown overboard. He'd left the account live in case the SFPD had any questions that he was willing to answer. He'd meant to close it as it had been a few weeks since Mr. Spinnaker's murder, but he'd forgotten. Now someone was trying to contact him. He sat at the keyboard for a while thinking through his options.

He could type 'yes' and nothing more.

He could ignore the question.

He could give a few more details like, 'yes we are'. 'We' implying there was more than one person behind the email.

He could give a quick response to let someone know that he was indeed looking, but then close the account as it represented a danger to Hermione, Ariana, and himself.

He could research who sent the email and how they knew James Spinnaker was searching for 'Hannah Sherwood'.

First, he'd tell Ariana, and then they would tell Hermione after school.

He was down in his watercraft garage preparing to head to Richmond and work, when he dialed Ariana, "Hey, how's it going?" He knew at this hour she was likely driving toward a meeting with one of her start-ups located in San Francisco.

"What's up?" She asked knowing that Damian didn't call just to shoot the breeze.

"I got an email on the account I set up to correspond with the SFPD about James Spinnaker's death. I left the account live in case they had some question I was willing to answer and then I forgot to shut it down. An email arrived this morning asking if I was looking for the parents of Hannah Sherwood."

"What are you going to do, research who sent it?"

"I debated what to do and then settled on that option. I should have just called you and saved myself the thinking time."

He heard her laugh on the other end of the phone and she replied, "Woman's intuition made that my first choice. You have the day to research, and then we'll tell Hermione after school, right?"

"Now you're scaring me since you're currently predicting my plan for the day. Besides women's intuition, what are you, a mind reader?"

"Yes, you're the genius, but I read minds, so we're a good combo."

"That we are. I'll give you a call if I turn up anything interesting."

"Thanks," Ariana said before ending the call. She liked that he now volunteered information rather than her having to ask for it.

Once Damian reached his office he spent a few hours working through problems that each of his projects were causing, as well as collecting any special space needs now that they were going to embark on a remodel. Fortunately, except for having a cleaning service clear the dust from the third floor, they could all very quickly move out of the way of the impending demolition for Pete's restaurant.

After lunch, Damian settled down to research the email. He'd sent the information about James Spinnaker to a specific SFPD detective he knew was assigned to the case. Damian assumed that detective contacted Homeland Security about James Spinnaker to notify them of his death and his illegal side hustle. So perhaps Homeland Security got his phone and email records and was able to trace that he was looking for Hannah Sherwood in an unofficial role and that person happen to contact the U.S. Marshals. It really could be that random. They inhabited the same building and at times had overlapping duties. Surely some of the agents crossed over to the other division in friendship. He was going to assume that was how the connection was made. So what to do with that? How did he make contact without losing custody of Hermione to someone other than her parents?

Should he respond 'yes' to the email and see what the next question was? He decided to check in with Ariana as they all had a stake in this.

"I'm thinking of responding to the email with a simple 'yes' and see what happens next," Damian said after she answered her phone.

There was silence for a minute while she thought about the consequences of showing their cards.

"Can they identify who you are?"

"No, just that we're having a conversation and I can send it in confidential mode and have the email self-destruct after it's read."

"That's pretty cool, the self-destructing I mean. If they can't trace who you are, then you could write them a book of poetry and have that self-destruct so be as verbose as you want. So now the question is whether to respond with more than a simple 'yes'?"

"Exactly."

"Hmmm. I think a simple 'yes' is really all you need to say, then wait to see where they go next."

"That was sort of what I was thinking, but since both you and

Hermione will feel the ramifications if I get this wrong, I just wanted to get your input."

"Type in 'yes' now and see what happens. Does the software that destroys the email give you any kind of a message of when it's read?"

"Let's see," Damian said, and Ariana heard him typing in the background.

There were a few moments of silence while Ariana continued to drive and Damian was watching his screen for some kind of reaction.

Finally, he said, "Nothing. Nothing is happening. I just have to assume that the message hasn't been read yet. I'll call you back if and when that happens hopefully before we pick Hermione up from school."

"Hopefully. You probably have to wait for someone in SFPD to see the message and then run it over to whomever in the Marshals Service and get their response. It's not like a police officer is going to share his email password with another agency."

"True," Damian said and they ended their call, while he checked the time. He had about an hour before he needed to leave to head over to Belvedere for Hermione's soccer game. Time to get some real work done, by checking in with his staff on what they were doing.

By the time he left to go across the Bay, there was no response to his email. He had no idea if the person that sent the message, assuming it was not the detective, had seen Damian's reply. Oh well, it was time to put the email aside and enjoy watching Hermione amaze everyone as a soccer goalkeeper. She was so good that they thought she'd be named to the all-region soccer team. Her soccer skills were definitely going to create scholarship opportunities for college.

Ariana and Damian were watching Hermione play and sharing information about themselves in answer to questions like, 'Who would you have lunch with, dead or alive, if you had your choice of anyone.' Damian felt his phone vibrate and pulled it out and looked at the alert to find a response from his earlier email.

'*Why are you looking?*'

Ariana was looking over Damian's shoulder at the email and asked, "Can you respond to the account with your phone or do you need to use your super-duper secret computer on your island?"

"Super-duper, huh? I don't recall that being on the list of specifications for my home computer," Damian said with a grin.

She nudged him and said, "Well do you?"

"No. It's more about where my email overall goes than the physical location on the island."

"Then respond now with, 'their daughter wants to talk with them.'

He did so awaiting another response. He imagined the recipient calling up someone in Homeland Security and reading the message then hanging up while they thought of an answer, somewhat like he and Ariana were doing. He put his phone away to watch the game knowing another email would be a while coming.

An hour later as they were eating dinner, the next message arrived.

'Does she have a birthmark on her right inside elbow?'

Damian read it aloud, and Hermione screwed up her face and said, "no, no birthmarks anywhere."

"Do you have any distinctive marks or scars?" Ariana asked since she hadn't noticed any.

Hermione pulled back her hair at her skull and pointed to a thin white line.

"I ran into a table as a kid and had to get stitches."

"That's a good scar. Your parents know you have it, but the average Joe on the streets doesn't see it or know of its existence."

Damian typed back a simple 'no' and waited.

The next message came back sooner, "Does she have any marks?"

"I'm going to ask a question of whoever is asking these questions. How about 'what food allergy does Hannah have and what are her symptoms?'"

Hermione and Ariana both thought about Damian's question and nodded their agreement. It was a question that fake parents wouldn't know. There were many popular food allergies that someone would guess first like fish or peanuts. Hermione's allergy of raw tomatoes would not even make it into the top ten probably. Damian typed the question without answering their question.

"I don't know if your parents are near-by whoever is sending us a message, so this might take them a while to get an answer. Let's put this aside for the night, but I'll contact you if we get a correct answer. We still don't know who we are dealing with or if they're in contact with your parents."

Hermione thought about what Damian said and felt a little deflated as she had so many mixed emotions in regards to her parents. She knew from the bottom of her heart that they loved her. They had even set up the second safe room to keep her safe along with all the precautions they took. However, always living on the run, limiting her after-school activities and friendships, had made for a lonely childhood. She was happy with where she was now. She was enjoying her high school sports teams and her classes and the vacations she had with Ariana and Damian. Then she felt guilty again for enjoying her life so much when she wasn't sure what was going on with her parents.

She nodded, and they returned their discussion about her soccer game, the skills of her teammates, and their standing in their league, as well as the statistics of the top high school players. Damian headed home thinking about how much he enjoyed the company of the two women. They expanded his universe.

CHAPTER 23

There was no response from the police email account with the answer to Hermione's allergy question. Either they didn't know the answer, or it took a while to reach the email and then reach the girl's parents, or perhaps on their end, they were debating what questions to answer and which of their own to ask. Regardless, Damian put the puzzle aside for the moment and decided to spend a few moments anticipating his date with Ariana in two days. Did he want to re-marry? Did he want to try and have a child with Ariana? She was in her late thirties, and so with a little luck they could have a child. Did he want a second family?

Really, they hadn't had a real date yet, and he had them setting up a nursery! What was wrong with him? It just didn't feel like an actual first date as he knew so much about Ariana. They had vacationed together and raised Hermione together. He knew more about Ariana than almost any first date couple on average did. He wouldn't go into this date wondering if he would like the person more or less as he grew to know them better; he knew he liked Ariana. Oh well, time to put that aside and concentrate on the areas of his life he could control.

Finally, on Friday, the date of Hermione's sleepover and Damian and Ariana's date, he had a response from the email account about mid-day.

'Hannah's allergic to raw tomatoes and her mouth gets itchy.'

OMG, thought Damian. Hermione's real parents must be in the background of this email. That meant they were alive. He felt a wave of depression roll over him at the thought of losing Hermione in his life, mixed with happiness for her to find her parents alive.

He dialed Ariana's number after looking at the time. He'd been so lost in thought, he couldn't remember whether it was day or night. It was just before noon, and he was in his office in Richmond.

"Hey. Are you calling to cancel our date tonight?"

"Ur, no. I got an email regarding Hermione, and I think her parents might be alive."

"Oh," Ariana said and then paused as if she was trying to construct her thoughts. "I'll say this only to you, I wanted the mystery of parents to continue. I enjoy being her pseudo-mom. What are our next steps?"

"Tell Hermione for one, perhaps after school today. Then I'll go about arranging a meeting, and I suppose we'll have to let her go," Damian said with sadness in his voice.

"Yeah, I suppose. How do we safeguard her if say the answer to the question was tortured out of her parents?"

Damian paused to think a moment and said, "We'll handle a call just like we did for the two people that weren't her parents. We could ask about the scar in her hairline – does Hannah Sherwood have any marks, and force the parents to answer live on the call. I would hope that since this connection evolved through the SFPD, that whoever is at the other side of the video call is not a Malaysian drug maker, or another group that wants the child of the parents that caused them financial distress," Damian said still thinking about the situation. Then he added, "Well they supplied the correct answer."

"Okay, let's go about arranging a call. The next three nights Hermione doesn't have soccer practice or a game. If this really is her parents, then they should be anxious to have this call occur. See you later, and I'll keep you posted if I get a response."

Damian found himself composing a response to the email a few moments later. He edited several times before settling on the reply.

We should arrange a meeting. I want to be sure that her parents are in a safe position to take care of her. I'd like to arrange a video call first. Hannah is free the next three nights after five. Please confirm a time.

It pained him to hit the send button. He had such fun being a parent to the teenager. He wondered if they would receive a response today or tomorrow? Meanwhile, the three of them would have the call hanging over their heads. He finished up his work day and traveled back to the island to head over to Ariana's later. Their date might be on hold depending on what Hermione's parents did and whether she still went on a sleepover.

Again they met Hermione at school. Seeing Damian in the car on a day she didn't expect him to be there meant something was up and she asked.

"I got an email today around noon with the correct answer to the question about your allergy. I think your parents might be behind whoever is emailing us."

Hermione was quiet in the back seat thinking she wanted to stay with Ariana and Damian. They were stable and protected her, and for the first time she had friends to do things with. She didn't want to go back on the run with her parents.

"Okay," was all Hermione could think of to say.

"Sweetie, that's exactly my thinking," Ariana said. "I'm happy for you that your parents appear to be alive, but I love you and love being a fake mother to you. Let's get through this call and then we'll worry about what's next."

"Ditto for me kiddo," Damian added to the silence.

Hermione thought for a while and then said, "Can I still do the sleepover at Megan's tonight or do you think the call will be arranged for tonight?"

Damian thought for a moment and then replied, "I replied about four hours ago and had no response. I told whomever to schedule a video call for any of the next three nights after five, so I think you're good tonight for the sleepover as I have no response. If push comes to shove, we can bring you back from Megan's house, but I don't think it's going to happen tonight."

"Why are we doing a video call? I thought you were convinced it's my parents?"

"I'm convinced your parents provided the answer which means nothing more than they're alive, but I want to watch them on a video call to determine if they are in a position to take care of you. If they're on the run, and hiding, then personally I think you're better off staying with us."

"You're not just going to arrange a meeting in a parking lot and turn me over to them?"

"No, they lost you once, and I need to make sure they won't lose you again, so that means that Ariana and I will determine if they're in a position that's safe for you."

"Okay. Good. If I have a choice, and if they are on the run from someone, then I'm going to choose to stay here. I'm making my mark on the world, and I don't want to have to disappear before I'm labeled the greatest high school goalkeeper in the State of California."

"Kid, hang on to your sense of humor. I think you're going to need it over the next couple of days," Ariana said as she reached back to fist-pump Hermione, while Damian smiled.

Thirty minutes later they were saying goodbye to Hermione as she walked five houses down to her friend Megan's. Ariana knew there were six to eight girls at the sleepover and Ariana rather felt sorry for Megan's parents. The teenage giggles would go on for hours that night. She rejoined Damian on her pool love-seat with two glasses of wine. He'd been outside playing fetch with Miguel while Hermione packed her bag for the sleepover.

"It's convenient that she's only five houses away."

"Yeah, this is her first sleepover ever, and she was both excited to be a part of the sisterhood and dreading admitting to the girls that she had never done that before."

"I don't remember doing that as a teenager."

"It's more a girl thing to do. We like to chat. While you boys were out hunting and gathering and killing meat, we women stayed behind, tended the fires, made bread and chatted. It's in our DNA."

Damian laughed out loud at the picture Ariana painted of herself as a prehistoric woman.

"Somehow, I think you left the cave and were out hunting yourself."

"Probably. You don't seem discouraged over the impending loss of Hermione."

"I've been thinking about the email and her response, and I don't think we're going to lose her. Her parents are in some kind of difficult situation, and I think Hermione is going to choose not to join them. It would be nice if we created an open line with her parents so she could contact them on occasion, but I suspect she's going to choose to stay here."

"Okay," Ariana said and then pausing for a few moments added, "So we're going on a date tonight?"

"Seems that way," Damian replied smiling.

She reached over and chinked her glass to his.

CHAPTER 24

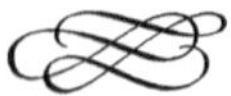

Deputy Marshal Cindy Gregory and Deputy Marshal Thomas Kinnear entered the apartment kitchen in Redwood City after they ended the call with their contact in the San Francisco Police Department. It was too bad they couldn't see the email trail. After the first disappearing email the SFPD had learned to take a picture of the email message. They had concluded that whoever sent the emails was tech savvy and likely had control of their protectees Jason and Amy Sherwood's daughter.

The Sherwoods looked up, and Amy asked, "Does the source have Hannah? Is she okay? When can we see her?"

Gregory and Kinnear briefly looked at each other before answering. They'd been paired together to take the lead on this couple. Attempts on their lives had been made several times and their daughter Hannah had been missing from the start. They were up against a pharmaceutical firm which was originally founded in the Ottoman Empire's Syria with their first drug deliveries made by camel. Now a $22B international company, they were one of the mightiest foes that the U.S. Marshals Service had had through their history. They had through their history, they had protected people with ties to the mafia, foreign agents, and drug cartels from Mexico, but never had they had such a wealthy sponsor with unlimited funds to hire hit-men or women. The government had almost lost them the previous year when they had been kidnapped and thrown overboard from a ship in San Francisco Bay. Now, the Marshals moved the couple around the State of California every week to secure their lives.

Fortunately, the college sweethearts had been collegiate swimmers and had no problem swimming ashore after untangling ties around their feet and arms. They had swum ashore, called the police and eventually had been connected to the Justice Department for the prosecution of the pharmaceutical mesh company and provided protection so they would be alive to testify at trial. The unknown for them this past year had been what had happened to their teenage daughter. They were sure she had sheltered in the safe room inside her bedroom, as they heard their kidnappers talk about it, but they heard nothing after that.

The marshals had visited their old house and used the code to unlock the safe room, but there had been no Hannah. There was evidence she'd been in the room, but no indication of where she's gone. Then the Justice Department caught wind of the murder at the Pier and its connection to a yacht owned by the very company they were prosecuting. The SFPD passed on the message linking the Homeland Security agent to the yacht owner to the Justice Department and Homeland Security to make sure that someone investigated it, and that was when it trickled down to the two marshals.

Their first effort was devoted to finding out who sent the message to the SFPD. After a week, the department made no progress. The email bounced off many servers before landing at the SFPD, and it disappeared after being opened. That was unexpected. However what was really crucial was the allergy of the kid. It was something that wouldn't be the result of a wild guess.

"We gave the right answer to the allergy question, and now

whoever is behind the email wants to do a video call," replied Marshal Gregory.

"We like that idea as it allows us to protect you two," added Marshal Kinnear.

"So you think it sounds like someone has Hannah and that's she's safe?" Amy asked with teary eyes. She'd worried about her daughter for the past year constantly asking herself what they could have done differently to keep their daughter safe.

"We do. Whoever is caring for Hannah says she's free after five for the next three nights. That implies the girl has obligations and a schedule. That doesn't sound like someone held in captivity. Furthermore, the message indicated that they were arranging it around your daughter's schedule and not that of the adults with her," Gregory said.

"I assume you two want to do a call. We're running out of time to make arrangements for tonight. How about if I ask for tomorrow at five in the evening? That will give us time to move you to a safe location to host the call. We can't conduct the call from here as it would potentially give away your location."

The Sherwoods nodded their agreement looking hopeful and fearful. Hopeful that they would find their daughter safe during the call tomorrow, fearful, that she still might be in a bad situation.

"Although the call will not be until five, we'll need to move you well before then. We're thinking of using our video conferencing facility at the San Francisco Courthouse. If the person that has sent us emails traces us to that location, it will be challenging for them to make arrangements to attack you two. The building has armed guards and great security. The only other place I think might be better is San Quentin prison. No one would be able to attack that facility to obtain your release!" Kinnear said.

"Personally, I'd rather call from a courthouse than the prison. I have nightmares about being accidentally left behind in prison," Amy said, shuttering.

"Okay. We'll plan to move you about eleven in the morning taking a circular route to the courthouse. Once there, we'll have time on our hands. We'll grab lunch there and attend to the call in a conference room. On our end, we'll be trying to gain information about the callers like who they are and where they're located."

Jason nodded, pleased with the plan. He wondered if ether Amy or he would be able to sleep that night, knowing their quest for their daughter was nearly at an end. They continued talking with the agents and were eventually left alone.

"Jason, who do you think is caring for Hannah?"Amy asked.

"I don't know. I don't even have a sense if it's a man or woman. Really all we know is the person is very technology savvy and they know the allergy detail about Hannah. We'll hope for the best tomorrow."

"What is the best?" Amy asked with a sob.

Jason reached over and comforted Amy, putting his arm around her. It had been a trying year from the moment they hadn't made it to the safe room, to their escape and the now endless boredom of being in protective custody. Furthermore, there was no end in sight as the trial was still two to three years off and they would have to remain in protection for some time beyond the end of the trial.

"I think the best for Hannah at the moment would be a safe location for her and a good set of foster parents. We could ask her to join us here, but if she is safe and happy elsewhere, then she should stay there."

Amy leaned back from Jason and looked into his eyes, nodding her agreement.

"I would love to have her with us, but this is no life for a teenager. When the legal proceedings are over, how would we record her high school classes? I suppose we could home-school her."

"Yes, but living with us restricts her from even going outside. It's not just that she would be home-schooled, but she would have to cut off all social connections except us. That's a pretty horrible experience for a teenager."

"She's always been a strong girl. She'll tell us what is best," Amy said.

"Let's just agree to be hopeful about the call tomorrow and not worry about anything else. All we want is for Hannah to be healthy and happy, right?"

"Right."

"Someday we'll have our life back. Once the trial is over, and the conglomerate is neutralized, we should get new names and plastic surgery and start a new life."

"How will we start a new life? We're young, and we'll need jobs. How will we get a reference? Where will the money come from? Do you think our house has been foreclosed on as we haven't written a check for the taxes or anything else?"

"I asked the agents to check for me maybe a month ago, and at the time, our taxes had been paid, and the utilities were on. Weird. I assume the Marshals Service is paying the bills, so we have something at the end of the trial," Jason replied.

"Oh, okay. I don't understand this new world of ours. It seems that while we have our personal safety, we don't have control of anything in our lives including our own daughter."

"Maybe that's for the better. We'd make dismal parents at the moment. If only I'd never gone to work for that company. You and Hannah would be safe and together."

"Com'on Jason, we've been over this already. Moping about making different decisions doesn't change where we are now or make this situation any better. Let's just move on and hope for great news from Hannah tomorrow. Besides it's the company I went to work for that's the problem now."

He leaned close to his wife grateful that she didn't blame him for their confinement. He hoped tomorrow would bring good news from their daughter.

CHAPTER 25

*D*amian had provided their mysterious contact with a number to reach them tomorrow, and so his work was done. It was time to enjoy the here and now on a date with Ariana. She'd seen him in every clothing imaginable from playing regular clothes to swimsuits as they snorkeled or taught Hermione how to play water polo. They had seen each other in every type of clothing except formal wear, and he'd bet she would look sensational in a fancy dress. He couldn't think of a time when she didn't look beautiful.

It was the first date that he'd rode in his date's car with her driving. Yep, Damian thought, he was going to be rusty at this dating thing. It was weird going on a date with a woman that at present was his best friend. How would the evening evolve from friendship to romance? He needed to stop thinking about the future and just enjoy the here and now. He had to stop his brain from its natural progression of what-if scenarios – something that it usually did all day.

Shortly they arrived at the first of perhaps the fifteen or so galleries lining Bridgewater Street. While they progressed down the street, they were also keeping an eye open for dinner. Ariana was casually looking for a piece for her house. She was tired of a watercolor that she had in her bedroom. She didn't know what she was looking for only that she would fall in love when she set her eyes on it. Damian was thinking of his house and couldn't remember if he had any.

"Do I have any artwork on my walls?" he suddenly asked Ariana.

She looked over at him with a deeply amused glance and said, "Why do you think I made this our first date? It was a subtle way to add something to your walls if we could find something that you like. Have you seen anything that catches your eye? Moves you? Has you looking at more than once?"

Damian smiled at her smile and said, "That bad, huh? Why do I need art when I have the best view in the world? Mother nature is my canvas."

"Touche! Perhaps though you would like a piece that takes you away from San Francisco Bay to another part of the world you enjoy?"

"Hmmm," was all Damian said. He hadn't seen anything yet, that fit Ariana's description.

He held out his arm, and they strolled arm in arm stopping at times to comment on some really awful piece of art in a low voice. Art was in the eyes of the beholder as evidenced by some of the prices that Picasso's works sold for. Edward Munch's 'The Scream" sold for over $100Million and yet Damian's only use for such a painting would be to put it on the cliff walls of his island to scare people off like a no-trespassing sign.

They ended their art gallery stroll with no purchase for either of them.

"I guess this isn't our night to find great art," Ariana said.

"Maybe I have bad juju for finding great art and that cast a pall on you finding anything as well."

"Sorry, but I've had days like this before, and in fact, I'm rarely successful in actively looking for something. I do much better accidentally falling on the perfect piece. Did you at least get any ideas of what you might want on your walls?"

"No. Mostly I now know what I don't want. I do think I would like something in black and white or sepia picture of something," Damian said.

"Have you looked through your pictures on your phone to see if there is anything there that might serve you – say from our vacation to the Great Barrier Reef?"

"That's a thought. I'll look there. Let's duck into this Italian restaurant. I'd love a great pasta tonight. Would that suit you?"

"Sure, they have good food. I've eaten here before."

Damian hesitated at her last comment and said, "Would you like to go to some place that you've never been to?"

"I don't know if there is such a place in Sausalito," Ariana said with a laugh.

Damian grabbed her hand, and they went inside and soon had a table overlooking the water. Sunset had already occurred, and so they enjoyed the view of the marina and its lights at night. There was a comfortable silence perhaps as each of them thought of prior dates with their spouses.

"I feel like it's rare for two people of the same approximate age to have lost their spouses and in my case, their children and meet, have an outside child to unite over and have lots in common," Damian murmured.

"Are you trying to sell me on why we should be together with all that in common?"

"No. Just commenting on the mathematical weirdness of us being together."

"The world's a strange place with random things happening all the time. I would say this is a random good thing, rather than the random bad things that took our spouses and children in your case."

"True. Forgive my moroseness."

"I don't think you're being morose, rather it's your brain calculating the rare odds of us being together. My advice is to let it go and run with the moment. We could lose Hermione tomorrow. Do you think we would stay together or go on a second date without her to care for?"

Damian thought for a while and then nodded, "Yes I do think we would stay together. Of course, I would also try to stay in contact with her if she's able to return to her parents. We could be a favorite aunt and uncle."

"Yeah, we could! Thanks for that thought. I'll admit I've been a little down myself thinking that Hermione might leave me. I enjoy my aunt role with my nieces and nephews, and I could add her to that category."

"Okay then let's focus on us. Since we vacationed together, fought killers together, and run a company together, we know a lot about each other, but let's use this date to find out new stuff. If you hopped on a plane tomorrow and had to tell the pilot to head to a location, what would that locale be?"

"Good question. Am I by myself, with you, with girlfriends, or is it the three of us?"

"With your girlfriends."

"We would head to Milan and eat, drink, and shop our way through Italy. Start at the fashion houses in Milan and the wines of the Lombard region, then move over to Venice for some glass and food, then head south to Florence for leather, park a few days in Tuscany before heading south to Rome for the flight home. Of course, we'd have a private driver so we wouldn't have to worry about drinking and driving."

"Wouldn't be my first choice, but I understand. Where would you direct the plane if it was just me on board?"

"I think we would head for somewhere in Australia to spend time scuba diving. There are many choices there, we just have to find one without sharks," Ariana said giving a shudder.

"Good luck finding that site."

"How about you? Where do you want to go by yourself and with me?"

"I might point the plane toward a destination that would allow me to see the Aurora Borealis if I was by myself. With you, I would head the plane to Salt Lake City to see the National Parks there and do some glam-camping."

"Is the glamorous camping for me or you?"

"Me. I don't mind tent walls, but I want to sleep on a regular mattress. After hiking or biking all day, the last thing I want is an uncomfortable place to sleep."

"Okay, my turn. You have a chef who will cook anything, what does he make for you for dinner?"

They continued the twenty questions through dessert and weaved their way back through the town to where her car was parked.

Arriving back at her house for a glass of wine, they continued their fun question game, until kissing took over. Damian had both wondered and fantasized what it would be like to take Ariana to bed, and hours later he admitted the real thing was better than the fantasy.

The next morning in her kitchen, they were making coffee to take outside and enjoy the day. Hermione was due home in a few hours from her sleepover and the three of them would head over to his island for the call.

"Thanks for letting me stay the night. It was wonderful," Damian told Ariana.

She nodded not saying anything in return with her eyes closed, but her face smiling while catching the first rays of the sun. About one in three days were foggy, and this was not going to be one of them. They planned to get a thirty-minute swim in her heated pool and clean up before Hermione was expected home. Then they were leaving early to head over to his island, making sure that everything was in place for the call. What happened after the call was anyone's guess.

CHAPTER 26

$\mathcal{I}$t was early afternoon, and the three of them were settled on lounge chairs with blankets as the February air was cold. While their respective homes were both located on San Francisco Bay, the temperature could vary as much as fifteen degrees. It seemed that despite the anxiety about the call later that day, everyone at the moment needed some extra sleep. They could have slept indoors, but the sound of boats going by made the perfect noise to create sleepiness.

They had a good half hour under their belt when Damian's cell phone began sounding an alarm. It woke all of them from their sleep, and Ariana and Hermione looked at him in annoyance as their naps had been too short.

He stood up gathering the blankets they used and said, "That alarm indicates there's an intruder on the island. Let's go inside and see what's going on. I'm glad we all came on my boat as it's inside the watercraft garage and that's locked up tight."

They hurried toward the door with the two cats and Miguel following them. They'd also been dosing when the alarm sounded. They soon entered the house and followed Damian down to his lab to see what was going on. He guessed it was probably just a weekend boater who couldn't read the sign that said 'private property, stay off Red Rock Island'. When he saw the video feed of his beach, he was appalled.

"Oh boy! Ladies, I'll need your help, until the police arrive, to defend ourselves."

"I'll make the call to the police while you organize what you want us to do," Ariana said using her cell phone to call the 9-1-1 operator.

"I'm ready!" Hermione said. "I've been practicing with a video game to shoot people with water cannons. Let me operate that station."

Ariana and Damian looked at each other and then at Hermione.

"I have a new technology you can try. I have a metal cord that shoots out and wraps itself around your legs or waist. There are fish hooks on each end to dig into clothing and make it harder to move your legs if it's around the lower body or move your arms around the upper body. The men need to be within about fifteen feet of the gun in the cliff, and so if you're keeping them away with the water cannon, you won't have a chance to try the cord."

"Maybe next time I visit the island, I can practice. I want to be Bat-girl!"

Ariana and Damian swallowed, hoping there would be a next time. It really all depended on that call later.

"Sweetie you have surprises every day," Ariana noted. Then she spoke to the emergency dispatcher that answered giving her a status of what was going on. Ariana could tell there was some disbelief in the dispatcher's voice, and so she offered to connect the dispatcher with the video feed inside Damian's lab. The dispatcher soon saw the same feed that featured armed men jumping off a yacht with automatic weapons in their hands. Ariana could hear her making background commands to get them some help.

"How soon do you think we'll see police here to help us?"

Ariana asked in a calm voice having every faith that Damian's building and tactics would keep them safe.

"The Oakland Air Patrol will be responding, and their ETA is ten minutes. San Francisco has a twenty minute ETA, and the Contra Costa County Sheriff is unable to respond at this time. I will stay on the line until police arrive and take command."

"Thank you," Ariana said. Rather than put the phone on speaker and distract Hermione and Damian, she used her Bluetooth headset to stay in contact with the dispatcher.

"Remember this house is reinforced and so we should be able to withstand anything short of a bomb being dropped. Guns won't have an effect on the house's shell. Let's keep them on the beach. I have a new technology I'm going to try – it's a few swarms of drones. I also have them loaded with canisters that will drop my pepper spray green dye on them. I put the mixture in pods like you see used for laundry detergent, but the plastic covering is more fragile, so it will bust open immediately. They'll be successful shooting down some of the drones, but I have the drones arriving from both sides of the island as well as from the mountaintop. I got the idea from the Independence Day shows that went from fireworks to drone shows."

"When this is over will you teach me to operate drone swarms?" Hermione asked.

Ariana teared up over the question, and Damian took a big swallow before saying, "Sure kiddo."

They crewed their stations with Ariana planning to aid Hermione. She knew nothing of Damian's drone swarms, but she could whack a mole with the water cannons.

Her earpiece indicated that help was being marshaled as she heard background communication with officers to be dispatched in boats. Ariana checked in with the dispatcher briefly to confirm that she could still see the feed on the cameras. She smiled when she had news that the Coast Guard was redirecting a ship toward the island.

"Okay, guys we need to hold the fort for about ten minutes before help arrives," Ariana announced.

Hermione grinned and said, "Game on."

Damian looked a little taken aback by the teenage warrior, but then he thought he shouldn't be surprised given what she'd been through in the past year.

Damian studied the yacht and decided it was the same one that had been parked at the Pier where they found James Spinnaker, so this must be that same drug company after him. He wondered how they found out where he lived? No time to ponder that question he needed to get the swarm working.

When he thought of the swarm being used for security of his island, he'd spent hours creating the computer program to coordinate multi-robots which essentially are what a drone swarm is. He took the swarms on a trip around his island for them to memorize the boundaries. He lost a few drones in that process to the cliff rock or the water. Then he created a reward for the drone by dropping its payload on a target. When he designed the program, he used rocks on the beach or bushes lining the cliff as the target. He now used those same concepts on the men trying to overrun his island. Hermione's actions with the water cannons confused and blinded the men and hid the sound of the drone swarm. All of the individual propellers made a particular sound – a swarm of bees, but that would be drowned out by the sound of gunfire or the water cannons.

Hermione was firing the cannons and letting out shouts of glee whenever she jammed one of the men's guns with a blast of water. She watched them drop a gun and grab another usually from the small of their back. Damian's swarms were coming in from the side, and they began unloading the little packets of green dye and pepper juice on the men still on the boat. He targeted the man at the helm first as he wanted to disable the boat's escape. Dammit, he wanted to be sure these guys went to prison, and he needed them stuck at his beach unable to see their way away from the island until the police and Coast Guard arrived!

Damian let out a cheer when he saw the first swarm drop their little pods on the men on the deck of the boat. He watched them suddenly grab their face, one falling off balance on the back of the yacht to splash in the water. As far he could see, he'd disabled everyone aboard the yacht except a man standing under a sheltered bridge. Fortunately, he seemed disinclined to back out of the island's harbor. He had his hands full controlling the yacht this close to the island and couldn't come to the aid of any of the men.

As soon as the swarm dropped their packages, he moved them away and around his island to save them from gunfire. Still he lost a few, not to gunfire, but instead, they got blasted by the water cannons. He parked that in the back of his brain to find a software solution for the two defensive items to co-exist. He checked where they were from an overall battle and directed the second swarm toward the fighters that were on his island. Two had made it up the hillside and were approaching his front door, and so he went after them first.

The two men looked up when they heard the buzzing sound and took aim, but fortunately, it was milliseconds after the swarm dropped their load on the men. A few of the drones were shot down as the men pulled the trigger just as they were blinded by the bursting bags landing on their heads. He made a second mental note to himself to blast music or something when the island was under attack to cover the sound of the drones. There was nothing he could do to quiet down the drone propellers.

He looked over at Ariana and Hermione to see if they were both doing okay and ended up smiling to himself that he had two warriors at his side.

"When's the cavalry arriving?" he asked.

"Dispatcher says we should be able to see the Coast Guard boat approaching from the south and the helicopter from the east. She wants to know if there's a landing pad on the island?"

"There isn't but they can still land on the island. The men that are now struggling with pepper spray in their eyes are likely in the way of a copter landing. I'm going to have to go outside and drag them out of the way."

He could hear Ariana relaying the information to the dispatcher.

"Damian, how are you going to stay safe outside? All the technology in the world won't save you from bullets."

"I know. There's no one else on the top yet and I don't want the drones in the way of the helicopter or sucked up in its draft, so I need you to keep those water cannons going. Ask the pilot if the officers aboard the copter will cover me while I move the men?"

Both Hermione and Ariana looked at him with worry, and Hermione asked, "Do you have a vest and helmet that will protect you from bullets?"

Damian gave it thought and said, "I made a jumpsuit from my magic fabric that will make me less visible. Tell the pilot that they'll see hands and feet moving the men, and to keep watch on the cliff and they'll be able to land once I have the men out of the way."

Ariana relayed the information to the dispatcher who said in disbelief, "You're telling me there's going to be an invisible man moving two men so the copter can land? This I got to see. Is there a camera that I can connect to the copter? This has been the weirdest operation I've ever witnessed."

Damian shook his head 'no'.

"There is but I don't want to take the time to make the connection right now. I need to get outside, and you two need to keep blasting with the water cannons."

Ariana nodded and said to the dispatcher, "Sorry only your crew in the helicopter will be able to see the invisible man move two men."

Damian was soon cloaked in his invisible jumpsuit, and with the face covering off, Ariana and Hermione smiled briefly at how funny it was seeing shoes, hands, and his face. Once he put down the flap covering his face, it was really bizarre seeing hands encased in blue medical gloves in midair. Miguel had scurried behind Ariana at the disturbing sight. She reached down to pet the dog and said, "It's okay, those are Damian's hands you're seeing." Not that the dog understood what she said.

"Good luck and don't scare your cats on the way out," Ariana urged as he left to go up the steps.

Hermione went back to watching the men on the beach approach the hillside and coordinating the exact moment to blast someone when they were off balance.

Ariana kept watch on the water cannons and the position of the intruders while watching two blue hands dragging a screaming man with his hands on his face to the side of the space that would be used for a copter landing. She could hear the helicopter, but not see it as it was above her camera line. The men were moved and then she saw the blue hands retreat to the front door. Damian briefly pulled up the face shield to operate the eye scan door lock of his front door, and he was inside again.

"Damian's safe inside the house," Ariana said out loud for Hermione's benefit.

"Ha! Take that you bad man!" she practically screeched like it was the final battle of a video game.

Suddenly the men were making a hasty retreat to the yacht. They jumped on board, leaving a few men in the water and tried to take off at full power to evade the incoming Coast Guard boat.

Hermione leaned back to give Ariana a high five saying "I win!"

Damian had been watching the various camera views of his island while he took off the jumpsuit. As soon as the helicopter landed, he opened the door and stood just outside waiting for the signal that the officers climbing out of the copter saw him and weren't going to see him as a threat.

He watched as one officer pointed to the men writhing on the ground and another pointed to Damian. One approached with his gun aimed downward. The copter blade noise and wind updrafts made it hard to hear.

Once the officer got close, he asked, "Are you Damian Green?"

Damian nodded, "My friends are down in my lab and called the dispatcher when we saw we were under siege by that yacht," Damian said pointing at the departing boat.

"I'm officer Travis Bishop, what's wrong with these men?"

"Ask your men to wear gloves. I hit them with homemade pepper juice mixed with green dye. The dye will take several days to wear off. If their eyes are rinsed, they'll regain their vision in six to eight hours."

The officer used his lapel mic to relay the information to his partners, and Damian saw the few officers that hadn't, pull on gloves. Two other men looked over the edge of the island to where the two men left behind by the boat, were standing with their hands in the air upon the command of another officer. Damian saw that they were taking steps to take the men into custody.

"The dispatcher indicated that you have this entire incident on camera?"

"Yes sir."

"That's some jumpsuit you're wearing. Where did you get it?"

"I'm an inventor. I've been experimenting with fabrics and materials that cloak by distorting visible light. I'm trying to find fabric that neither adsorbs nor reflects light."

"Looks like you achieved that goal. We couldn't see you in the helicopter."

"If I put it on and stood next to you, you could see me. The fabric only works to cloak me from a distance, so it's not ready for commercial purposes yet. I've been working on it for almost a decade."

"Okay well, what you have so far is impressive. You could sell it now on the Halloween market."

"That's not my target market. I'm designing it for law enforcement and military use. The technology would aide in crime in the hands of the common person."

"True," Officer Bishop said.

CHAPTER 27

Throughout the whole attack, Hermione had been giving surreptitious glances at the time. She was worried that they would miss the call with her parents. On the hundredth time she glanced at the clock, Damian put her out of her misery by saying, "Hermione, I've seen you take many glances at the time this afternoon. Don't worry, we won't miss the video call with your parents. If I have to, I'll lock the police and crime scene staff outside of the house so that we may make the call in private. I haven't forgotten the call."

She visibly relaxed saying simply with a small smile, "Thanks."

First, several officers had invaded Damian's lab to watch a replay of the attack. While it played back, Damian kept an eye on the officers to make sure they didn't touch anything, and he didn't hesitate to admonish an officer he saw reach out to touch something with, "This is a working technical lab, please don't touch anything."

After that he observed no one else letting their hands stray. Hermione had taken delight in demonstrating how the water cannons worked. Damian showed them a pepper juice packet that he had the drone drop. After getting a copy of the video footage, the officers were back out of his lab organizing the transport of their prisoners to jail in Oakland. The two other men were transported to the hospital for eye care before their transfer to jail.

Officer Bishop relayed that the Coast Guard had caught up with the yacht just under the Golden Gate Bridge, apprehending the five men on board. They assisted the police by towing the yacht back to a police dock and turning the men over to the police for booking on attempted murder.

Damian looked at the swarm of officers and the battle that had taken place there and realized his island, and his identity no longer would have any privacy. It was an end of an era for him, and he mourned the loss of his privacy.

Ariana seemed to sense what he was feeling and sidled up to him putting an arm around his waist and whispering, "It will be okay. People still won't be allowed onto your island, although there are enough young fools that might want to brave the water cannons for the fun of it. You and this island will be known by this attack, but I think the vast majority of people will be amazed and approve of how you've set up your defense systems as I am. I see our company getting calls to set up security systems for other people. We may need to add that to the company's portfolio."

Damian chuckled and said, "You're probably right about that. Thanks for that unappealing vision of setting up security systems for the rest of my life."

"No problem," she said with a grin. "Although I do think you'll need to make an enhancement soon. I really do see scores of idiot young men trying to land on your beach to take on the water cannons. I think you need to re-aim them so that people get blasted in their boats and don't get a chance to come ashore."

"That's a brilliant idea! Gives me something positive to think about in the near future as I mourn the loss of my privacy."

"Buddy, you've done so many good things recently that I don't think you could stay in the shadows no matter what you tried."

"I just wish there was a car chase or a brush fire somewhere to take those damn news copters away from this island. Why couldn't there be bad news for journalists to chase rather than my story."

"Next time I know your island is under attack, I'll hire someone to do a freeway chase. How's that for a plan?"

Damian chuckled at the thought of that altercation. In his years, he'd seen some weird freeway chases like a fifty-foot recreational vehicle being chased by four Highway Patrol cars. It's not like the RV could hide anywhere, or the vehicle could get to high speeds or cut sharp corners. No, it was a slow chase until the RV ran out of gas.

"Just make sure it's a lumbering RV."

"What?"

"I don't want a sexy car-chase, just a slow one that will take an hour and not hurt anyone."

"Ah... okay. A special order crime. Hmmm."

"We have about an hour before our call," Ariana said. "Is the video camera all set up?"

"It's still good to go. Fortunately, there's no crime scene there for the technicians to destroy."

"When do you think they'll be done?"

"I'm hoping they're done tomorrow. In total there are eight men that they have to prosecute and so they have to collect evidence for those individual cases. They'll run out of daylight and need to return tomorrow."

"Yikes, two houses to clean from crime scene dust. Hermione and I will help you clean up the outside tomorrow. Fortunately, you don't have stuff to clean on the inside. All they want from inside is digital copies."

"I checked the weather forecast for tomorrow, and it's supposed to rain in the afternoon, so I'm thinking the rain will wash everything away, and the crime scene techs will be motivated to finish and get off my island."

Damian was interrupted to answer another question by a

detective. Finally, he was sure they had run out of questions, and so he said, "I've got an hour-long video call at five, and I need to not be interrupted. Do you have everything you need from inside the house? I'm not worried about the outside you can stay as long as you like."

"We are done on the inside of your house, and it's going to be dark soon outside, so our techs will likely return in the morning to continue collecting evidence. I assume if we need video footage of something we haven't thought of yet, that you'll be able to supply us with that something going forward?"

"Yes, I'd like to cooperate as best I can. We would have been dead if I didn't have defensive systems set up on this island. No fault of yours, but it takes a while for law enforcement to come to our aid."

"I understand sir. To add to this distance problem, this island is under the jurisdiction of three counties, so you get help from whomever can reach you first. This time it was the SFPD and the Coast Guard, and hopefully, this will be the last attack."

"I'm afraid that if this plays out on the news, I'll have idiotic young people trying to breach my water cannons. I've been thinking about what I can do to discourage that behavior and I'd appreciate any suggestions you or any of the other officers have. Don't be surprised if the next time, there's an attack on my property that the California Highway Patrol is involved with a freeway chase. Anything to move the news copters away from my island."

"I understand," the officer said and paused thinking about his answer, "Maybe we could invoke a no-fly zone over your island, though they would probably just use long range photo lens."

After a few more conversations, the officers left Damian's island and finally there was peace and quiet as the three of them sat in Damian's living room. He had business cards to follow up with people from the various agencies if he needed to. He sighed and leaned back closing his eyes and says, "Ladies, a long distance high-five for your work today. I don't have the energy to give you more kudos than that."

Before he knew it, he felt both sides of his sofa cushion sink, and he felt two sets of female arms wrap around his neck for a hug. He opened his eyes and returned the hug.

"Thanks, ladies. Let's just relax here for another twenty minutes or so, and then we'll retire to the lab for our phone call. It's all ready to go, so if we go down there now, we'll just sit around and look at each other."

Ariana got up and walked into Damian's kitchen to open a bottle of wine. She looked over at Hermione and said, "If this island were located in the Mediterranean Sea and was a part of Italy, you would routinely drink wine. This has been a stressful day so we'll pretend we're in Italy and I'll offer you a glass of wine."

"Seriously?! Bring it on!"

Damian didn't say anything as he thought it was a brilliant idea and if they were going to lose custody of Hermione after their call tonight what did it matter if they allowed her to have wine with them. Maybe if they still retained custody of her, they would travel to Rome on spring break and have a drink at the Piazza Navona. Then Damian thought, the kid would probably rather go back to Fantasialand.

Soon the three of them clinked wine glasses, but before Hermione was allowed to sip, Ariana took a moment to explain how she should evaluate the wine. After hearing about legs, color, smell, and taste, she took her first sip.

Damian and Ariana watched her for a reaction.

"What?!" Hermione asked when she caught them watching her. "I did what you said!"

"Sooooo, What did you think of the taste?" Ariana asked.

Hermione took a second sip and said, "It's unique. I've never tasted any juice or soda that comes close to this taste. Beer's a different color, so I assume it tastes very different from this wine. What's its name?"

"We'll have you try beer at a different time and yes it's a very different taste from wine," Ariana said. "The wine you're drinking is a Barbera, a sweet red wine. When you first start drinking wine, start with sweet and drink your way toward dry wines. They all have nuances that give them unique flavors. We'll give you a wine lesson later - grapes, fruit juices, oak barrels, cold or hot climates - it all makes a difference."

"Okay. I will say you drink this differently. It's a swallow at a time rather than how I might drink a soda or water. I can't see chugging it. I guess it's like hot coffee that you have to sip."

They sat chilling with their wine for a while, each in their own thoughts. Finally, Damian leaned forward, and said, "Let's go down to the lab."

He finished his wine and set his glass on the breakfast nook surface before heading downstairs to his lab and the ladies copied his actions.

Once they got down there, he explained the set-up which was the same as the previous call to James Spinnaker. Hermione's face would be a distorted picture of herself from two years ago. Once they established that her real parents were on the call, then Damian would do a reveal so they could see their real daughter and then he didn't know what was going to happen.

Damian checked his watch for the tenth time and noted they had two more minutes before the call and his mind was drawing a blank over what to say. Ariana must be having the same problem as she also seemed mute.

Hermione broke the silence with, "Are you two dating?"

Damian said, "What!"

As Ariana simultaneously said, "huh?"

Both adults looked like deer caught in the headlights, but before they had no time to fabricate an answer as the phone rang.

Ariana and Hermione paled, so Damian gave them a quick hug before answering the phone.

Damian answered the video call after everyone was in their place. Hermione was out of range of the screen while her hologram was in the air next to Damian. As the other end of the video call came into focus, there was a man sitting at a table with no one else in view of the screen.

Damian said, "You are not Mr. Sherwood."

The man replied, "Hannah Sherwood is next to you but she looks a little off."

Suddenly a woman lunged into the screen and said "What's wrong with Hannah? Hannah?"

Damian waved Hermione over, clicking off the hologram and bringing her into the call.

Hermione had heard the voice and said, "Mom is that you?" with breathless excitement.

Suddenly, Hermione's father entered the screen to look into the camera, while Hermione said, "Dad?"

Ariana joined Hermione to look at her parents.

"Mr. and Mrs. Sherwood are you in a safe place? Are you being held hostage? Is there anything we can do for you?"

"This is U.S. Marshal Thomas Kinnear," and he held his badge close to the camera so they could read it. "Who are you and what are you doing with Hannah Sherwood? Why did she look different at the start of this call?"

"I'm Damian Green, and this is Ariana Knowles. We've been caring for the Sherwood's daughter since about a week after they were kidnapped from their home. I live on an island in the Bay, and Hannah lives with Ariana in the city of Belvedere. She attends high school there."

They could all see Hannah's mother crying in the background.

Suddenly the teenager said, "I have a new name and identity, and Damian and Ariana have kept me safe from the bad people who are after you. We also changed my appearance so I wouldn't look like I used to – my hair is different, and I wear glasses that have clear lens. We changed my appearance because they've come after me too. My name is now Hermione Knowles, I'm Ariana's long-lost niece or something."

"Back-up. What do you mean men have been after you?" the agent asked.

Damian said, "Let me give you a quick summary of the last year or so. Hermione escaped from her parents' house and went to the marina in hopes of getting on the family boat, but the boat wasn't there, and she was so exhausted she fell asleep in my skiff at the marina and awoke when I approached my island. I called my friend Ariana as I was unequipped to take care of a teenage girl.

"I verified Hannah's story by visiting your house, and so we gave her the choice of calling the police so she could enter the foster care system or being raised by us until you folks reappeared."

Jason Sherwood said, "Thank you Damian and Ariana. Hannah looks in good health and happy. You say she's been attending school?"

"Yes, and," Damian said before Hermione cut him off.

"Daddy I'm going to high school near Ariana's home, and I've played water polo, I was on the swim team and now I'm the soccer goalkeeper. I also have good grades, and I hope to work at Damian's company this summer, and I went to Fantasialand two weeks ago!"

Damian watched the parents melting down with both joy that their child was happy and safe and sadness that they had missed some of her milestones.

"Where is this call originating from?" asked Kinnear.

"My island in the Bay. I believe your call is coming from the Justice Center in San Francisco, correct?"

"How do you know that?"

"I'm a scientist and inventor, so I have my phone system

bouncing off satellites around the world whereas my technology shows that your call is from an IP address in the Superior Court building. May I presume that Mr. and Mrs. Sherwood are in protective custody by the United States Marshals Service and that you're protecting them from a pharmaceutical billionaire intent on killing the family?"

"I think we need to end this call, now that we have verified the existence of Hannah Sherwood so we can research who you are," Kinnear said.

There were anguished moans from Hermione's parents as they both tried to block the agent from ending the call.

Damian understood the agent's angst, so he said, "Look, go ahead and have your department research Ariana and myself, but I think we need another call once you know we're good people. The child deserves to talk with her parents," Damian urged.

Kinnear nodded and said, "I'll set up a follow-up call once we investigate you people."

And just like that, Hermione's parents disappeared from the screen.

CHAPTER 28

"**W**ell sweetie, I don't think you're going to be reunited with your parents soon. I wouldn't be surprised if we have some U.S. Marshals personally visiting us over the next few days," Ariana said.

"Yeah, I was thinking I'd make it easy for them by giving them our names and addresses, but I don't like using that SFPD email account, so I think I'll wait for them to contact us," Damian said.

"My parents look different. I think they must have had their appearance changed just like I did, but I am so excited to see that they are still alive! I was so convinced they were dead last year when I escaped our old house. I mean they looked dead when I watched them dragged out in bags on the video monitor in my safe room. Why was there a marshal on the phone call? What do they have to do with my parents?"

"The Marshals Service usually guards key witnesses in important court cases. When the government was trying to bring down the mafia, and key witnesses were killed at the beginning, they found they had to keep them in protective custody so they would be alive to testify. I think the Marshals Service has been around for a few hundred years," Damian said.

"So what do I do next? Should I go to school on Monday? Do you think they'll meet us in person?"

"We really don't know," Ariana said. "If I were them I would secretly watch the three of us for a while. You may have a choice to make later - live with your parents in protective custody and be home-schooled, or stay here and communicate with your parents by phone."

"Really? You think I will get a choice?"

"You're old enough to make choices, so if I were your parents, I'd let you make the decision if they determine that you're happy and safe staying with me. I assume the Marshals Service after they take a look at the history of us protecting you, would rather you stay with us than them. They don't want responsibility for another person, especially one that won't testify in court. They just need to make sure that whomever your parents are testifying against can't get to you to influence them by holding you hostage."

Hermione thought for a little bit about Damian and Ariana's words. She loved her parents, but her world would be cut-off if she went with them into seclusion. No more soccer, or swimming, or water polo. Her entry into college might be affected by a home-schooled record, but then again not. She'd have no friends her own age, and she wouldn't learn to drive a boat or car or get a summer job at Damian's business. She'd have to give up her entire life to live with her parents. She loved living with Ariana and Damian, and they did as good a job and probably better at protecting her than the Marshals did as she had the freedom to play and travel.

"I love my parents, but if I'm a given a choice, I'd rather stay with you guys. I have so much freedom here to attend school, play sports, visit Fantasialand, get a summer job. Is it expensive to take care of me? Maybe I can get a job sooner so I can help with my costs."

At that last sentence, Damian and Ariana closed in on Hermione and said, "Sweetie, we have plenty of money, and you're not a burden. We are enjoying being fake parents and cheering you on. If you decide after you talk with the Marshals and your parents some more, that you want to continue living with me until they leave custody, you can do that. That might be one of the questions you ask the Marshals – if you join your parents in protection, how many years are you talking about? Certainly, they would need to protect you up to a trial and perhaps for a few years after. I don't really know how that works."

"Hermione, we've always wanted the best for you, and it's your decision, but I think you'll have a better life living with Ariana and I. You would likely be safer with the Marshals as they keep you under lock and key and I suppose someone could go after you at school, or at a sleepover, but I think we covered your tracks."

Hermione let out a loud yawn and said, "Boy am I tired. I didn't get much sleep at the slumber party, then I used a lot of energy operating the water cannons, and finally seeing my parents for the first time in almost a year! It's been a pretty cool day."

With that, she got another hug, and Damian said, "I think we're all tired after the busy day. Do you want dinner here, at Ariana's, or take-out from somewhere?"

Hermione let out another jaw-cracking yawn and said, "Let's go home, and I'll help Ariana make spaghetti, and Damian you can do garlic bread."

Soon, Damian had everyone loaded on his boat, Miguel laying down on the floor of the boat while he navigated in the dark across the bay. It was a clear night, and the three of them admired the beauty of the San Francisco skyline lit up. Soon they were back at Ariana's house, and they all helped with dinner preparations.

"I'd open another bottle of Chianti to go with the spaghetti, but we had enough wine earlier, and we don't want the Marshals to find a house full of drunks when they arrive," Damian said.

"Yeah, water or tea for us," Ariana agreed.

"Do you think Mom and Dad get wine when they're in protection?"

"I have no idea, and I hope never to find out, but you can ask them on your next call," Ariana said.

Hermione beamed and said, "Yeah, there's going to be a next call."

"We don't know when you'll get that call, but I would expect that it will take them a few days to a week for them to check us out. At least your parents, I think were reassured that you're doing well under our wings. I would expect that several agents will check out Ariana and I. If they're smart, they'll investigate how you're doing at school as that's a reflection of well we treat you at home."

Hermione nodded thinking about Damian's and Ariana's words, "That seems like the fair and smart thing to do. I guess you two could be related somehow to this drug cartel and you threatened me to get me to say good things about you on camera."

"Exactly sweetie," Ariana said adding noodles to boiling water for their pasta. "Look at how many have already tried to kidnap you. I don't know if we know the full scope of who your parents antagonized. That yacht that chased us down on Damian's island appears to be different from the Malaysian pharmaceutical drug king that was after you last year, or maybe they're all related through a far east alliance. Regardless I think we'll have to await an explanation from the Marshals to understand the full situation and the danger you and your parents are in."

Damian had put a loaf of french bread in the oven sprinkled with butter and herbs and was now working on a salad. Now that they had time to relax, he found he was starving. He was also more optimistic that he and Ariana would continue to have this wonderful teenager in their lives. What parent looking at the home life that he and Ariana provided would want their child to give that up to live in protected isolation with them? Sure if the child were an infant or otherwise young enough that only the mother would do, you would leave the child with them, but not in the case of the active teenager. They would just have to wait and see what the week brought.

"When's your next soccer game?" Damian asked.

"Wednesday. Are you coming?"

"Of course. I was thinking we might record parts of the game for your parents."

Damian watched the first tears form in this stoic teenager's eyes. She hadn't had a tear the entire time they were fighting off the evil men from the yacht, and yet here she was tearing up over the thought of her parents watching her in a game.

She had her head down as though she was praying while she got herself under control, and then she asked, "Could you just record the entire game? Sometimes the ball moves so fast that it's hard to turn the camera off and on."

"Sure I could record the whole game," Damian said. "Your parents could always forward through the boring stuff to just watch when you're in action. If your teammates are doing well, then you could take a nap because most of the action is at the other goal line."

"I might get a lot of action this week as we're playing the best team in our division."

"Okay, well we'll film the whole game, but don't get hurt diving through the air as that might bring a quick end to our guardianship of you," Ariana urged as she began placing bowls of food on her table. "Let's eat and change the subject. How was your sleep-over at Megan's house? Did anyone give you any grief about not being on one before now?"

"I never admitted it was my first sleep-over. I just followed whatever Jenna did and no one seemed to notice that I was having a weird experience. Mostly we gossiped about people in high school or on TV. Actually, I gave everyone a different opinion of one girl on my soccer team. Megan didn't like her, because she thought she was stuck up, but really she's just quiet and listens a lot, so I felt pretty good about coming to Whitney's defense in her absence. I even said we should invite her for the next sleep-over. Oh, and I volunteered to host it here."

"Seriously?" Ariana asked. "I'm scared to be around five hormone driven teenage girls."

"Don't look at me," Damian said with a smile. "Your posse is not coming to my island. I'm dumping this all on Ariana." Looking at her, he said, "Good luck with that."

"Wimp!" Ariana exclaimed.

"You bet. I'm not strong enough to serve as a referee for teenage girls," Damian agreed.

"You guys are funny. My friends aren't that bad. We were asleep by just after the Tonight Show ended. They had Ariana Grande, on and we wanted to watch it."

"Seriously, you can't have a sleepover at my island. There isn't room, there aren't enough bathrooms or showers, It's too far for your friends to go. Sometime I might be willing to teach your gang to fish, but that's it."

"How about the water cannons? Operating those cannons is like a video game for my generation."

"No."

"Alrighty then, I think I'll do a little reading then head to bed. It's been a long day, and it was so good to see my parents again. I'll sleep better knowing they're in good hands. And you two can discuss me without me listening," Hermione said as she stood up putting her dish in the sink before heading to her room.

"Sweet dreams sweetie," Ariana smiled at the teenager. "Good job today."

"Just don't tell your classmates that you want to be a water cannon operator when you grow up, okay?"

Hermione returned to the table and fist-bumped Damian and ran her fingers across her lips as though they were zipped tight.

She left the room with Ariana and Damian smiling at her as Ariana called out, "She's such a ham."

They waited until her door closed, then Ariana said, "Let's go out to my fire pit and enjoy the cool night. I have some blankets we can take out with us."

He nodded and followed her, settling into a chair so that he was facing the bay and she could see inside her house. Ariana wrapped herself in a blanket and stared across the fire at Damian.

"What a day! If I were to describe it to someone else no one would believe me."

"Even for me, it was a pretty far-fetched day starting with waking up next to you. We'll have to circle back to that once we're on solid ground with Hermione and her parents."

"Yeah, now is the not the time to be answering Hermione's question about whether we're dating."

"Do you think the Marshals Service will be here tomorrow inspecting our homes?" Ariana asked.

"I don't know the division of labor in that service. I would think they want to do deep background checks on us and maybe those kinds of people don't work weekends. If I were them, I would collect data on us and check on Hermione through the school. If they check the police departments for action at our two houses, then they'll get an earful that might take time sorting through. They may not know that the SFPD has people in custody related to some Asian Big Pharma company. Imagine their surprise when they find out how well we've protected Hermione. We probably could do a decent job protecting her parents, but I'm not attached to them like I am their daughter."

"Yeah, I know what you mean about the parents. I'm kind of angry with them for shortchanging Hermione of many normal teenage things like sleep-overs. At this point in her life, I think we're better parents than the real ones are."

They spent a few more minutes chatting before Ariana turned the fire off and took the blankets inside. She and Damian got a quick kiss in, and then he was off, across the bay to his island home.

CHAPTER 29

Sunday was a quiet day after all the hyperactivity of the day before. Damian expected another contingent of crime scene technicians arriving at his island early as rain was forecasted for the afternoon. He hoped they would finish and leave so he would have some time to clean before the rain hit. He wanted to rake the beach to cover the green dye and pepper juice in hopes that any wildlife sunbathing on his small beach or island cliffs would not be threatened by it. He assumed that the crime scene people would remove any bullets or shell casings as evidence. He supposed there were even empty magazines on his island, but he'd be the first to say he didn't know the correct terms for parts of a gun. He'd love to get an early start on the clean-up. But really he was afraid to step outside for fear of damaging any evidence. He called Officer Bishop to see what the day's plans were and was assured they would be there soon and likely not spend more than an hour or two on the island.

He decided to go down to his lab and get some work done on his GPS crystals. He was aware of the microchips that pet owners used, but he wanted something smaller and better for parents. Something that wouldn't have to be removed when they reached a certain age but rather would expire and stop sending signals after five years of use. Pet chips also worked via radio-frequency when scanned. His assumption with children though was they needed to be tracked to find them rather than be able to scan them once they were found. So maybe he needed a solar battery in the chip that would recharge itself so that it could emit a pulse say once every thirty minutes for five years. So he'd need a battery that would pulse 90,000 times then disappear. Since he saw it being applied like a tattoo and lying on top of the skin, it just needed to fade away. He also needed it to be invisible so that child abductors wouldn't slice the skin off the child trying to get rid of the transmitter. What a gruesome idea, he thought.

He was startled from his thoughts by the alarm going off. He quickly scooted on his rolling chair over to his security terminal and saw the approach of law enforcement in a patrol boat. He put aside his thought of emitters and went outside to talk to them from atop his cliff. After a shouted conversation, he learned that they had everything they needed close to the house and would only be collecting evidence from the cliff side and beach. That explanation gave Damian the go-ahead to clean up the upper lawn of his island. He dropped the green dye and pepper spray packets, and he spent a few moments thinking about what he wanted to do about it. The incoming rain would help dilute the potion, and as the soil was fairly sandy beneath his lawn, he'd add some sand from down below, and then cut his grass sooner than usual to see to the disappearance of the neon green.

He was finishing up when the techs came up the hill to ask him questions.

"We would like to film the operation of your water cannons and drone swarm as evidence."

Damian thought, how do I get out of this? Again he didn't want the news media showing coverage of his island's weapons on the evening news.

"I'd rather not do that. Could I create a computer graphic to demonstrate my system? Of course, that's in addition to the footage I gave the police yesterday of the real fight we had here. Is that enough?"

"Why don't you want us operating your equipment and filming that?"

"Frankly I don't want my equipment damaged by amateur operators."

"I heard you had a teenager operating the water cannons."

"Yes but she's trained and plays a video game that shoots water off an island like this. What's your training?"

"I admit I neither play video games nor have I used water cannons. I guess we'll have a go with your computer graphic, but we reserve the right to come back and try your technology in the future."

Damian nodded and walked them down to the beach where their boat was anchored, carrying a rake and shovel to see what he could do to clean the place up. He'd let out a sigh of relief when he saw the boat heading back toward San Francisco. No more visitors other than guests he invited to his island in the near future. He stood looking at the hillside and sandy beach with its sea of green dye splashes, then he looked towards the clouds in the sky and checked the weather. He had at most two hours before the rain hit, so he got to work raking the sand. When the color was more even to his satisfaction, a pale lime, he moved over to the hillside and looked at the damage there and indeed it wasn't bad. He surveyed his island once more and decided he'd let Mother Nature cure the remaining problems with a little rain.

The cats had been keeping him company outside and now returned with him indoors, perhaps sensing the impending rainstorms. They always said pets could detect changes in the weather better than their human owners could.

By the next morning there was no word from the Marshals Service, and so the three of them treated the day as if it was a regular Monday. Hermione was at school, Ariana had business with one of her start-ups and Damian was at his office in Richmond chatting with staff.

He and Lily were chatting about molecules and how to make the kid tattoo work. He was expecting Pete at any moment with the final plans for his restaurant and bar. Pete wanted to share them with him and his staff as he figured they were the first customers that would need to be satisfied. The whole gang was excited to see what he planned, and so when he showed up mid-morning, everyone dropped what they were doing and gathered around. They were pleased to see he would have more taps for craft beer. The space his original restaurant had was limited, and he had nowhere to expand the taps as he lacked the space for the kegs; besides when he'd opened the first restaurant, craft beer wasn't as popular as it was today. No one could think of anything to add other than a special occasion room, but Pete had no desire to expand his bar and restaurant in that direction. Damian sat back a moment thinking about how his life had changed over the past year or so. He felt so lucky to have found the employees he had, in addition to Ariana and Hermione.

After Pete left and everyone was back at their desks, he got an email from Natalie that provided information about Olivia Roth. The family was putting itself back together. Jennifer Shields pleaded guilty to child abduction charges and would serve three years in state prison and pay a $10,000 fine. Stupid woman. If she had just given Olivia up after a month or so, she'd be back to her regular life now. While she hadn't physically hurt the little girl, she had kept her away from her family for five long years.

Damian had a quiet night, checking in with Ariana and Hermione to see if they had any unexpected guests or perhaps felt that someone was watching them. In theory, the Marshals Service could go into Hermione's high school and just take her to live with her parents. Damian was glad they hadn't had to suffer through that so far.

Wednesday rolled around, and Damian affixed a tripod to the

top of a small set of bleachers that were available on the field. He checked the view and was assured he could see the entire field. He waited for the game to begin so he could hit the record button then take a seat next Ariana. Soon he forgot he was recording the game and became caught up rooting for Hermione's team. Hermione was correct in that she would see more action at her side of the field. She'd blocked five kicks already. Each time, the ball had gotten too far in front of the girl kicking it so she was able to step out from the net and kick it as far as she could and then hope her own forwards would take it to the opposite net. After the halftime, she saw a switch in strategy for Hermione's team that meant all the action was at the opposite net.

As usual, after a game, they waited for her to clear the locker room, and then they left for burgers at a restaurant in town. Hermione was entranced with the video that Damian had made. It was better than the one the coach made as it was higher up. She studied it intently making remarks.

"Are you thinking of making a career in broadcasting?" Damian asked.

"Huh?" Hermione asked.

"You're narrating the game like a commentator."

"Oh, sorry. It's just so easy to see where we didn't excel in this game. I'm going to email the video to our coach. I'd email it to my teammates, but I guess that I should let the coach do that."

"Yeah, you should let the coach do that," Ariana said. "Sharing film is a coach thing to do. Also, you don't want to take the lead to criticize all of your teammates – let the coach do that."

"Yeah, I know. It's just I can see our mistakes so well with this film unlike I've been able to before. I guess the coach hasn't recorded from that angle perhaps because he was afraid his cell phone would be stolen since he can't keep an eye on it and us at the same time. Can I volunteer you to film all of the games?"

"Sure kiddo. If I'm not able to attend one of your games,

Ariana can do the same thing with her phone, and I'll leave the tripod I used here with you."

Hermione smiled her thanks and said, "I noticed some guys in suits at the school today. They didn't talk to me or seem to be staring at me, but they looked a little overdressed compared to everyone else. Maybe they were checking my records at the principal's office."

"I think they would have to have a search warrant for that," Ariana said. "Not that they couldn't get one, but your records are private, and only Damian and I are supposed to be able to view them."

"We still haven't heard a peep from the Marshals Service. They could have looked in the school yearbook for information about you – that's public information. It would have your pictures from the sports teams you've been on as well as a school picture. I'm going to send the link for your soccer game video to the original account for your parents to watch and I'll be able to see the number of views but not necessarily that your parents are viewing it, but I don't know why the Marshals Service wouldn't share it with your parents. It shows that you're talented and happy."

"Cool," was all the teenager said around a mouthful of burger.

Damian had to give the kid credit, she was good at letting go of things she couldn't do anything about and enjoying the here and now.

Once they returned to Ariana's house, Damian said goodnight to Hermione as she walked down the hallway to her bedroom to do the night's homework. She had straight "As" and seemed intent on continuing academic success.

Damian spent some time talking to Ariana about plans for the remainder of the week, Hermione had another soccer game that Friday and they were on the watch for any action the U.S. Marshals might take. Dating was on hold until they had clarification of Hermione's status. With an extended goodbye kiss, he was striding down the dock to his boat with a promise to be back on Friday for the game.

On Thursday, he received some much-needed information from the SFPD. His single question had been how did they know who he was and where he lived? He was grateful that the same attack hadn't occurred at Ariana's house as she didn't have the defenses that she did while she did have a faster police response. If they hadn't reached the end of corrupt pharmaceutical companies from Asia trying to kill Hermione's parents, he would have looked at some angles to protect her property.

In a plea deal, someone on board the ship revealed that there were surveillance cameras on top of the yacht and they reviewed the footage because the police arrived so quickly after the dead body was found. His identity and location had been discovered through the call letters on his speedster boat captured on the camera footage. It was registered through the Department of Motor Vehicles, and it had taken a while to track him to his home in the bay. He received his mail through a P.O. Box in Richmond, but they had tracked him beyond that post office box. He was glad, he hadn't been attacked at his warehouse in Richmond which also didn't have any defensive systems. The yacht owners must have concluded that he could get help much sooner in Richmond than he would on an isolated island in the Bay.

He and Ariana were back at a different high school soccer field on Friday, this time an away game. Fortunately, there were again a set of bleachers that he was able to set his phone up on a high point to capture the match. The coach had briefly thanked him before the start of the game for the excellent recording of the previous game, and other parents had asked to see it, so he was going to begin posting it to a site they could all reach and watch. As they had only a day of practice between games, Damian wasn't hopeful that there would be an improvement but who knew what miracles a coach might create.

He was surprised to see some improvement. It was as though

each girl had more faith in her teammates having seen their skills on video, and there was less clustering near the ball. Hermione's team had another decisive win and Damian and Ariana checked the high school schedule for playoff dates to add to their calendar. Admittedly, it was still early in the season, but they were undefeated.

Damian posted the game video sending everyone links including his SFPD address that seemed to reach Hermione's parents. They had another quiet weekend with no word from the U.S. Marshals. Damian thought them rather slow, but then he'd gone to great lengths to protect his privacy which would make them suspicious of him.

CHAPTER 30

$\mathcal{A}$riana had just finished dropping Hermione off at school, and she was returning home to get her boat to head over to Damian's Island where they would commute to the warehouse for her to get some work done on site in Richmond.

There was a strange car parked on the street close to her driveway. It was a sedan, but usually, there wasn't a car parked in that location. After her recent bad experience with her stalker, she had the full security system on which meant that if the vehicle followed her car on her driveway with open windows, its driver would be sprayed with pepper juice. As the system turned off with a sensor from her car, she was curious as to whether it would come back on immediately and spray the car. She thought a nanosecond about warning the occupants of the car, but then decided they hadn't called and made an appointment, and so she would keep her defense systems up until some identification was shown. If the driver got sprayed, well then she hoped he wouldn't lose control of his brakes and crash into her house. Then she thought of Miguel in the house and knew she didn't want him hurt by an out of control car, so she turned off the security system and sighed over the worthless internal argument she'd had with herself.

She pulled into her garage and then waited for the approach of the sedan just at the edge of the door. She could see there were at least two people in the car.

As they exited the car, she held up her cell phone and said, "I have my local police station on the other line, one at a time, approach and show me your ID," then she said into the phone, "There are two people that got out of a car and one is approaching with her identification, please hold."

When the woman was within five feet, she held up a badge that said, 'FBI'. Ariana had never seen a badge before but thought it looked real. She said into the phone, "The badge says FBI, I'm going to end our call now, but send an officer out in ten minutes if I don't call back and say everything's okay." She pretended to listen, then hit a button on her phone as if to end the call. There was no reason to reveal to these two that the call had never been connected in the first place.

"Are you always this suspicious of people?" the man asked holding out his identification.

"I'm Special Agent Mark Tauscher, and this is Special Agent Susan Abbott."

"I am. I have reason to be. My person and my home have been attacked in the past year or so. What do you want?" Ariana asked in her most unfriendly voice.

"Are you Ariana Knowles?" Abbott asked.

"Yes."

"We're here to conduct an investigation about a child by the name of Hermione Knowles," replied Special Agent Abbott.

Ariana was unexpectedly scared by the question. When she and Damian went down the path of taking care of Hermione, she'd never thought of the moment of being interviewed by the FBI about that decision. Now she knew she looked and felt like a child abductor.

"So, what's your question?"

"How long has the child resided at this location?" asked Special Agent Tauscher. His sunglasses were hiding any expressiveness of his face.

"Almost a year," Ariana aimed to keep her responses as short and as vague as possible.

"She attends school near here?" Abbott asked.

"Yes, she attends high school. It's where she is now."

"We know. Frankly, this is the strangest case we've ever investigated. On the surface, it appears that two rational adults took in a teenager on the run and didn't report her to the police or foster care system."

"Actually, her guardian lives on an island in San Francisco Bay, and as there's no school's nearby, I agreed to care for her after her parents died in a car accident. She's attended school in this district over the past year."

"We know, we checked out the yearbooks at her school last week. She's a member of the National Honor Society which means she has good grades and she's on the swim team."

"Also the water polo and soccer team," Ariana added with pride in her voice.

"Why does she have your last name?" Special Agent Abbott asked.

"We started out with her original name, which is Sherwood, but that got too hard to be constantly comparing her last name to mine, so we changed it."

"How did you do that? I see she has a passport issued in your last name, but I could find no change of name in the Marin County Court records for that name change," Tauscher said.

"I'm not going to answer that question."

"It's against the law to lie to us," Abbott said.

"I haven't lied. I've said nothing."

Abbott and Tausher looked at each other and passed some message between them.

"May we see where the child stays?" Abbott asked.

Ariana looked at the time on her phone and calculated, "Hermione's class hasn't started yet, let me see if she'll give you permission."

Ariana texted Hermione explaining the FBI's appearance and them asking to see her room. Did she grant them permission?

Ariana waited a beat, and Hermione texted back, 'Yes, call me on my next break between classes.'

Ariana looked at the two agents and said, "She's given her permission."

She let them inside, and Miguel let out a growl at the two strangers. Ariana reassured her pet that all was well, but loved the unwelcoming glare the dog continued to give the agents. She walked down the hall and showed them Hermione's room. They looked inside and nodded.

"Why was Hermione held at knife-point a few weeks ago? This doesn't sound like a safe environment from what I read in the police report," Tauscher commented,

"If you read the police report then you know that the knife holder was released from prison and stalking me. As Hermione and I came home from school, he was near my garage, and I didn't see him hiding there. I have an excellent security system, but he came by boat and then used the opportunity of me leaving to drive to school to pick up Hermione to move onto my property. I turn the system off when I go up and down my driveway."

"Why do you turn off the security?" Abbott asked curiosity in her voice. "Is it a shrieking alarm?"

"No. I debated leaving the security system on for you two, but I didn't want to risk my dog."

"I don't understand. Why would your dog be at risk?"

"My security system would have spayed the driver's side window with pepper spray. If you lost control of your car, because you couldn't see, you had the potential to crash into my living room where Miguel might be lying down taking a nap."

"So why do you have such a strange security system?"

"Because since Hermione has come to live with me, we have had multiple attacks on ourselves. This time I was the target."

"Have you been on vacation with her?" Special Agent Abbott asked changing tactics.

"Yes, we've been sailing to Papau New Guinea and Australia, London for a week to watch several soccer games, and Fantasialand."

"What's she going to do in the coming year? New skills, vacations, etc.? Can you brag about her?"

Ariana's mind was racing a million miles a minute trying to protect Hermione and herself, yet demonstrate that she was in a loving home and happy. This last question seemed to be out of left field.

"At school, I think her soccer team is going to go to the state championships – they're really that good. In the spring she'll be back on the swim team, and she made the regional qualification last year. In the summer, she wants to work at Damian's business, so we're going to teach her to drive a boat so she can reach his island or the Richmond dock and then she'll get a car service from there to work. We're working on a program for kids to grow them into inventors like Damian. I've filed paperwork with the state so we can hire kids. We'll also take her somewhere on vacation. Next fall will be her junior year. She has her eye on UC Berkeley, she wants to swim for them and get a degree there. Maybe if she's really a good swimmer, she might go to the Olympics in 2020. How's that for bragging."

"She sounds like a good kid with a good life and someone that loves her," Abbott remarked.

"We do love her. Isn't that a part of what any child needs to thrive in this world?"

"Where is this island in the San Francisco Bay that Damian Green lives on?" Tauscher asked ready to move the conversation on to the next interviewee.

"Would you like him to come here? His island is too far from here to see from my dock. It's about fifteen minutes by boat."

"We would like to go there. Is it possible that you would take us?"

"Just a moment, I'm going to have a conversation with him, he may already be at his office."

With that Ariana walked down her hallway to her bedroom and shut the door and locked it, then went into her bathroom and closed the door. Then she called Damian.

"Hello," he said when he answered.

"Hi, back at you. The FBI was here when I returned from school. I don't think they believe our story of how Hermione came to live with me, but they have nothing to counter it. Now they have asked me to take them to see you. Are you still on your island and what do you think?"

"I want Hermione to be approved by them to continue living with us. I don't want either of us to be arrested for not reporting her appearance last year to the authorities. I hate having anyone on my island, but after last week's shootout, it probably doesn't matter. They've probably seen the tapes from the SFPD with agency cooperation. I'm still here, so go ahead and bring them over. I'll meet you at the dock. How's your interview gone so far?"

"It's been weird. The agents asked why Hermione's name was changed from Sherwood to Knowles and I explained, and they said they could find no record of us filing a name change with Marin County. Then they asked to see her room and what our hopes were for her for the coming year. Weird. They also asked how she was held at knifepoint and remarked that I have a weird security system. Wait until they see yours."

"So I should expect some weird questions. Okay, I'll see you in about twenty minutes. Text me when you're five minutes out."

"Will do."

CHAPTER 31

It had been a rough crossing of the bay, and both agents were looking a little green by the time they slowed to approach Damian's dock. He was standing outside looking like a man ready to defend his castle from invaders. He assisted Ariana tying up the boat and helped her off of it, then let the two agents stumble without assistance onto the dock. As Damian raised and lowered the dock, it wasn't as solid feeling as the average dock, and he secretly smiled watching the agents move on to land as fast they could.

Introductions were performed, and Damian studied their badges and used his cell phone camera to take a picture of each.

"Why do you need a picture?" Special Agent Tauscher asked.

"I don't know you from Adam, and I don't know if your badges are real, so I'm going to check you out."

"We have guns, are you sure you're safe?" mocked Special Agent Abbott, in a bad mood after the bumpy and nauseating ride to this remote island.

"I am. This entire island is full of modifications, and I could have you screaming in pain in no time," Damian said in a hostile voice.

Ariana thought to bridge the gap and said, "But you won't pull your guns, and he won't cause you pain. Let's get on with this."

Tauscher regathered himself and asked, "Where does Hermione stay when she visits you on the island?"

Damian said, "Follow me and don't touch anything as you walk by."

The agents were so busy looking around that they barreled into each other when Damian stopped at Hermione's room at the back end of his lab. Ariana had to cover a laugh when that happened.

"There's not much room here for the teenager. And she has no window."

Damian hit a button, and the "window" showed the choppy waters of the bay outside and the sky above.

"Wow. Why doesn't Hermione have a real window?" Abbott asked trying to imagine the layout of the island.

"My lab is surrounded by stone. When she came to live with me, I only had the single bedroom upstairs. So with her agreement, I added this room downstairs as well as a toilet to the lower level."

"Ah," was all Special Agent Abbott could say as though she understood how hard it was to build on this island.

"Let's see the rest of this place. We would like to make sure it's safe for a teenager. How do you keep her away from stuff in this lab? You just warned us not to touch," Special Agent Tauscher said.

"She's a smart kid, she doesn't touch anything I haven't shown her to be safe," Damian said implying that the agents weren't smart.

Ariana thought score three for Damian. The wobbly dock, the lab, and now the comment about brains.

Damian steered the agents upstairs to the main living level of his house. The agents saw a door to a bedroom open partially, a kitchen and a living room. It was a million dollar view no matter the weather.

"How often does she stay with you Damian?" asked Special Agent Abbott.

"Perhaps once a month, whenever Ariana is out of town for business. If she stays with me more than that, it adds twenty-five minutes to her commute to school."

"How often does she see you each week?"

"Depends on our schedules but at least twice a week. Ariana and I are at all of her sporting events, plus parent-teacher events."

"Has she ever spent a night away from both of you?"

"Once," they both said at the same time and smiled at each other. "She had a sleepover with a girlfriend down the street last week. The first in her life," Ariana finished.

"Have you joined vacations with Ariana and Hermione?"

"Yes. I organize our vacations."

"The SFPD mentioned that she operated water cannons when your island was attacked recently. Is that appropriate for a child?" asked Special Agent Tauscher.

"No, but then it isn't appropriate for Ariana and I to have to defend ourselves against a shipload of hooligans, right?"

After a brief pause, the agent replied, "I guess not sir."

"Would you mind waiting a few minutes while Agent Abbott and I step outside and talk?"

"No, but knock hard when you want back in. The door won't open for you," Damian said.

The agent looked puzzled by Damian's comment and stood staring at the door briefly after they exited.

After the door closed, Ariana and Damian looked at each other, and Ariana said, "This is the weirdest verbal dance I've ever done. If we could be straight with them and not hurt our guardianship of Hermione, I would just come out and say what I really think."

"Yeah, I know. This is the largest elephant in the room that I have ever tried to talk around."

"So what do you think our next steps are?"

"Let's see what they say when they come back in. They're trying to do a background check, but I have them blocked on all angles if they do a computer search. They can't prove that Hermione isn't exactly who we say she is."

Ariana looked over at Damian's phone which showed the camera view of the two agents outside. First, they chatted, then Special Agent Tauscher called someone on his cell and turned his back on the camera. Special Agent Abbott stood looking towards the Golden Gate Bridge, perhaps reliving the rough boat ride to the island. After about ten minutes he ended the call and turned back to Abbott saying something to her and then the two of them turned to knock on the door.

They could barely hear it inside and the motion was superfluous as unknown to the two agents, they'd been watched on video the entire time they were outside.

Damian approached and opened his front door and the two agents returned with a gust of wind behind them.

Special Agent Tauscher said, "We just spoke with our contact in another department of the government about investigating you two and the child. That department assures us that the kid known by the name of Hermione Knowles is really Hannah Sherwood. However, after a week of trying to check you two out on our various computer systems, we are coming up with a big fat zero on how you came to be her guardians. We know who both of you are and your background. We know that you've both lost spouses."

"And children," Damian said grimly.

"And children in your case, Mr. Green. We think the two of you are hiding the child's real identity, but likely for good and altruistic reasons. We feel fairly sure that Hannah Sherwood is well cared for, happy, and doing well in life. What we can't determine is whether you're a threat to her parents."

"Contact the SFPD officer handling the attack on this island last week. I think you'll find if you read the interviews of the men arrested from that boat, that their target was Hermione, not Ariana or myself. If we were a risk to her or her parents, we would not have kept her safe through multiple attacks over the past nine months. Take a look at those records and interview Hermione. She might provide some insights to you. She's a smart kid."

"So are you admitting that she's Hannah Sherwood?" asked Abbott.

"No. She's Hermione Knowles," replied Damian.

The two agents sighed and said, "We'd like to interview her. When is she free today?"

Ariana pulled out her phone to look at her calendar and said "School's over at 3:30, but she has soccer practice after that. Why don't you return to my house at 5:30 this evening and you can speak with her."

Abbott asked, "Is there a way to return to our car that doesn't involve getting on your boat?"

Ariana smiled and said, "Not really. Damian has a little speedster boat that seats two and he could get you to the Richmond side in about five minutes on smoother water, but then your car is in my driveway, so one of you needs to come with me to move it."

Damian added, "I could brew you some mint tea before you go and keep your eye on the horizon to reduce your nausea."

Abbott sighed and said "I'd appreciate some mint tea. If you have a go-cup, I'll leave the cup with Ms. Knowles once I return to her home."

Damian took a few minutes to brew both agents some tea and then he saw them off his island and cruising back to Ariana's home. They should be grateful that Ariana had a pontoon boat as it actually usually reduced the seasickness compared to other boats. He'd follow her across the bay later today to be on hand for the interview with Hermione.

CHAPTER 32

*D*amian was at his desk in his office in Richmond when he got a call from Ariana.

"How'd the ride back go?" Damian asked.

"They both sipped your tea while facing ahead and looking at the horizon and there was no puking. They managed to make it to my dock a little less green than on the way over."

"Good. Does Hermione know about the interview?"

"Yes, and you know her. Game on."

"Did you caution her about saying little as far as we were not her real parents?"

"Oh yeah. She's happy living with you and I and doesn't want that changed. It was her opinion based on the call last week, that where ever her parents are, they're confined in some way, and she would rather not join them in their confinement."

"Like we told the agents, she's a smart girl," Damian said. "I wonder if she'll at some point get to see her parents in person if she chooses to stay with us."

"Certainly, they could land on your island and spend some time together before any bad people had the chance to reach them out in the middle of the bay. Even if those bad people got word of where they would be, your island defenses are such that the parents would be safe there."

"The least they should do is set up a permanent line of communication with her. I could give the Marshals Service an IP address for a satellite which would provide cover for their physical location."

"The next few days are going to be interesting. They could go horribly wrong, or perhaps be incredibly boring if we don't hear anything after the interview. I'll make a pitch to the FBI agents about landing on my island, and we'll see where that goes."

After they ended their call, he looked around the office assessing things. He had a huge smile over what a weird life he had currently. He was sort of dating a woman he really liked and could see a future with. He got to be a knight in shining armor to two women he swore to protect, and he got to do an awkward question and answer dance with two FBI agents. What more entertainment could a man want?

Soon his brain was back to the problems his staff was having with their projects. While Lily was in charge of his temporary tattoo with GPS for children, she knew he was also working on the item of how to get the tattoo to melt away after five years. They kept their notes on what they tried on a spreadsheet online, so he took some time to update what he'd worked on in his own lab on the island. He read her notes, and liked the direction she was going. Between the two of them, they'd solve this question and very soon they could significantly reduce child abductions nationally.

He checked on other projects that his staff was working on and then went to see Haley regarding the drone software. He'd learned a few things while steering the drone swarms during the attack on his island and he wanted to incorporate those insights into her project. After an otherwise intellectually stimulating day at the office, he left to return to his island and on to Ariana's house to support Hermione in her upcoming interview.

They were waiting outside her school when she exited the girl's locker room. She opened the door and got in the back seat of Ariana's SUV.

"I like that whenever I'm facing any kind of problem, you two show up together behind me. You don't tell me what to do rather, you lurk in the background letting me know you're with me. Kind of like my soccer team."

Damian watched Ariana try to drive while gulping back her emotions at Hermione's insight.

"We wouldn't have it any other way," he said. "Both of us have never raised a teenager before, so most days we're walking through the wilderness while trying to do the best job possible."

"Well, I'd have to say you've been spot on. In fact, you're so good that some of my friends wish they had you two as parents."

"Wow, with compliments like that, I'd think you were buttering us up to get a car or something," Damian said with a laugh.

"Seriously, I want to have a party at Ariana's house, and share you with my friends, then perhaps you two could melt away before you do something that shoots my opinion of you all to pieces."

The two adults laughed out-loud at that piece of teenage wisdom, with Ariana adding, "You bet kiddo."

Damian could see that the last comment had allowed Ariana to move on from her earlier tears. They were approaching her driveway, and the agents weren't parked there at the moment. They had Ariana's phone number and would call her before attempting to drive down her driveway.

Hermione dropped her backpack in her room and then joined Damian and Ariana in the kitchen asking, "I don't suppose you'd offer me another glass of red wine with the FBI on its way?"

"That would be a big fat 'no'!" Damian said. "I've returned to my embarrassing parent behavior."

"No problem. What should I say to these guys?"

"Tell them the truth," Damian advised.

"Should I admit to being Hannah Sherwood? Won't that get you guys in trouble?"

"Unless they do a DNA test they cannot prove that you're not Hermione Knowles, and I hope you're too young to testify against us in court. So you might take the tactic of asking them if they're recording this conversation, and asking them not to. You can tell them the truth, but also tell them you'll never give the explanation again to anyone other than Amy and Jason Sherwood,. That puts them in a bind, but allows them to do their job."

"What is their job?"

"I think they were sent by the Marshals Service to investigate Ariana and me to determine if we are a risk to your parents or to you," Damian suggested.

"You're not a threat to me, as you could have given me to that Malaysian businessman months ago. You're not a threat to Mom and Dad, as it's not the way you live your life unless they were threatening me, which they wouldn't do as they're my parents."

Damian saw Ariana wipe another tear from the side of her face as she turned to putter around the kitchen.

"You can tell the agents that if you like," Damian said.

"Can I also make them go outside and leave their phones in their car to make sure they are not recording the conversation? Do you still have the device that searches for bugs, so I can scan them?"

Damian laughed and said, "Hermione, you been living with us for too long. You've become too dependent on technology solutions. I don't have my bug detector with me, so just ask them politely to comply."

"Ok. What's for dinner? I had to run more today, so I'm starving."

"How about chicken piccata with a salad?" Ariana replied having regained her emotions.

"Sounds like a plan," Hermione said fidgeting and looking at the time.

Ariana saw the movements and said, "If you want to study, we'll call you out when the FBI arrives."

"I can't concentrate on homework at the moment. Damian, will you play Fortnite with me? That'll take my mind off these people."

"Sure, I'll open up the program," he said going over to the game consoles and Ariana's TV in her living room to start the program.

"Don't let me win," Hermione advised wanting the fierce concentration of trying to beat the game king that Damian was.

"I won't. You know I always play to win. It's better to practice losing with Ariana and me, then to lose for the first time with your friends."

"Maybe when I have my friends over, we can all play this game and see how impossible it is to beat you. That would be fun."

"Do all of your friends play Fortnite?" Damian asked not wanting any of her friends excluded.

"Okay, I have to say that you're clueless, Damian. Of course, we all play," Hermione said with exaggerated superiority in her voice, but a smile on her face.

"Game on then!"

Damian and Hermione were so involved in their game, they didn't hear Ariana's cellphone ping with the text from the agents, nor notice when they came in the door. She let the game go on a little longer then said, "Guys, the FBI agents are here."

They both looked back at her, game consoles in hand, disappointment on their faces at having to end the game early. They paused the game, then they both stood up. Ariana said, "Why don't you three go outside on the deck to chat? Hermione can turn on the outdoor heater if you're cold."

Damian and Ariana watched the three settle outside and then saw Hermione spring up to turn the propane heater on. It was probably fifty-five degrees outside so not exactly warm, but Ariana wanted to be able to see them through the windows.

She grabbed Damian's hand and squeezed saying, "This is it."

"It will be fine, you'll see. Hermione somehow convinced two rational adults, you and me to take her on in secret and we did. She'll have those agents eating out of her hand in no time."

They turned and settled in the kitchen to await the outcome.

CHAPTER 33

*H*ermione reached for the switch on the outdoor heater, and then sat down asking, "Who are you? Are you recording what we talk about?"

First one then the other agent leaned forward showing her their ID. She studied each one and then sat back on her sofa and waited for them to proceed.

"We left our phones out in the car, so we're not recording you," said Special Agent Tauscher.

"Are you Hannah Sherwood?" Special Agent Abbott asked.

"My school name is Hermione Knowles."

Abbott sighed and muttered, "You're as difficult as those two inside."

Hermione beamed like she'd just been paid a compliment.

"What's your life been like for the past nine months?" asked Tauscher.

"School's been good, I love living with Damian and Ariana, we've had some fantastic vacations, and we fought off bad people after one of the three of us."

"There have been other battles you've participated in besides the stalker and the recent island attack?

"Oh yeah! There were a group of convicts after Damian, and there was a Malaysian man who was trying to kidnap me to use me as a hostage to find Mom and Dad."

"There's been another incident besides the recent attack on Damian Green's island?" asked Abbott. From the sound of it, this kid had been through a lot but hadn't broken as of yet.

"Yeah, dad worked for a pharmaceutical company in Malaysia, and there was a man hired as a private detective from that country who was supposed to find and capture me. The government was holding his old parents hostage to make him chase me. Damian protected me and freed the man's parents, so we're good."

"What are your plans for the future? Are you planning on going to college?"

Hermione never blinked at the change in conversation and instead responded to the question.

"I have an A grade average, and I've already skipped a grade. I hope to go to UC Berkeley, and I want to compete on the swimming, water polo, and soccer teams. I'll probably only get to do one sport, but I have two and a half years before I move on to college, so I hope to have a good reputation in one of the sports. This summer I'm going to work in Damian's company helping his employees invent stuff."

"Do you feel safe in Ariana's house?"

"Yes." Weird how she could feel safer in a house without a safe room than in a home with one. Maybe it was because Ariana and Damian had taught her how to fight back in a non-violent way. How to use her brains to outsmart the bad guys.

"Do you think that Ariana Knowles and Damian Green are a threat to your parents? That is if you admitted that Amy and Jason Sherwood were your parents."

"They have no need to be a threat to my parents. They have everything they need without threatening others to get someone else's share..... Does that make sense?"

"Yeah, it does, and it's a good closing conclusion for our report. Will you show us the way out?"

Hermione stood up and started toward the french doors into the house, then she turned and asked, "Would you give this to my parents if you see them? It's a recording of my last soccer game."

Special Agent Abbott had hated this assignment from the get-go, but no more so then at this moment with a child asking her to pass on information to her real parents.

"I will."

The front door soon closed behind the two agents, and Ariana looked out the front to see their car back up the driveway. She reset her security system and hoped they wouldn't change their mind and come back and then she walked into her kitchen.

"The chicken is done, Damian, you finish the salad, and Hermione, take care of the rice pilaf. We should be able to eat in about fifteen minutes."

"Do you want to know what they asked me?"

"Only if you want to tell us," Damian said.

"Well, it's not like it's a secret and they didn't tell me to zip my lips. They asked if I felt safe here and what my plans for the future were."

"Did they ask you if you were Hannah Sherwood?"

"Yeah, they did, and I told them my school name is Hermione Knowles. That way I avoided telling a lie."

"Good job!"

"They also asked if I thought you were a threat to my parents. I said 'no' as there's nothing my parents have that you want and because you're not like that."

"Oh sweetie," Ariana said hugging the girl.

Hermione looked over Ariana's shoulder at Damian and rolled her eyes at the snuffling sounds she heard Ariana making. He just smiled, and soon they returned to making dinner as though it were any other night.

"Oh one thing, I gave them a CD with the footage from my last soccer game so they could get to my parents in case they didn't get the link. I think they'll be amazed at what I'm doing."

"Good idea. If I'd thought of it I would have copied all of my coverage of you in your various sports over the past year," Damian said. "I suppose I still could. I'll make a CD for all three of us, and whoever sees the agents next will be armed with a copy to get to your parents. I didn't video your water polo games from beginning to end, but I've got video clips and pictures of your events."

"So what do you think is going to happen next?"

"I think they'll give a report to the Marshals service and then it could go one of many ways. At worst case, they could remove you from this house because we never legally were assigned to take care of you. They would have a difficult time doing that as they don't have proof that you're not exactly who Ariana and I say you are. I think they will say that you're well cared for here and happy, and...."

"Yes I am,"

"And you're safe. What I don't know is whether they would allow you to visit your parents on occasion. They may still view you and us as threats to your parents. I also think they could enter in the middle of the night and snatch you if your parents demanded it."

"Should I move over to the island until this is finished?"

"Good question. Maybe we should do that for the remainder of the week. I think we'll know something by Friday. I can take you to the dock at Tiburon and arrange for a car service to take you to school. That would cut down your commute time and take you to a place not expected. Ariana, I don't think you're at any risk, but you could move to a nearby hotel with Miguel."

"I think I'll stay put. I don't feel like I'm at any risk as you say. I'll see you guys tomorrow, and Thursday evening for soccer games, then on Friday, Hermione will likely return home."

"Okay then Hermione, pack your bag for four days of school clothes, and we'll return to my house tonight. We'll swing by

Tiburon, so we know how long it will take us in the morning to drop you off there and then tomorrow you'll just come home with me after the soccer game. Sounds simple for a few days."

They followed their plan for the remainder of the week. Ariana had no disturbances, and no one tried to snatch Hermione on her way to and from school. They heard nothing from the agents going into the weekend and so planned to go back to their normal routine on Saturday.

CHAPTER 34

my and Jason Sherwood were allowed to read the report prepared by the FBI about the couple that was raising Hannah. They had a decision to make. The FBI could snatch the girl from these two adults who seemed to be doing an excellent job raising their daughter. The Marshals Service wanted her to stay with the couple, but it was really up to her parents. They had sacrificed a lot on behalf of the government to be the star witnesses in a ten billion dollar lawsuit against a pharmaceutical firm.

They could decide to keep Hannah with them or not. The downside for the child was she faced homeschooling and no school sports if she stayed with her parents. They had watched two soccer games their daughter had starred in, and they were impressed with her goalkeeper skills. If she joined them, she'd have to leave the team, even though she clearly excelled as an athlete. As former Olympic swimmers, her parents were proud of her accomplishments

"It seems like it's in Hannah's best interests that she stay where she is. She's with two adults who have apparently keep her safer than we did and yet have somehow given her more freedom."

"These years of high school are so important to her future. They said the trial will be over in three years, but I don't know this criminal enterprise enough to understand if we walk free after the court case is over or if we'll need to stay in custody for a while after that," Jason said.

"I hadn't thought of that! I had in my mind that we would be free at the end of the court case. To think this could go beyond that is an awful thought. Do you think we could arrange a monthly or even quarterly meet-up with Hannah? I'd really like to hear from her in person and alone to make sure we're making the right decision. Maybe they could bring her here to this safe house," Amy proposed.

"Let's ask. That's an excellent suggestion! It's our daughter's future at stake, and we want to hear directly from her to feel good about making the decision to leave her where she is."

When Marshal Cindy Gregory entered the living room later to chat with the Sherwoods, they proposed meeting Hannah in person, pleading that as parents they needed to feel solid about making the decision to leave Hannah where she was.

"Let me talk with the Service to see what we can arrange, and I'll get back to you. I think if we brought your daughter here, then by our policy we would have to move you permanently to a new location, which is a lot of work. Let's see what we can work out."

Amy nodded and watched the marshal leave.

"I wish you had never gone to work for that company. It's nearly killed our daughter and us, and we're losing time with her as she's growing up."

"You know I agree with you. I thought we would be safe and I thought we would build a nest egg for ourselves. I thought we would be safe at home in the United States, half a world away from that company. I was wrong."

They had been over this ground many times, and nothing good could come of re-thinking decisions already made. All they could do was hope for a meeting with their daughter.

Marshal Cindy Gregory briefly discussed the Sherwood's request with her partner Marshal Thomas Kinnear.

"Does the one parent live on some island in the bay? If it's big enough, we could land a helicopter there and have the meeting occur on the island. From the report I read, it's a very secure location as the island has security and protective equipment," Kinnear suggested.

"That's what I was thinking, but our service doesn't have a copter, and I don't know if it's in our budget to use one. Maybe the Coast Guard could take us out there. Their officers carry firearms and know how to use them. Besides they would keep quiet about the meeting."

"Let's suggest both to HQ and see where that gets us. From a budget perspective, I think it's cheaper to ease these parents minds with a meeting, then to add an agent to care for the teenager if they demand she joins them as a condition of testifying."

They put in the call to HQ and made the request with suggested alternatives. Then waited for a response. They knew someone would run it down within their service as strange arrangements were made all the time for the comfort and security of the witnesses they protected.

A week later they heard back from HQ, and the Coast Guard agreed to the assistance with the meeting. They requested a night meeting as rescue calls were rare at night on San Francisco Bay. There might be a worst case scenario where they would have to pull away from the island to assist a boat in distress, but it was unlikely. After HQ read the report of the attack on the island by the yacht, they felt confident that if that happened, Mr. and Mrs. Sherwood and the agents would be safe until the boat could return. They planned for an hour meeting on a weeknight on the island. Now all they had to do was tell the island's owner that they were coming.

CHAPTER 35

Two marshals were waiting in their car at Damian's warehouse in Richmond. They had his photo and were awaiting his arrival at work. They watched occupants get out of their cars, and none matched the photo of Damian Green. They looked up the Department of Motor Vehicles and had found a truck registered in his name, and so far there was only one truck that had arrived, and that man was nearly half a foot shorter and bald as compared to Mr. Green.

A half an hour after nearly everyone else arrived, a white Ford truck pulled into the parking lot, and the marshal saw that this was the man they were sent to speak to and so they quickly exited their car.

"Mr. Green, I'm Marshal Jonas Hill and this Marshal Charlie Morton, may we speak with you?"

Damian was surprised by the approach of the two men and immediately thought they were reporters than he realized they were dressed wrong for that profession. His next thought was more FBI agents. Hermione had returned home late last week, and they assumed the immediate threat of her being kidnapped was over, now he was worried again.

"Is something wrong with Hermione? Have you taken her? Did you harm Ariana?" he asked taking out his cell phone.

The marshals were a little surprised by his response and quickly said, "To our knowledge Ariana Knowles and the teenager you call Hermione Knowles are safe. Certainly, we've had no report of anything."

"Okay," Damian said trying to slow his thundering heart.

"Look we've been sent here to arrange a meeting. We have two guests that would like to visit your island around ten tonight. We would like Hermione Knowles to be on your island at that time."

"Are you taking Hermione away?"

"That's not the plan that we been informed of. The party that will come with us, will leave with us, with no new guests expected," said Hill.

"So this is just a face to face meeting between Hermione and the Sherwoods."

"I can neither confirm nor deny that statement," Hill said.

"Okay. We'll be there. How is your party arriving?"

"I'm unable to provide that information, sir."

"Okay, well there's a spot to land a helicopter on top of my island. If you come by boat, you'll need a gang-plank to get from the boat to my beach. I'll turn the lights on for either approach."

"Sir, please don't do anything different from normal. It sounds like the lights are off normally, so leave them off."

"Actually the lights are on a sensor. If it's a foggy night, the lights are on, so someone doesn't hit my island in the dark. If the night is clear, there's a single high light to again prevent boats from hitting the island in the dark. At this moment I don't know what the forecast is for tonight, but I'll just plan on the sensor doing its work. You say ten tonight?"

"Yes, though the time may vary."

"Try and not be too late. This is a school night, and Hermione needs her sleep. She has a soccer game tomorrow."

"I'll pass that on sir. I can make no promises about the time."

With that, the two marshals departed, and seconds later the entire brief conversation felt like a mirage to Damian. He shook his head and entered the building trying to switch gears and greet his employees without betraying the urgency of calling Ariana to tell her of the night's plan.

Thirty minutes later he closed the door to his office and called Ariana.

"What's up? I'm doing a little grocery shopping after dropping Hermione off at school."

"I was just visited by two U.S. Marshals, and.."

"Is Hermione going to be taken from us?" Ariana interrupted him with urgency to her question.

"I don't think so. It was a weird conversation with some missing facts, but at around ten tonight my island is going to be visited by two guests. We're to have Hermione on the island. I don't know if they're coming by air or water, and it might not be at ten."

"Okay," Ariana said with the word drawn out while she thought. "So probably her parents are being granted a visit to see her in person. The kid will be excited by the opportunity. Do you think they'll take her home with them?"

"I don't think so. The agents said they were departing with two guests."

"Hooray for that! That's the right thing to do for Hermione."

"Yeah, Why don't you come to the island right after school. I checked the weather, and it's clear and rather cold tonight, not too much wind. You can stay overnight or leave once they leave. I cautioned them that tonight's a school night and she has a soccer game tomorrow so they should try and not keep her awake too long."

"You didn't?" Ariana laughed.

"Well, she does have school tomorrow and a game," Damian said defensively.

"You must have sounded like a cool customer with that reply."

"Actually, when they first approached, my heart thundered as I thought they had taken Hermione and possibly arrested you and were just coming to arrest me. So I moved fast to the point that Hermione had school tomorrow."

"Oh my! It sounds like you need to go to Pete's bar for lunch and have a large mug of beer to calm down after that encounter."

"I might do that. I had to walk into the office as if nothing special occurred in the parking lot. I'm running out of energy for my cool customer facade."

"Poor baby! We'll prop you up tonight. Though I think you and Hermione should probably play Fortnite so you can both take your minds off the coming meeting."

"That's a good suggestion. We'll need to give her some time for homework, I'll cook a meal, and then I'll just wait for my security system to alarm when someone approaches."

"Have a calm day, do go to Pete's and we'll see you around five or six tonight."

Damian took Ariana's advice and went to lunch early at Pete's. In fact to take his mind off the coming event that night, he took his entire crew there for lunch. The effort of talking to his staff would take his mind off the meeting.

He worked the rest of the afternoon on a variety of projects and left early to pick up some chicken for the barbecue along with a key lime pie for dessert. He was putting stuff away when he got the text from Ariana that they were five minutes out from his island. He went down to his garage and awaited the approach of Ariana's boat. He tied up the pontoon boat, glad the bay was calm at the moment. They followed him into the lab and dropped their overnight bags just inside the door. Their use would depend on when the meeting ended as to where they would spend the night. Following him up the stairs to his main lab, Hermione waited until then to ask questions.

"Ariana said two guests would be arriving tonight probably at ten by air or sea, correct?"

"Yes."

"Do you think it will be my parents?"

"Either them or the President and Vice President of the United States. I'm sure they want to meet you on this secret island under cover of darkness."

"I'd rather it be my parents."

"So would I."

"Do you know why they're coming here?"

"I don't, but if I were them, meaning parents that love you, I would want to meet face to face with you to assure myself that you're safe and to explain my decision."

"What decision?"

"Whether you stay with us or retreat with them."

"Don't I have a say in this?"

"No, not legally, but I can't believe your parents would ignore your wishes. I also think they want to meet Ariana and me to have a sense of us despite what the FBI may or may not have said about us."

"Okay. Do you need help making dinner? Ariana mentioned we would get to play Fortnite again after I did my homework. If I can have thirty minutes down in my room, I think I can get my homework done."

And just like that, the teenager switched topics. Damian still wasn't used to the lightning changes in what the teenager was focused on.

"Go ahead kiddo. We'll call you up for dinner in forty-five minutes in case you need a little extra time."

They watched her head downstairs to her lower level bedroom slightly amazed she could work on homework at a time like this.

Damian shook his head and said, "I don't know how she stays so even emotionally despite teenage hormones probably raging through her."

"Sounds like life on the run with her parents has made her cope in that manner, take the punches as they come and move on."

"I feel that way about her parents. Even though I saw the video of their kidnapping, I still want to punch them for nearly getting the girl killed, forcing her to survive by herself. She's incredibly lucky she ended up with us instead of a sex trafficking ring, or other perverts out there looking for girls her age."

"You sound like a father," Ariana said with a smile.

"I guess I am and I do. It's complicated. I feel as protective towards her as I did for my two daughters that were murdered. Maybe I'm trying to redeem myself through her."

"No, you're just a man with a strong moral core."

"Let's change the topic, or I'll be crying on your shoulder soon."

"Did I blubber badly on Hermione's shoulder?"

"She did roll her eyes over it, but she was touched."

"Will you teach me some tricks on Fortnite? I'd like to play her without getting slaughtered."

"Sure, let me put the chicken on the barbecue, and I'll show you a few tricks."

An hour later, they were all sitting around eating dinner and checking the clock out.

"It's about three hours now before the guests arrive although the agents said we should consider it an estimate not an absolute of the arrival time," Damian said.

"How will we know when they're here? It's really dark out there."

"I have my usual security cameras on, though we won't get much warning with a helicopter approach. I'm also trying a new technology I invented last weekend. I'll put two drones in the air around nine and have them look for invaders. They have a longer range than the island's cameras, and they'll be able to see what's above the island."

"Wow, you're always thinking Damian," Hermione said. "It sounds like you created this thing with the drones before you knew you were going to have special guests. What made you think of that?"

"Actually I don't know what made me think of it. I guess I was looking for more drone uses."

"Okay then let's play Fortnite. Ariana, are you going to join us?"

"I will this time. Maybe Damian will distract you enough that I'll be able to beat you."

"Ha! Game on!"

Within minutes they were all deeply engrossed in building their worlds and trying to kill each other in the video world. They were surprised when an alarm sounded on Damian's phone. He quickly exited the game and opened the phone screen to see what the alarm was. He heard Ariana and Hermione shutting down as well and all three of them looking at the time.

"My drone has spotted an incoming boat, rather large, with at least twelve men on board, but not a yacht. Let me have some cameras focus on it, the shape looks familiar."

There was silence in the room waiting for Damian to get a better handle on the boat.

"It's the Coast Guard. At least we're not under attack. I wonder what they're doing here, or maybe they're bringing the special guests."

Damian's cell phone rang with an incoming blocked call.

CHAPTER 36

"Hello."

"This is Captain John Dumas of the United States Coast Guard. We are approaching your island. Where do you advise we send our rigid inflatable boat?"

"Captain, this is Damian Green of Red Rock Island, you will find a beach at Geo-coordinates 37,92901 -122.432096. It's the northwest side of the island. I have your vessel on approach and suggest you turn your ship slightly to the left."

"How are you tracking my ship?"

"I have a drone in the air off your bow, I'll pull it back to my island."

"Ah, I'd wondered what the blip on our radar screen was. We'll see you shortly."

Damian asked the two women to stay inside while he went out to greet the boat. As it was dark and he still had his chairlift at that cliff, it was likely the best way to get people up on top the island.

"I want to come with you," Hermione said.

"Look there are people holding guns out there, and if I were them, I would search me, then come to the house and search you guys and make sure it's safe for their guests to step on the island.

It will go faster if you stay inside and I won't have to worry about some gun-sight being on you, okay?"

"Okay."

Damian grabbed his jacket and a flashlight and walked down the hill toward the craggy cliff and its beach below.

As he approached the hill, he saw people on board the 110-foot patrol boat and the inflatable boat being launched. He suspected the marshal would climb out of the boat and inspect the island then come back for their guests. He was curious to watch what happened.

He dropped his flashlight to the ground and held his hands in the air and yelled about the noise of the boat.

"Hello, I'm Damian Green. Welcome to Red Rock Island. There's a chairlift that will lift you up the cliff. There's the seat in the rocks straight ahead and you'll see a green button that will move you up here, or you can scale the cliff. I'm going to put my hands down and stay still until you arrive on top."

Damian felt like a fool shouting out suggestions, then standing there waiting for someone to arrive and frisk him, but really it was just as he told Hermione. The marshals were very intent on keeping their guests safe.

When they were finally cleared, Hermione and Ariana came to the cliff's edge to watch her parents leave the Coast Guard patrol boat and come ashore in the inflatable then take the chair up the hill. Hermione/Hannah hugged first her mother and then her father. The patrol boat idled off his coast. The three marshals escorted everyone inside Damian's house.

Damian was surprised when after introductions were performed, Mrs. Sherwood gave him a fierce hug for saving, then protecting, then encouraging her daughter in school and in sports. Damian was embarrassed and was happy when she turned to Ariana and likewise praised her for taking on her daughter and the small acts of kindness like taking her to school.

"Look, Hermione has school and a soccer game tomorrow, and

I somehow don't think that you folks plan on being overnight guests here. There's an unopened bottle of wine of the counter and glasses. Ariana and I are going downstairs to give you privacy. The marshals are welcome to come with us, or you can stand outside my front door, or wait in my bedroom. Holler down the stairs when you need us."

They also left Miguel with Hermione as he was a calming influence on a fraught situation.

Ariana and Damian retreated to the lower level. Distracted as they were, they tried to get some business done but were called back upstairs after about twenty minutes. The Sherwoods were satisfied that they had the whole story of Hermione's adventure from her, and they now understood the power this genius and inventor had in saving her life.

"We wanted to hear from our daughter and then from you that you would be pleased to continue being her parents for the next few years. You've likely managed better than we did and she's happy and thriving, and you've kept her safe. We are entangled in this court case we're told for at least three years or by the time she's ready for college. We don't know if once the case is over, that we'll immediately be free. We could bring her with us into protective custody, but she'll have a better life here," Jason said as Amy continued to wipe her tears.

"I'll speak for both of us and say we'd love to continue to be her fake parents as we call ourselves. We're grateful you raised a daughter who hasn't flaked out on us in her teenage years. She rarely thinks we're stupid to our faces and someday I'm going to beat her at Fortnite."

"I'll add that I can create a secure way for you to communicate with your daughter over the coming years. I have my own communication satellite in orbit, and you can use that to bounce off of while not giving away your physical location. Perhaps someone in the Marshals Service IT department can investigate to assure your safety."

"That would be cool especially if they could watch one of my games or swim meets live instead of waiting several days to get a link to a tape," Hermione said.

"We're going to have to get used to calling you Hermione instead of Hannah because by the time we come back into your life you'll have had the name for several years," Amy Sherwood said. "I assume you chose that name from Harry Potter, it was always your favorite book."

Hermione nodded.

"I also like your new look. I remember you begging me to make those changes, and I wouldn't allow it, but you're a very pretty young lady."

Hermione just blushed over her mom's praise.

The marshals had been standing near the door during this part of the conversation, and they spoke, "Mr. and Mrs. Sherwood, we need to leave now for your own safety. The patrol boat is waiting, and we need to descend the cliff. We'll have our IT person contact you, Mr. Green, about that connection. It sounds like a great idea, and it would give the Sherwoods some peace of mind to be in more frequent communication with their daughter."

Ten minutes later, Hermione stood at the cliff's edge waving goodbye to her parents long after she was still able to see them on the boat in the dark.

"Well sweetie, we need to get back across the bay and get to sleep. You have a long day tomorrow."

As Damian reached to open his front door, she grabbed him and pulled these two wonderful adults in for a hug.

"Thank you."

The hug went on for a while, then Damian said, "I'll be rolling my eyes soon over your head at Ariana."

"Haha. Open the door, and we'll get out of your hair. Did you teach Ariana all the Fortnite secrets?"

"No, because then she would beat me, but she'll definitely conquer you when you next play."

Damian carried their bags to Ariana's boat and looked at an app on his phone. It was always a good idea to check the weather for weird wind changes in the wintertime. They should have a smooth sail across the Bay. They were off in no time, and twenty minutes later, he got a text that they were safely tied up at her house.

EPILOGUE

*A*ll three were surprised when they slept through the night. Damian arrived the next afternoon to cheer Hermione on during her soccer game. Her school had won again, and there was real talk about going on to regional finals.

Hermione chose take-out from a Thai restaurant as her post-game calorie load.

"Do you think we'll get a connection to my parents?"

"I think so. The Marshals should have their IT person check out my idea, which I know to be sound."

"Won't you know where my parents are when they call since it's your satellite? Not that I don't think you can be trusted."

"No. I'll give their IT person space on my satellite to set up their own protocol. Once they do that I'll be locked out of that part of my satellite."

"Sounds like a plan! Can I have some more red wine with my Thai food?"

"No," both Ariana and Damian said at the same time.

"Kiddo, we're not going to let you drink wine every night. Let's save it for special occasions."

"Isn't today a special occasion? I know my parents are alive and well and we won my soccer game."

"Your parent thing was yesterday, and you win every game so today's not a special occasion. It's an average day. Besides any wine connoisseur would tell you red wine doesn't go with a spicy chicken dish, a Riesling would be a far better pairing."

"Oh well, thought I try. Maybe the next thing I can learn is which wine goes with which dish."

"No, you won't be learning that until you're twenty-one. We're not turning you into a wine connoisseur before you're legally allowed to drink," Ariana said.

"Now you sound like my real parents."

"I'm sure they would be very pleased to hear that," Damian said as he gave a fist bump to Ariana.

THE END

If you liked this story, please leave a review at Amazon

ABOUT THE AUTHOR

I reside in Northern California with my rescue dog and cat. I love to travel, play sports, read, and drink wine and beer. I enjoy the diversity of the world and I'm always watching people and events for story ideas. All of my stories are generated by my imagination, I don't use AI to write books.

If you would like to sign up for my bi-weekly blog and announcement of new books, please follow this link: https://www.AlecPecheBooks.com

While you're waiting for the next story, if you would be so kind as to leave a review for this book, that would be great. I appreciate all the feedback and support. Reviews buoy my spirits and stoke the fires of creativity.

Readers that sign up for my blog receive a free prequel novelette for the Jill Quint Series.

* * *

Author Profile on Goodreads

Author Profile on BookBub

* * *

ALSO BY ALEC PECHE

<u>Jill Quint, MD Forensic Pathologist Series</u>

Time's Up (prequel short story)

Vials

Chocolate Diamonds

A Breck Death

Death On A Green

A Taxing Death

Murder At The Podium

Castle Killing

Crescent City Murder

Sicilian Murder

Opus Murder

Forensic Murder

Return to the Scene of the Crime (short story)

Embers of Murder

Ashes to Murder

Mint Death

<u>Damian Green Series</u>

Red Rock Island

Willow Glen Heist

The Girl From Diana Park

Evergreen Valley Murder

Long Delayed Justice

<u>Michelle Watson Series</u>

Now You Don't See Me

Where Did She Go?

How Did She Get There?

<u>Dog Humor</u>

Eat, Play, Poop: Letters to my parents from camp

<u>New Urban Fantasy Series - Stephanie Jones</u>

The Awakening at Lake Tahoe (short story)

Witch's Medicine (2024)